Hostile Eyewitness:

Serena Manchester Series Book One

Hostile Eyewitness:

Serena Manchester Series Book One

Tyora Moody

www.urbanchristianonline.com

Urban Books, LLC
97 N18th Street
Wyandanch, NY 11798

Hostile Eyewitness: Serena Manchester Series Book One

ISBN 13: 978-1-62286-800-1
ISBN 10: 1-62286-800-5

First Trade Paperback Printing April 2015
Printed in the United States of America

10 9 8 7 6 5 4 3 2

Distributed by Kensington Publishing Corp.
Submit orders to:
Customer Service
400 Hahn Road
Westminster, MD 21157-4627
Phone: 1-800-733-3000
Fax: 1-800-659-2436

Hostile Eyewitness:

Serena Manchester Series Book One

by

Tyora Moody

DEDICATION

This book is dedicated to my dad, my uncles, and my paternal and maternal grandfathers. It's been a blessing to be raised by and surrounded by these awesome men, and to be living with their legacy.

ACKNOWLEDGMENTS

Readers, whether you met Serena Manchester from reading the Victory Gospel Series or she is a new character to you, I hope you enjoy her journey in this novel. She's a character who has been with me for a number of years, and it was time to let her tell her own story. At some point in our lives all of us come to a crossroads and have to make a decision about whether to go left or right. Like Serena in *Hostile Eyewitness*, I have been guilty of choosing the wrong direction, because I wasn't tuned in or listening to God's voice. God is always there, quietly urging us on to the next step on our journey. Sometimes years may go by before we really hear Him. Sometimes a tragedy or a particular event reveals God's purpose to us with such intensity that we are forced to pause and reflect.

Joylynn Ross, thank you for always being available for my questions and for pushing me as a writer in the editing process. I've learned so much from you and the Urban Christian family. Thanks to Robin Caldwell for listening to my thoughts and rants about my characters.

Thanks to my parents, my sister, my friends, and my clients for always being supportive during those times when I have been super-focused in order to meet my deadlines.

I don't like to post names, because I have come across so many people due to the world of social media and my travels to events. I want to take a moment to acknowledge the people who helped me promote my first book series, Victory Gospel Series. To family and friends, book reviewers, bloggers, online radio hosts, book clubs and readers, thank you for your support.

I'm looking forward to bringing you more Soul-Searching Suspense with Serena Manchester as the main character. I have always had a feeling that once I let her tell one story, she would have more stories to share.

Train up a child in the way he should go:
and when he is old, he will not depart from it.

Psalm 22:6

CHAPTER ONE

Wednesday, April 15, 10:00 p.m.

I had always had a knack for being in the wrong place at the wrong time. It usually was my fault and was due to my insatiable desire to stick my nose where it didn't belong. For many years, my curiosity had led me to award-winning stories. But that life as Serena Manchester, the investigative reporter, was in the past, thanks to a serious knock to my hard noggin.

It was that almost fatal injury that changed my life forever.

I sank down lower into the couch. The living room had been my usual spot for several weeks now, as I obsessed over what happened to me a year ago. At least I'd finally graduated from being in the bed, with the covers over my head.

I'd been known to attract crazy men, but it was still hard to believe that last year a madman tried to kill me. Funny, I didn't remember much about my tumble down the flight of stairs. I was thankful to be alive, but some days I didn't recognize myself. I just hadn't been the same. It had been a scary journey, but I wouldn't dare admit this revelation to anyone. So for almost three months I'd been playing hide-and-seek in a town that I had sworn I would never return to. The goal really was to have no one find me or know I had returned.

I had my demons and issues wrapping their arms around me daily. It was so frustrating to me that my brain wanted to occupy itself with memories from years past, when I couldn't seem to grasp what I had been thinking about even thirty minutes ago. So the reality of my life slapped me in the face over and over again.

I was forty-two, with no kids, was twice divorced, and was currently unemployed. I could say I left my job as a television reporter out of sheer frustration with my own work performance. I couldn't conduct a decent interview or keep my thoughts together for a story. I had grown deeply disturbed that the up-and-coming, wannabe hot-shot reporters were getting the best stories. Twenty years ago that was me; I was the "it" girl. I still wanted to think I was a hotshot, but the past year had melted my ego. I wanted to go back to investigative reporting, but the way life had treated me, I wasn't sure if any television station would take me.

I felt my age and sometimes older. Whenever I looked in the mirror, I was shocked by the pain in my eyes. Some of it stemmed from the consequences of my head injury, but most of my pain welled up from a deep place inside me. I thought I had shoved the past far enough away that I would never have to deal with it again. Looked like I was a fool, thinking I had that kind of control.

No. I didn't like my state of mind. Not at all.

I was not sure what day it was currently. The days really ran together in my head. What I did know was that my sweet tooth seemed to be driving me crazier than I already felt. I managed to convince myself it would be okay to come out of hiding. I could run to the store, and no one would notice me.

I dressed quickly in my normal uniform for leaving the house: jeans and a T-shirt. I peeked at myself in the bathroom mirror and rubbed my hands across my chopped natural hair. The woman looking back at me had dark circles under her eyes, making them appear even larger. In my past life, I had worn weaves and make-up and had dressed up for the camera. I was surprised I didn't miss that part of my life. It was weird at first, but my natural face, void of make-up, wasn't all that bad. My milk chocolate skin was clear of the blemishes that came from following the regimen necessary to look good for the camera.

I walked to the front of the house, still amazed about how I had made it my home. This house was owned by my father's sister. Claudia Robinson, better known as Aunt C, had been my salvation while I was growing up. She was the one person I could trust. As an adult, I didn't come to visit her as often, but we stayed in touch. When Aunt C died in January, no one was more surprised than me to find out I had inherited her house. It was almost like she used the opportunity to draw me back home.

That woman had always had a plan.

My companion, Callie, a big fat calico cat, stirred in the corner of the living room as I strolled through. The large green eyes seemed to be asking, "Is it supper time yet?" I had never owned an animal, but this cat had become mine. Actually, it was more like I became her human. She had lived here before I did, and she merely tolerated me as the new person charged with feeding her and taking care of her other feline needs.

I scratched Callie under her chin and then grabbed my keys. "I will be back in a few minutes," I said to the cat, as if she understood English.

The sun had gone down a while ago, so it was dark out. I opened the front door and winced as the screen door squealed in protest. Gnats were buzzing around the porch light. I was grateful that this light worked by motion detection, since I would forget to turn it on if that were not the case. I sucked in the evening air, raising my nose to sniff the Atlantic Ocean. As I climbed into my Honda Civic, I thought that the only good thing about my South Carolina hometown was its proximity to the ocean, a benefit I had missed all the years I lived in Charlotte. I felt free, despite being back in Georgetown County. From the time I was a preteen, I had felt like a prisoner within these rural town limits. As I drove, like an alcoholic seeking a drink, my mind began to stray from my mission. The corner store was about three blocks from the house.

I turned into the convenience store parking lot and then checked my gas meter to see if the gas tank needed to be filled. I smirked. The tank was three-quarters full. It wasn't like I was planning to go on a road trip anywhere. I'd really become a bit of a hermit, the only exception being when my sister and her daughters came by. I welcomed the company since my relationship with my sister had become strained over the years. I ticked off the days in my mind, determining that this had to be a Wednesday evening since I hadn't talked to my sister since Sunday. I could count on my younger sister nagging me persistently to attend church with her and her family every Sunday morning.

I swung the car into a parking space and jumped out. I still kind of missed my SUV, but I had decided it was best to go with a more economical car. I was living off savings now. I noticed that parked on the other side of my car was a dark Ford Crown Victoria. Having hung out around investigators and law enforcement most of my career, I knew that vehicle had been a popular car with the police for years. I didn't stop to observe if anyone was in the car. I was on a mission.

As I entered the store, I glanced over at the cash register and noticed the attendant. I stopped and waved like I was some beauty queen. "How are you doing, Marty?"

Marty Davis was an older guy. I estimated he was between forty-five and fifty. His hair was gray around the
temples, and he wore it in a small Afro. He was a short
man, but was definitely not slim. He looked tall and men-
acing behind the counter. I came in the store enough for
him to know my face, so he seemed liked a gentle bear
to me. Tonight, when he looked at me, his smile seemed
tight and his eyes darted behind me.

I wasn't in the mood to start a conversation, but I felt
compelled to ask Marty, "Is everything okay?"

Marty blinked. "Yes. I'm just tired. It's been a long day.
How you doing today, ma'am? I haven't seen you in a
while."

"I stay busy, Marty." *I stay busy trying not to lose my
mind.* "Please don't call me ma'am. I'm not that old."

He laughed, but I noticed his eyes were still focused on
something past me, outside the window. I had this insane
feeling that I should leave the store. I started to turn,
but then I thought that was silly. I blamed my head for
playing tricks on me, and the fact that Marty was exuding
nervous energy didn't help matters. I wanted to get what I
had come for and get back home. Temptation had called,
and I was hooked.

My head started to pound slightly as I walked down the
candy aisle. I had this crazy urge to eat chocolate. There
were rows and rows of different kinds of chocolate. I
grabbed a chocolate bar that had peanuts and one that had
caramel. Then I looked over at some chocolate-covered
raisins. Yep, a chocolate binge was coming on strong.

Just as I reached down to grab another candy bar, I
heard the bells above the store door jingle. It shouldn't
have been a big deal, but my eyes slid toward the back
corner of the store and up to where a big round mirror
hung. The hairs on my arms stood up. My eyes were fixed
on the mirror as I watched two, no, three young males

enter the store. One of the boys sauntered down the aisle behind me, while the other two stayed near the front of the store. I couldn't see their faces.

As a habit, I noted that one of the boys wore a hoodie over a red baseball cap. While the temperature had been a balmy eighty degrees earlier today, last night it dipped down to the fifties. The hoodie didn't bother me, since I had a similar one in my closet. It was when I saw the back of the jacket one of the other boys was wearing that my senses went on full alert. I forgot about the last candy bar and decided to scoot around to the end of the aisle. I bent down, as if I was tying my shoe, hoping no one had noticed me.

Is that why Marty was acting nervous? I didn't see the boys when I entered the store, but they could've arrived after that. Had they come by car on or on foot?

I was not into the profiling thing, but my years of investigating criminal cases had taught me to be on the alert. That jacket said "creepy" to me, especially about the person wearing it. It wasn't your ordinary high school varsity jacket, even though it had a similar shape and style. The jacket was red, with a large white skull on the back. There were images around the skull, but from where I stood, observing in the mirror's angle, I couldn't make out the details.

I heard the tremble in Marty's voice when he inquired, "Can I help you boys with something?"

My breath caught in my throat when I heard the boy with the jacket answer back, "Old man, I need you to empty out the register."

I gulped and shook my head. "No, no, no," I said softly under my breath. This could not be happening. My life had already flashed before my eyes a year ago. I peered up at the mirror, willing Marty not to play the tough guy and to just give the boys what they wanted. I also hoped that behind the counter Marty had a button connected to an alarm.

Marty's voice was strong but nervous. "I don't want any trouble. You boys need to leave. The police will be here any second."

I watched the boy reach into his jacket and pull something out. "You don't tell me what to do. I told you what to do." He stepped closer to Marty. "Now do it or die."

Do it or die. Looking into the mirror, I couldn't tell if the boy had a gun in his hand, but my instincts said he'd just reached in and pulled out a weapon. I also realized I would be in a perilous situation if they saw me. All the progress I had made, despite the obstacles I'd faced, would be wasted if I got shot and killed. I could only hope that God would spare my life again. I didn't deserve the second chance He had given me last year.

As that thought passed through my mind, I heard a loud bang. A flash in the mirror drew my attention. Horrified, I clasped my hands over my mouth as I watched, and the chocolate fell to the floor.

Marty yelled, "You don't have to do this."

I watched Marty stab at the buttons on the cash register in an effort to open the money drawer.

What happened next felt unreal. Another shot rang out, and I saw Marty's body fly back and fall behind the counter. My hand was still over my mouth, and I sought to stifle the scream that had risen up in my throat. Why did the boy shoot the gun a second time? I wondered. It had looked like Marty was giving them the money. My body was frozen as my mind tried to figure out what to do next.

Then I heard the panicked voice of the boy who had walked down the aisle. "Man, why did you shoot him?"

The boy with the jacket swung around toward the boy down the aisle. That was when I saw the gun. The boy with the jacket was definitely the ringleader, and he was wearing shades. He had purposely tried to hide his features. He yelled at the boy in the aisle, "Shut up, or I will send you to the same place I just sent this dude!" He turned around to face the boy in the hoodie. "Let's finish this. Get the money before the cops come."

I wanted so badly to stand up and get Marty some help. I watched the boy in the hoodie reach across the counter and inside the open cash register, stuffing cash into his hoodie pockets, while the boy who did the shooting waved the gun around, scanning the store. I was glad I had ducked down.

The boy in the aisle seemed to be backing up to the end of the aisle, away from the front. It occurred to me that he would see me, so I scrambled around to the other aisle. I looked around at my surroundings, trying to figure out what to do. I turned my attention to the mirror to observe the approaching boy. He seemed to be scared and not sure of himself.

It suddenly dawned on me that if he turned around and looked up, he would be able to see me in the mirror. The mirror was angled in such a way that he might be able to see me crouching down like a hopeless idiot. As I attempted to steady my rapid breathing, distant police sirens sounded outside the store.

The boy wearing the red jacket shouted, "Let's go! Now!" Then he headed out of the store, the boy in the hoodie running after him.

The boy who was down the aisle didn't move as fast, and he turned his head as he went, as if looking for an alternate door through which to exit the store. As I crouched on the floor, pain shot through my calves. But that pain didn't rock me as much as the glimpse I got of the boy in the aisle. Despite the dark blue Charlotte Bobcats cap hanging over his eyes, when he turned, I saw his face in the mirror.

I know him.

I sucked in my breath sharply as I watched the young man finally decide to run toward the front of the store. As he exited the store, in the back of my mind I hoped he didn't get caught. If he was who I thought he was, I felt for sure that young man was in the wrong place at the wrong time.

I waited a minute or two, and then I stood, feeling sharp pains up and down my legs, especially the leg that had the broken ankle a year ago. I limped to the front of the store, almost tripping over my own feet.

"Marty! Marty, can you hear me?" I shouted.

I peered over the counter, catching a glimpse of blood spatter across the tile floor and on items behind the counter. Marty lay in a pool of blood, which appeared to have formed around his head. That boy had aimed directly at Marty's head. The second shot had been unnecessary, and so vicious. The boy had shot to kill him.

Why was the boy in the Bobcats cap with them?

From the corner of my eye, I could see flashing blue lights as a vehicle pulled into the store parking lot. I would have to figure out what to tell the police when they came inside. I hoped with all my heart that I was mistaken about whose face I had seen. He was family. My family had a reputation is this town, which was one of the many reasons why I had left.

CHAPTER TWO

Wednesday, 11:15 p.m.

I leaned up against my car, trying to shake the images of Marty's body in the pool of blood from my fragile mind. Just what I needed for my already sleep-deprived life.

The female paramedic came over and asked again, "'Ma'am, you sure you don't want to go to the hospital?" I had told the officers I was fine, but my limping hadn't convinced them that I wasn't hurt. The paramedics were certainly not needed for Marty.

"Yes, I'm sure." I glanced away, wishing she would leave me alone. I really didn't need to be bringing attention to myself. Besides, I wasn't hurt. Despite the fact that I had sustained no injuries, I was shaking like a drug addict going through withdrawal. I had wrapped my arms tightly around myself, but the night air had penetrated my T-shirt, which felt slightly damp from sweat.

I wanted to go home, but the police wanted to question me. I looked nonchalantly for the boys amid the growing crowd of onlookers, but they appeared to be gone. That was good, but I still would have liked to get a closer look at one of the boys. He had seemed so familiar to me. I hoped my brain hadn't been playing tricks on me. It wouldn't be the first time when what my eyes saw and what my brain deciphered didn't quite connect.

I glanced to my right and saw two men walking toward me. Having worked around law enforcement, I was pretty sure the white man and the black man in suit and tie were investigators from the City of Georgetown Police Department.

The white man, the taller of the two, stepped in front of me. He towered over me, but he had a kind face and a gentle voice. He said, "I hear you witnessed what happened here, Ms.—"

"Serena Manchester," the other investigator said, finishing for him. He seemed to flex his muscles, which were definitely huge under his jacket

I was a bit shocked that the man had just identified me. His face could have been handsome, but right now he was staring at me like he was ready to haul me into the station. I wouldn't go without a fight, because I had seen all I could handle for one night. I narrowed my eyes. "How do you know who I am?"

The investigator replied, "I'm from the Charlotte area. I remember seeing you report the news. WYNN News, right? What brings you down to this little town?"

I hoped my face didn't display the disdain that was seeping through my mind. Who knew coming out to the corner store would cause me this much upheaval? I scolded myself for my chocolate weakness. If I'd stayed in the house, I wouldn't be an eyewitness to a crime and I wouldn't be forced to respond to questions about my recent exodus to my hometown. I managed to quell my emotions a bit before answering, with what I hoped was a pleasant smile."I don't believe you two gentlemen have introduced yourselves."

The taller man responded, "So sorry, ma'am. I'm Investigator Oliver Baldwin. This is my partner, Investigator Malcolm Moses. We're from Georgetown CID."

Criminal Investigation Department. I was familiar with criminal investigators. I nodded but didn't look at Investigator Moses. I had no intention of letting him know why I was here in Georgetown. What did that have to do with the crime that had just been committed, anyway? Besides, I still wasn't sure why attending my aunt's funeral back in January had resulted in my extended stay.

What I did know was these men wanted my eyewitness account. "I came out to tonight to get some snacks. A few minutes after I entered the store, two . . . I mean, three young men entered the store."

Investigator Moses stepped closer to me. "Can you describe them?"

The face of the boy I thought I had recognized flashed before me. I couldn't be sure. "I can't describe their faces. I was in the back of the store, trying not to be seen."

Investigator Moses said, "You said you were trying not to be seen. What prompted you to want to hide?"

I hated to admit what I had been thinking at the time. "I guess the way the boys walked in the store just felt odd to me. One of them had on a really creepy jacket. It had a skull on the back. I wouldn't think that would be something a kid would wear around here."

The two investigators glanced at each other.

Investigator Baldwin nodded. "I'm not familiar with that jacket, but there are certain clothes and colors we look for in certain crimes. Given these perps are younger, it's quite possible tonight's robbery and shooting are gang-related crimes."

I stared incredulously at the men. "A gang? Here?"

Investigator Moses shook his head. "Believe us, it's been a challenge, because no one expects the types of crimes that used to be only in inner cities to take place in a small Southern town."

As a reporter in the not so distant past, I really shouldn't have been surprised, but in the back of my mind an uneasy feeling started to form. What if the boy who came down the aisle saw me? I wondered. I thought I had recognized him, but maybe it wasn't the boy I knew. That boy was a good kid. There was no way he was part of a gang. I also knew that I didn't want to get caught up in this mess if a gang was involved. That type of harassment I didn't need. I suddenly wanted to head home and lock myself up in the house.

Investigator Baldwin asked, "Were the boys wearing anything else that stood out to you?"

A baseball cap came to mind. It was the dark blue cap with the Charlotte Bobcats insignia on the front. What else was he wearing? *No, no, no. I can't say what he was wearing.*

I knew how important what I had witnessed was in helping the police. I simply wasn't sure of what I had seen. "I'm trying to remember."

Investigator Baldwin leaned forward. "Take your time, Ms. Manchester. You can do this. You said there were two or three boys?"

No, I can't. I focused my mind back on the mirror in which I had seen most of the action inside the convenience store. What had the two boys in the front of the store worn? "I told you about the jacket. I think the other boy was wearing a dark hoodie. I couldn't tell if it was black or dark blue. His head was covered. I think he had maybe a red baseball cap, definitely a cap, underneath the hoodie."

"Okay, that's good." Investigator Baldwin declared as he jotted down notes in his notebook.

I was past shivering now. I looked around at the crowd again for any signs of the boys. I thought I glimpsed some boys watching me, but I really didn't know if they were the same boys or not.

Investigator Moses jolted me from my thoughts when he barked out, "Anything else you can tell us?"

"They were probably all wearing jeans and sneakers, but I can't say for sure. I'm sorry I can't be more helpful, but I need to go." I rubbed my hands down my arms, feeling goose bumps. I bounced from one foot to the other, as if I had to run to the bathroom.

Investigator Baldwin held up his hand, as if to comfort me. "Please, just a few more minutes of your time. I know this had to have been a shock. How much did you see of the crime? What about the store owner? Anything you can help us with would be appreciated."

I willed myself to stand still, but my body had the shakes. I suspected the cold air wasn't the only reason. "I heard Marty exchange words with the boy wearing the red jacket. He sounded like he could have been the ringleader. He was shouting the most, telling the other boys what to do. Anyway, Marty warned them to leave, but then I heard a gunshot. I guess it was to scare Marty, but then the boy fired the gun a second time."

I closed my eyes, remembering the scene I saw in the mirror. I had arrived at many crime scenes in my life to get a story, but I'd never been close to a crime being committed. That bullet had landed in Marty's forehead. Why had the boy been so trigger happy if all they wanted was money from the register? Marty had opened the register for them. Did Marty have a gun behind the counter? Had the boy felt threatened? I had missed something due to my position down the store aisle. Something had felt odd about the entire incident from the moment I walked into the store.

I swallowed as once again I saw the image of the boy's familiar face in my mind's eye. I tried to continue to answer the question for the investigators. "I don't understand why they killed Marty. He seemed to be cooperating. Anyway, the boy with the jacket told the boy dressed in the hoodie to get the money. I saw him reach in the register and take the money out. Marty must have triggered some kind of alarm behind the counter, because I heard police sirens very quickly. Then they were all gone."

Investigator Moses stepped closer to me. He asked, "You didn't see anyone's face?"

I wanted him to step back. While his cologne smelled good, now was not a good time for me to be inhaling it. I moved backward and shook my head. "I was in the back, and I saw most of what I just told you in the store's rear mirror. I was more concerned with not drawing attention to myself. Now I'm freezing. Can I go now?"

"Of course. We're sorry to keep you. You have been really helpful." Investigator Baldwin smiled slightly. "Maybe we can touch base tomorrow, after you get some rest. There might be something that comes to you tonight."

That isn't going to happen!

I was heading back to my hiding place, and I would think long and hard about coming out again. I opened my car door and climbed inside. Once I slammed the door shut, I looked over at both men. Investigator Moses had his eye on me, while Investigator Baldwin was strolling back toward the crime scene. I started the engine and drove off as quickly as I could without making my tires squeal.

As I drove away, I looked through the side windows of the car, as if I suspected someone was watching me. The sense of safety I'd enjoyed for three months seemed to have slipped away in a few short hours.

CHAPTER THREE

Thursday, April 16, 12:05 a.m.

It was after midnight, but I decided not to go home. My decision was partially influenced by my growing paranoia that the boys could follow me home. I had to admit it didn't make much sense, since they were probably long gone and I hadn't really seen anything that was helpful to the investigators. Most criminals were set on getting away, not sticking around the crime scene. That is, unless they were just that brazen.

Not wanting to take any chances, I found myself a corner booth in a nearby Huddle House. It was quiet, with only a few other patrons. They appeared to be travel-weary tourists. Vacationers from all over would soon be passing through this area to get to the beachfront that stretched from Myrtle Beach all the way down to Charleston. Georgetown was right in the middle.

As I flipped open the colorful, though small menu, I realized I needed some human contact after seeing a man die at the hands of some crazy kid. As I tried to get my thoughts together, I couldn't stop wondering why Marty had acted the way he had when I walked into the convenience store. What was he nervous about? Had Marty sensed what was about to happen?

I really didn't remember seeing anyone outside when I walked into the store. I chided myself for not saying anything to the investigators about Marty appearing to be on edge, but maybe running a convenience store at night had sometimes made the man extra paranoid.

A voice jolted me from my thoughts.

"What will you have, hon?"

Without looking up, I said, "I will start with a cup of coffee."

"Rena, is that you?"

I glanced up from the menu to look at the waitress. I narrowed my eyes as I stared at her. She had burgundy-colored micro-braids and cocoa-brown skin, and she was smiling at me. Her heart-shaped face seemed familiar.

She said, "You don't remember me, do you?"

I turned my attention to her name tag. "Iris? Iris Jenkins?"

"That's me. Oh, my goodness. I can't believe you're here."

I shook my head and tried to force a smile. Stopping in here might not have been a good idea, after all. Iris was my first ex-husband's cousin. Iris had been nice to me, even sympathetic, as I quickly got out of my marriage to Doug Jenkins. I had learned an important lesson from that marriage, which had lasted barely one year: it paid to take people seriously when they showed their true self.

When I hooked up with Doug, I was nineteen and was still reeling from the loss of a boyfriend who had been shot dead the year before in Charlotte. I quickly found comfort in a man who was dangerously charming. I had to learn the hard way, but it took only one punch in the face for me to know I had married a man with a crazy temper. I should have stayed single and concentrated on my career.

Iris had been talking as memories that had been buried rushed forward in my mind. I shook my head and tuned back in to hear her say, "I'm just glad to see you went on with your life."

I assumed she was talking about me walking away from her cousin. I nodded and said, "I'm really cold. Can I get that coffee now?"

"Sure! I'm so sorry for running my mouth. I just haven't seen you in so long."

Iris went behind the counter. A few minutes later she returned with a coffee cup and a steaming carafe. After she poured the coffee, she asked, "What else can I get for you?"

Thoughts of the scene I had just left swirled in my mind. I just couldn't have a meal after seeing a man killed. It was late at night. Maybe this wasn't a good idea.

I must have had an odd look on my face, because Iris touched my shoulder. "Are you all right?"

I shook my head, not trusting myself to say anything. I didn't want anyone to know what I had just witnessed. I knew small-town gossip too well, and I couldn't afford to make myself so conspicuous. I held up my hand. "It's late. Let me just do coffee."

She eyed me. "Are you sure?"

"Yes." I placed the menu back in the holder.

After Iris walked away, I sipped the strong, hot coffee, thinking sleep might not come tonight. Nothing unusual. Insomnia had become a part of my life.

I pulled out my phone and saw that my sister had texted me a few times tonight. *Great!* She probably thought I was ignoring her, which I did have a tendency to do. I decided to ignore the messages and contact her in the morning. I could always say I was asleep, even though she would know I was lying. My sister, like Aunt C, knew me too well.

I drained the cup of coffee. It was time to head home. I walked over to the cash register and paid for the coffee. After I received the change, I returned to the table to leave a dollar tip for Iris. As I swung around, my eyes caught a man as he walked through the door.

I sucked in my breath.

I'd been avoiding church, despite my sister's persistent invitations, but surely, God wouldn't do me like this. Not tonight.

At first I thought the man was my second ex-husband, Benjamin Manchester. As the shock wore off, I realized that it was not him and that the man bore a striking resemblance to Benjamin. The man must have felt me staring, because he turned.

A huge grin broke out on Trey Evans's face. "It's that you, Rena?"

"Hey, Trey. I almost . . ."

He walked over to me. "Mistook me for Benny, right? I know. I decided to shave my beard, and now everyone keeps telling me how much I look like my half brother. I still don't see it."

Despite my weariness, I felt a smile tug at my face. Trey was the half brother of my second ex-husband, Benjamin "Benny" Manchester. The two men had grown up in separate counties and didn't know the other existed until they played high school football. They were both top athletes, and people couldn't help but talk about their similar looks. Neither boy had a problem catching the ladies' attention. I had always thought Trey was more intelligent and more of a gentleman than his brother.

I grew up with Trey and had the biggest crush on him back then. By the time I became involved with Benny, Trey and I had long grown apart, I had been married and had divorced, and I was enjoying my career in Charlotte. When I thought back on it, I had to wonder if I had been on the rebound from my first marriage when I fell for Benny. Or had I been looking for something I'd always wanted?

Trey certainly was looking good. He appeared to be as fit as he was in high school. "You're wearing a beard.

Seems like at one time you couldn't grow one." He'd always had a bit of a baby face, with his round cheeks and dimples.

"Ouch. You sure haven't lost your sharp touch, Rena. I'm much older, and that beard has a bit more gray in it than I expected. Goes to show, it has been a long time since I've seen you."

"Yeah, well, life moves by pretty fast."

His smile disappeared, but his eyes were warm, reminding of the time long ago when I would hang on his every word. He said, "I imagine your Aunt C passing brought you back home. I'm so sorry. Everyone loved your aunt."

My aunt was something of a town treasure, since many people either were in her fourth- grade class or were at McDonald Elementary School while she was the principal. "Yeah, it's weird but comforting to be home." I hadn't admitted that to anyone else.

"Well, it's good to see you. What has you out this late?"

The brief euphoria I had experienced from seeing Trey faded. My first thought was to say something snappy, like "What are *you* doing out this late?" Now wasn't the time to hide behind my sarcastic shield. I didn't want to run Trey off, so I pretended to yawn. "I just needed a change of scenery, but I do need to head back home now."

"Where are you staying?"

Suddenly conscious that we were standing at the front of the restaurant, I wanted to bolt. I glanced over at the booth where I had sat and saw Iris staring at me. *Or is she staring at Trey?*

I looked back at Trey. "My aunt's house. It was good seeing you. Maybe we can catch up another time."

He smiled. "I look forward to seeing you again." He reached over and opened the door for me. "Be safe out there."

My cheeks felt awfully warm as I brushed by him, catching a whiff of his cologne. Another good-smelling brother in only an hour. What was going on? At least this experience was more pleasant than my conversation with Investigator Moses and Investigator Baldwin. After the night I'd had, I didn't mind running into an old friend who was pleasing to the eye and the senses.

As I hurried to my car, unwanted thoughts of my marriage to Trey's half brother invaded my mind. That marriage had lasted five years. As far as I knew, Benjamin was up in the Richmond, Virginia, area now and was married, with two kids. He probably had a dog too.

I climbed in my car and started the engine. Before pulling off, I looked through the front window of the Huddle House. Trey had walked over to talk to Iris. She beamed up at him. I wondered if they were together. Maybe he was out this late to come check on her.

Then I remembered. How could I forget? Iris had been a cheerleader in high school, and she and Trey had been *the couple*. I had put high school behind me and had moved on, but here I was, almost twenty-five years later, still unnerved by seeing Trey with another woman. It was just like me to set my sights on a man who was not meant for me. It was a pattern for me.

I had subconsciously sworn off relationships, especially in the past year. Men brought with them complications, and I was already a screwed-up chick, thanks to one bad choice after another.

I pulled out of the parking lot, more ready for bed that I had thought I was only minutes ago. I just hoped sleep would come quickly and I would not have to stare at the ceiling another night.

CHAPTER FOUR

Thursday, 7:00 a.m.

I hadn't sleep well. I'd kept pushing the REPLAY button on the store shooting. I rubbed my eyes and blinked. This sleep-deprived limbo had me feeling like I had aged ten years. I eventually got out of bed and went into the living room. A quick peek through the blinds told me it was a gloomy, gray sky. Perfect weather for going back to sleep, if I could shut my brain off. Funny how I couldn't remember what I wanted, but all the bad memories and thoughts jumped right to the surface.

I turned from the bay window and looked around the room, noticing the shadows in the corners. Since the sun was hiding behind the clouds, I reached for a nearby lamp to add some light to the room. Then I held my hand to my forehead and breathed deeply. The pleasant scent of lavender, which Aunt C was known to stockpile, filled my nostrils.

As I exhaled, memories from my childhood slowly began to unfold in my mind. Even though the house was mine, I didn't know what to do with my aunt's things. I had left everything in the same spot. I'd spent a lot of time in this house when I was younger, but some days I felt like a stranger in my aunt's space. Since her death three months ago, I had been trying to decide if I wanted to keep her house, but for now it was my safe haven.

First, I needed to set my mind at ease about what I saw last night.

Aunt C had a stack of family albums on a nearby book-shelf. I grabbed a few of the albums and plopped down on the couch. As I turned the pages, I smiled and laughed out loud at some of the photos. I had been looking through the albums for some time when I came across a photo of Aunt C and my dad, Dallas Robinson. Aunt C had been more like my dad's mother than his sister. She had always looked out for him. Right up to his passing the week before my fourteenth birthday, Aunt C had been the one checking on him and making sure he was comfortable.

Dad was a decent, fun man, but he had a love for his cigarettes, booze, and women. He was a handsome man with hazel eyes and a grin that when I was a little girl, I saw made grown women turn giddy. Despite my parents being apart, I saw Dad sometimes when I visited Aunt C's house. It was usually the only time I saw him sober and in good spirits. Aunt C had that effect. You straightened up around her, at least for a little while.

By the time anyone realized my dad was really sick, the lung cancer had run its course. Tears stung my eyes, and I flipped away from the photo. I had been on the go for so many years that I had stuffed many parts of my life into deep compartments. The doors to those compartments had been flung wide open, and I was not enjoying these reminders of my childhood.

On the next page was a rare photo of my mom and dad together. He held her in his arms. I was struck by Mama's smile, since it was rarely seen these days. I loved Mama, but we had a complicated relationship. Her relationship with my dad had been even more intense. Something about their split had broken my mama. Despite having divorced many years before, Mama had taken my dad's death harder than anyone. I did not understood why, since he was the one who had hurt her.

I rubbed my fingers across the photo of my parents and stared for a while longer at the expressions on their faces. They loved each other in this photo. It was a travesty the way love came and went as it pleased. I finally turned away from that photo. The sun seemed to be peeking through the clouds now, so I decided a coffee break would do me good. Callie had been lurking around the living room as I flipped through the albums. The cat strolled in front of me as I walked toward the kitchen.

"I guess you want to be fed," I said to her.

The cat vocalized her response with high-pitched meows. Once inside the kitchen, I grabbed a bag of dry food from the cabinet and poured some into the cat's bowl. I started some coffee and pulled back the kitchen curtain as I waited for the coffee to percolate. Spring would soon be here, and I would need to decide what I wanted to do with the house. The house was old but had been well maintained. Right now, the yard had that neglected look, and to my surprise, the grass was tall in certain places. I had lived in apartments and town houses in Charlotte, so I wasn't the gardening type.

I poured myself a cup of coffee and headed back to the living room. It wasn't until I was midway through the last album that I stopped. I sat up from my slouched position and stared at the photo in front of me. This was what I'd been looking for. A sense of dread twisted my stomach.

The photo had been taken at some family event in Aunt C's backyard. Standing next to her was a boy who might've been twelve years old. His baseball cap was slung to the side, and his smile was just as crooked. Christopher Robinson was my cousin Leon's son and my godson. Leon was Aunt C's only child. Growing up, Leon and I had been pretty close cousins, despite the fact that he was four years older. Since we had long grown apart, I always wondered if Aunt C had put her son up to asking me to be Chris's godmother. I was flattered, but it wasn't like I kept up with my cousin.

No one could keep up with Leon. It still was a shock that last year he was fatally shot, allegedly by one of his own friends over something that no one could ever articulate. The investigation had never led to an arrest. I couldn't make the funeral, because I was in the hospital with my own injuries. At the time, Aunt C had long retired from Georgetown's school district, but she still worked occasionally as a substitute teacher and was active in church missions. After Leon's death, she stopped working completely and her health seemed to deteriorate rapidly.

I said out loud, "Chris, was that really you?" The poor kid didn't have the best male role models, but he had a praying grandmother. Aunt C used to always brag about how well Chris was doing in school. I could tell her grandson was her last hope for the men in the family.

I pulled the photo from behind the protective film and flipped it over. I recognized Aunt C's loopy handwriting. She'd written "Robinson Family Reunion, 2012" on the back. My sister and my aunt had tried to encourage me to come to the family reunions, but I had always found some excuse. I would take the time to attend a funeral. I was even a part of my sister's wedding as my own marriage crumbled. But I did not want to do the family reunion thing.

Now, as I looked at Leon's teenage son, I was realized I didn't know some of my own family, and it was my fault. This boy was my godson, but I hadn't been good about being a part of his life.

"He could be in some serious trouble," I whispered.

Then I thought about what the investigators had told me last night. How did a good boy and a good student end up hanging with gang members? I wondered. What had changed to make Chris an alleged accomplice in a convenience store robbery and a shooting? I had gotten the impression that Chris was surprised by last night's events. Like he'd been hanging around these boys just to be cool. Or had he veered that much off track since his father's death?

This was one of those times when I truly wished Aunt C was alive. She had had a heart of gold, but she hadn't played. Maybe someone needed to talk some sense into the boy. I knew Chris lived with his mother, Alecia Robinson. Alecia and I were best friends in high school. I knew losing Leon had been hard for her too.

I didn't have any time to think about my plans any further, because the doorbell rang. Someone leaned long and hard on the doorbell. I slapped the album closed, knowing that signature front door announcement meant I needed to brace myself.

CHAPTER FIVE

Thursday, 9:00 a.m.

I took a deep breath before opening the door. My younger sister, Beverly Lawson-Matthews, who was just Bev to me, had a determined look on her face, and she had come armed today. I looked down to see my sister's two daughters, Brittany and Tiffany, grinning at me through the screen door. Brittany was the oldest, at age eleven, and was blossoming into her preteen years. Tiffany was slightly overweight, but at age nine, she was almost as tall as her older sister. Both girls wore their hair in two strand twists that touched their shoulders.

As soon as I unlatched the screen door, the two girls sprang forward and wrapped their arms around my waist. I staggered backward but laughed along with the two giggling girls.

"What are y'all doing here?" I asked.

I watched my sister step into the house and close the door behind her. She turned and looked at me, not saying a word.

I said, "Why don't you girls go see if you can find Callie?" The cat wouldn't be pleased, but I sensed my sister had an agenda. She always did when she showed up unannounced. Just then I realized that I had forgotten to look at her text message from last night. Had I read it, I probably would have been warned of her arrival with the girls. I faced her after the girls ran toward the kitchen.

"It's Thursday. Is it some holiday or teacher in-service day?"

Bev shook her head. "You really don't listen, Rena. I told you the girls and I would be on spring break this week."

"Oh, okay. I guess that explains . . ." Although I doubted the boys I had seen last night had spring break activities on their mind. They had intended to commit a crime. I rubbed my hand across my head. I caught Bev studying my face. "What?" I asked her sharply.

Bev was shorter than me by about four inches. She lifted her chin and stared at me. "Are you okay?"

"I don't need you scrutinizing me."

"I just asked a simple question, Rena."

There was nothing simple about her question. She'd been on me since I had decided not to look for a neurologist while I was here in Georgetown. I had had enough of doctors in the past year.

I cooled my temper. "I'm fine. I was just looking at some old photo albums before you gals showed up." I walked back into the living room and scooped up the albums in my arms, as if they were sacred.

Bev had treated Aunt C like her aunt, and Aunt C had been equally as fond of Bev. The two women would unite when they both agreed I needed to be told a thing or two, but they weren't related by blood. Mama had married the man who would become my stepfather when I was five years old. They had had Bev about a year later. My stepfather and Aunt C never did like each other. That suited me just fine, and it explained why this house I had inherited was like a second home to me.

I often felt like my mom had married Reverend Thomas Lawson because she was lonely and was trying to fill some void my dad had left in her life. My dad had been a bit of a ladies' man, not one to really commit for long. On the other hand, Thomas was a deeply religious man, and while he provided, he was a hard man to live with sometimes. No, that was not true. Thomas was a curmudgeon, and he was one of the top reasons why I left home as quickly as I could.

I loved Bev. She was the only sister I had, but she was her daddy's daughter, and while he was no longer living, Bev seemed to have picked up where he left off. She was more subtle, though.

I placed the albums on the coffee table. "So, what brings you by today?"

"The girls wanted to see you today. I believe they have something to ask you."

"Oh?"

Behind me I heard giggling. Brittany was holding Callie. The cat didn't seem to mind that she was being carried around and was hanging across the girl's shoulder like a limp rag. Tiffany rubbed the cat's head and ears.

I sat down on the couch. "You girls want to ask me something?"

Tiffany jumped in front of me. Her eyes and her smile were bright. I couldn't help but feel the joy radiating from her. "Aunt Rena, can you help us with the Easter egg hunt?"

I glanced over at Bev, who had sat down on the couch, her eyes focused on a spot on the floor. I returned my attention to the girls. "What do you need me to do? Paint eggs?"

Brittany spoke up. "No, we don't need to do that. We have plastic eggs to fill up."

Tiffany added, "Then the eggs will be hidden, and all the kids have to find them."

I cocked my head to the side. "Well, won't you be at an unfair advantage if you know where the eggs are hidden?"

Bev responded, "They will help fill the eggs, but only grown-ups will hide the eggs."

"Sounds like fun!" It wasn't like I had anything else to do with my time. I enjoyed any time I could spend with my nieces.

As the girls continued to play with Callie, I looked at my sister. Something else was going on. She was too quiet. I expected her to be tearing into me about being in the house, still in my pajamas. Most of the morning was almost gone. I admitted to myself that I was in a funk. I was still mourning Aunt C. In other ways, I was mourning the life I had left behind in Charlotte.

My throat tightened as I opened my mouth. I swallowed and faced my sister. "How's Mama? Is she coming to the Easter egg hunt?"

Bev wouldn't look at me. She spoke softly. "I always ask her, but she usually says no."

That figures! I almost said it out loud, but I kept my mouth shut.

Bev sighed. "Mama's in trouble. Real trouble now."

I frowned. "What kind of trouble?"

She turned toward me, and that was when I saw the wetness around her dark lashes. "She needs help with the house."

I held up my hands. "Is it money? I told you I could help. I saved up money over the years. I rarely took a vacation. . . ."

"Rena!"

My sister's sharp voice ripped into me. I glanced at the girls. Both of them looked at their mother with alarm in their eyes. If Bev wanted to go off on me, I would go right back at her, though I wasn't comfortable doing this in front of the girls. What kind of examples would we be, arguing with each other?

I sensed my sister's high frustration level. "Okay. Tell me what's going on."

Bev shook her head. "You need to go see her."

I stood. "I told you I would when I'm ready." My relationship with our mama was complicated.

"She needs help. I can't do this alone."

I crossed my arms. What could I say? I'd been gone for years.

Bev jumped up from the couch. "You both are the same. Both of you are stubborn."

My cheeks grew warm as I shot a look at my sister. Now, I was trying to be nice, with the girls being here. It wasn't like I'd invited my sister over for a fight, but she knew I resented the comparison. Before I could respond, the doorbell rang.

I narrowed my eyes and said in a low voice, "Saved by the bell."

Whoever was at my door, I was grateful, because maybe it was time that my sister went her merry way. I would miss being around the girls, though. They had brightened my day.

I peeked through the peephole as the doorbell sounded again. I stepped back. My anger toward my sister had turned to something close to panic. I took a deep breath and opened the front door.

What is he doing here?

Standing on the front porch, with his baseball cap to the side and that crooked smile, was my godson. My mind wasn't playing tricks on me. As my mind flashed back to last night's shooting, I recognized the cap Chris wore.

Does he know I was at the store last night?

CHAPTER SIX

Thursday, 9:30 a.m.

I should be nominated for an Academy Award the way I opened the screen door and smiled at Chris. My sister and her girls were here, and I didn't want any trouble. "What's up, Chris? This is a surprise."

Chris grinned at me, but something about his smile was uneasy. "Hey, Rena. I hope you don't mind me stopping by."

"Of course not." I thought I should warn him I had company. "My sister, Bev, and her girls are here. You want to come in?"

He shot me an anxious look, but it lasted only for a second. Chris shook his head. "No. I just remembered Grandma liked her grass cut as soon as it started to grow. I didn't know if you wanted me to do the yard, you know, now that this is your house."

I had expected to hear some bitterness in Chris's voice. This was his grandmother's house, and I knew how much Aunt C had loved this boy. Being that he was her only grandson and her only child's son, I was sure Chris knew he was special, and he probably missed her. "That would be sweet of you, Chris. I haven't cut grass in years. I would love your help."

"Great! I will get started."

I watched as he walked around to the side of the house. Chris was a good boy. Maybe I was mistaken about who I saw last night. I surely hoped so, because I wasn't feeling good about sitting on information that could possibly help the police find Marty's killer. As soon as the investigators mentioned gangs last night, I knew that took the shooting to another level. While I was a reporter and was determined to reveal the truth, my last major story had planted seeds of fear in me.

I had prided myself on being a take-no-mess investigative reporter and hadn't really let anything stand in my way of getting a story. Even if it had meant stomping on folks to get it. This was different. This was family. Maybe after Bev and the girls left, I could talk to Chris.

"Was that Leon's son?" a voice behind me asked.

I forgot I was mad at my sister. I turned around and faced her. "Yeah, but we need to talk about why you seem bent on annoying me. Do you want me to leave and go back to Charlotte?"

Bev closed her eyes. "Of course not. I just want you to take care of yourself. Making contact with a neurologist here won't hurt."

I rolled my eyes. "Who's not listening now? I told you my doctor said they have done all they can do for me. My brain will heal over time, and I may always have short-term memory issues. I've been doing better."

I walked back through the living room to the kitchen. I heard Bev following behind me. I wanted to see what Chris was doing. As I peered out the window, I could hear Bev chattering behind me, but my own thoughts were filtering out her voice. Did Chris really just drop by to cut the grass? I wondered if his mother had sent him or if he had come by for some other reason.

"When will you go by to see Mama?"

I swung around to face my sister, who stood with her arms folded. I said, "You know I have seen Mama since I've been back."

Bev eyed me. "Yeah, when she was at my house. You haven't been to her house."

Now, this was a subject I clearly didn't want to deal with now. "Why? What does it matter?"

I watched my sister swallow and blink. "I need you to support me on something, but you need to go see Mama at her house."

Bev knew I didn't like *that* house. My intentions were never to step foot in that house again. Even though my stepfather was deceased, I just couldn't bring myself to go to that house. I had tried to get Mama to move, but she had refused.

I crossed my arms. "Is there something you're trying to tell me?"

"You have to see for yourself, Rena. I know you think I'm just being the annoying little sister here, but I need your help. I've needed your help for a while, but you had your career, and then you got hurt." She sighed, looking close to tears. "I'm glad you're back home."

Home. The word felt strangely comforting to me. I straightened my shoulders and really looked at my sister. Her long hair was pulled back in a ponytail. This was the same hairstyle she'd worn since we were girls. Her big brown eyes looked large and luminous behind her dark brown glasses. We both resembled our dads, but we had Mama's high cheekbones. I hadn't been paying attention before, but now I realized that Bev's face, though she was six years younger, looked as weary as mine.

Of course, she was a wife, a mother of two girls, a school guidance counselor, a Sunday school teacher, and whatever else she did at her church. I knew she hadn't worked for a while prior to deciding to go back to work in the local school district a few years ago.

I glanced over my shoulder to see Chris pushing the lawn mower across the yard. That kind of settled me a bit.

I sighed. "Okay, fine. I guess you're going to want me to go to church with y'all too."

Bev rolled her eyes. "It's Easter, Rena. Everyone tries to go to church at least on Easter Sunday."

I laughed. I wasn't a church person. I had missed a lot of Easter Sundays. But I was alive. God had looked out for me this past year and probably more times than I could count. That I couldn't deny.

"We got to go. You can come by the house on Friday to help us with the eggs. If you don't mind helping us hide them, we will do that early Saturday."

"How early?"

Bev touched my arm. "You will have fun." She called out to the girls as we entered the living room. Both of them had been engrossed in the photo albums. "Girls, let's go. Aunt Rena will hang out with us this weekend."

Both girls ran over to me.

Brittany asked, "Aunt Rena, why don't you have your photos on a computer?"

Tiffany said, "Yeah, like, you can put them on Instagram."

I laughed. "I don't think we want to post those photos online. Some of those need to stay private."

I walked Bev and the girls to the door. After I closed the door behind them, I walked over and picked up the photo albums from the coffee table. The girls did have a good idea. I should take some time to digitize some of the photos. These were the only copies of many of these photos, especially the ones with Dad and Aunt C.

I placed the albums back on the shelf and started to walk toward the kitchen. Maybe Chris needed something to drink. I wanted to talk to him about last night, although I wasn't sure how to broach the subject.

"Hey, godson, were you with a gang last night? Did you know you could be an accomplice to an armed robbery and murder?" I said silently.

That would break his mom's heart, especially after what his dad put Alecia through during their marriage. Chris might be a good kid, but his dad, Leon, was no role model. While I didn't keep in touch with Aunt C the way I should have, I was aware of how heartbroken my aunt had been over her son's demise.

The front doorbell rang again just as I reached the back door. I looked through the window, but I didn't see Chris. Had he finished mowing the lawn already? I had talked to Bev for a while, and the backyard wasn't huge. Still, he had the front yard to do too.

I walked back toward the front of the house, thinking maybe Chris had experienced some trouble when he started mowing the front yard. I swung open the door and then gasped.

The two men at my front door were certainly a surprise. As I looked through the screen door, my thoughts turned frantically to Chris's whereabouts.

CHAPTER SEVEN

Thursday, 10:00 a.m.

I was really starting to grow weary of people showing up at my front door today. It was like something out of the twilight zone. It was enough to make me run away, but of course, wasn't that the whole reason I had returned to this place? To run away from the life I had known for years, a life that had suddenly crumbled around me?

I opened the screen door. "What can I do to help the city of Georgetown's finest?"

Investigator Baldwin smiled. "We were hoping we could talk to you today." I had to admit I liked the tall, lanky man. His Southern twang was low and comforting.

I looked over at Investigator Moses. He stared at me as if I had something growing on my face. I got the impression that Moses played the bad cop part, while Baldwin was the good cop. *Too bad.* Moses could really be a decent-looking guy if he got rid of the scowl. A little too muscular for my taste, though. I imagined he lived at the gym when he wasn't harassing someone like me.

I invited the two men to come inside and took a quick glance around the front yard, searching for signs of my godson. I closed the door, and both investigators followed me into my living room.

I asked, "Can I get either of you something to drink?"

Baldwin responded, "No thanks."

Not so with Moses. He responded, "I would love something to drink."

I had figured he would say that. I had a feeling he wanted to snoop too. Why, I didn't know.

At the moment, however, I needed to know if Chris was outside. I needed to question him, and the cops being here wasn't helping. I walked into the kitchen and then reached inside the fridge to grab a bottle of water. Before I headed back to the living room, I peered out the window. The grass appeared to be cut, but there were no signs of Chris or the lawn mower. I wondered if the police car, though unmarked, had run Chris off.

I shook my head. This wasn't good. I had doubted my memory, but now the boy was acting way too suspicious. I quickly headed back to the living room, anxious about what the investigators would ask me.

Both men were standing where I had left them. Baldwin seemed to be transfixed by a painting behind the couch, while Moses didn't hide his interest in the bookshelves behind him. I handed him the bottled water.

"Thanks," he said.

I stretched my hand toward the chairs. "Shall we sit down, although I don't know how much help I will be today?" Aunt C's face flashed in my mind. My aunt had fiercely protected the males in the family. My dad. Her only son. If Aunt C was looking down from heaven, had she witnessed what her grandson had got into last night? If she had, I needed her to whisper a word to God to help me right now. I wasn't a praying woman, but right now I wished I had the faith other women in my family seemed to find so easily.

Moses eyed me like he was trying to see through me. "If you don't mind, can we go over the events from the shooting last night?"

I kind of did mind. I had replayed last night's shooting too many times. I wanted to go back to how things were before, and I mean way before last night. Despite the protests in my mind, I restated what I had seen at the store to the investigators. After I finished, I hoped they would leave.

Moses continued to stare at me. I stared back, this time not hiding my annoyance. "Are we finished? That's all I have for you gentlemen."

I turned my attention to Baldwin, who seemed to have more tact than his partner. The man was scribbling in his notebook. Finally, he looked up and smiled. "We appreciate your time. Maybe you wouldn't mind looking at some photos or working with a sketch artist?"

Why did it feel like the investigators were convinced that I wasn't telling them all that I knew? Most eyewitnesses weren't helpful and didn't remember what they had seen. People weren't usually paying attention to their surroundings. I was a bit different from the ordinary person. I didn't miss details, or at least I used to not miss details.

Was it that obvious that I wasn't telling the whole truth? I couldn't exactly tell them what I wasn't sure I saw. The reporter part of me knew I needed to have my facts in order.

I narrowed my eyes. "I don't think I can help you. I didn't see any of the boys' faces clearly." *That isn't a lie.* At least that was what I told myself. I wondered whether Chris was still outside. If he decided to knock on the front door, I wasn't sure if I could hold it together.

Then a sudden thought jolted me. If Marty was able to set off the alarm system, surely the store had a video surveillance camera. What if these investigators already had their evidence? I had to ask about a camera. "I imagine you have footage from the store's camera," I said. "Can't you get what you need from that source?"

The investigators exchanged glances.

Moses responded first. "We're looking at the surveillance camera for clues."

I narrowed my eyes. "So you will be releasing images for the media?"

Moses snorted. "Of course. We want to identify these perps. A man died last night."

Baldwin stood and reached into his pocket. He handed me a card. "Ms. Manchester, if you do recall anything, please contact us."

"I have told you all that I recall." I needed Baldwin and Moses to be on their way, like, now.

After I opened the front door for the investigators and they stepped outside, I latched the screen door closed and watched the men walk to their unmarked car and climb inside. As soon as they pulled off, I shut the front door and sprinted to the back door. I threw open the door and ran into the yard. The doors to the shed were open. I crossed the yard, inhaling the scent of freshly cut grass.

The lawn mower had been pushed into the shed. I could see grass clippings around the edges of the mower. I looked down and saw footprints in the mud around the shed. They were similar to a pattern commonly found on sneakers. Chris had been wearing sneakers. I looked at the footprints and saw that they went up to the side of the house. I followed the prints up to the bushes that lined one corner of the house. The footprints stopped there. I looked up toward the street.

Tears flooded my eyes. Chris had got spooked by the investigators. I needed to find my godson. Aunt C would have wanted me to help him. It was the least I could do after all these years. I felt almost like I owed her.

CHAPTER EIGHT

Thursday, 12:30 p.m.

It took me some time to get myself together, but I knew what I had to do. I drove my car through streets that were only slightly familiar. So much had changed over the years. As I passed the elementary school where my aunt had worked for most of her life, I started to get my bearings a bit more. When I found the house I was searching for, I slowed down and turned into the driveway. It was an older brick home with a carport. A black Audi was positioned behind what appeared to be an older white Chevy pickup truck.

I parked beside the truck and shut off the engine. I recognized the truck as a vehicle Leon had owned. I had arrived at Chris's home unsure of what I was doing there. I gripped the steering wheel for a few moments. The boy technically hadn't done anything. Maybe he hadn't known what was going to happen. Still, he would be considered an accomplice. *Would he snitch on his friends?*

If he did cooperate with law enforcement, Chris might get some type of deal or leniency for not having a prior record. It was really doubtful that Chris would be a snitch. His appearance at my house and then his disappearance when the investigators arrived made me think he was scared. Or was he following the orders of someone who had seen that I, too, was there at the convenience store at the time the crime was committed? I had a feeling that if my sister hadn't been at the house and if the investigators hadn't arrived, Chris would have asked me what I knew about the robbery and shooting.

I stepped out of the car and walked up the driveway, toward the front door. Not seeing a doorbell button, I tapped lightly on the door. When there was no answer, I banged my knuckles harder on the door's wooden frame.

A husky female voice answered from behind the door a few moments later. "Hello. Who is it?"

I answered back, "Serena." Then I thought for a split second and added, "I mean, Rena."

The door opened, and Alecia Robinson stared at me through the screen door. At first, I didn't think she would open the screen door, but finally she did. There was a smile on her face, but her eyes were red, as if she'd been crying. She stared at me. "It's good to see you, Rena. I haven't seen you since . . ."

"Aunt C's funeral," I said, finishing her sentence.

"I'm surprised you're still here in town."

"You and me both."

"Come in." Alecia stepped to the side to let me through.

I stepped inside the home, feeling its warmth. My eyes were drawn to the family photos that hung on the dark gold wall in the foyer. I noticed that most of the photos were of Chris at various ages. There was one photo of Leon that reminded me of my dad. They had the same gorgeous eyes that could convince a woman to do something foolish.

I turned around to face Alecia, who was definitely no fool. Alecia and I had been best friends from middle school until high school. She was a tough girl who still looked as athletic as she had when she played basketball. Chris had gotten his height from both sides of the family.

Interestingly, Alecia hadn't really had a boyfriend until she hooked up with my cousin. Leon was older, but Alecia had fallen hard for him, and he had seemed drawn to her, even though there had been other women clamoring for his attention.

"What brings you by, Rena?" Alecia asked.

Before I could respond, a familiar male voice boomed from the other room. "There's no telling with Rena."

I know my eyes widened from the shock of hearing Trey's voice. I whirled around to watch as he came from the room, which appeared to be the living room. It was hard for me to believe I was seeing him again after just running into him last night at the Huddle House.

He looked even more handsome in the daylight that was pouring through the hall window and playing across his face.

"Sorry to disturb your conversation." I sputtered. "I didn't know you had company."

Alecia waved her hand. "Girl, you know Trey is hardly company."

I knew Alecia was right. Trey was Alecia's cousin, and they were really close as kids, looking out for each other like a brother and a sister. In fact, we were all quite the trio when we were in school. It weighed heavily on me how much I had let go of people who were really important to me at one time. My focus had been to get out of this town, and looking back hadn't been an option.

Trey grinned, showing his pearly whites for a few seconds, before shifting his gaze toward Alecia. His eyes seemed to indicate that he was concerned.

I cleared my throat, wanting to focus on my reason for coming by. "Is Chris around?"

Alecia folded her arms. She looked over at Trey and then back at me. "Why are you asking?" Her words were sharp and accusatory.

I shrugged, still trying to be appear nonchalant, despite the churning in my stomach. "He came by earlier to cut the grass. I assume he was paid in the past by Aunt C, but he took off before I could pay him."

Alecia frowned. "He cut your grass, and you didn't ask him to?"

"That's right. I appreciate it too. I guess he remembered Aunt C used to ask him to cut the grass this time of year. I imagine he misses her." I stopped rambling, realizing the room was awfully quiet. Trey was watching Alecia, who suddenly seemed to be preoccupied with the floor.

What am I missing here? Did they already know about Chris's involvement in last night's armed robbery and shooting? Would Chris tell his mother about it? The reporter side of me decided to stir the pot a bit. "Did you hear about the robbery last night?"

Alecia whipped her head up and stared at me. She finally answered, "More than a robbery. Marty was killed."

"This being a small town, I guess you knew him," I said.

Alecia narrowed her eyes. "Oh, I knew Marty, all right. He used to hang with Chris's father. I used to tell Leon that Marty and that whole crowd were just bad news. He didn't listen. Marty may have gotten what he deserved." Alecia choked out that last word and then walked into the next room, leaving me standing in the foyer with Trey.

I knew Leon had been dead for almost a year, but given the way Alecia had just reacted, it was like my cousin had been shot last night instead of Marty. Leon was the love her life, but I wasn't expecting her to react the way she had when the subject of Marty came up. I turned to Trey and asked, "Did I come at a bad time, or did I just get the impression that Alecia doesn't care about Marty's shooting?"

Trey looked back and then stepped closer to me. I inhaled. *This man smells so good!* I clutched my hands into fists in a futile attempt not to focus on his closeness.

Trey's eyes were warm and familiar. "You may not know this, but certain people still think Marty was responsible for your cousin's death."

"What? How? I mean, I heard Leon was shot over some squabble with someone close, but I never did get the details."

"I don't know any of the details, either. There have been a lot of rumors, and those rumors always seem to point toward Marty being the one who pulled the trigger."

I couldn't imagine that the man who had been shot last night was the person responsible for Leon's death. He had seemed, well, like a sweet man, although I had sensed that he could be tough. Of course, people's personality could change in a heartbeat when they had a gun in their hand.

"Why wasn't he arrested? Did the police bring Marty in to be questioned?" I asked.

"Yes. Marty was questioned, but he must have had a solid alibi. Me, I never bought that Marty killed Leon. Alecia and I have disagreed many times, but Leon and Marty were really tight friends. They had disagreements, but what friends *always* get along?"

I had been gone a long time, and I didn't remember Marty. Then again, Leon was older than me, so I probably didn't know most of the people my cousin had known.

I felt woozy as the last image I had of Marty appeared in my mind. I felt my body sway.

Trey reached out and grabbed my arm. "Rena, are you okay?"

"Yes. Sorry." I touched my forehead, as if I had a headache. "Stupid head injury."

"Maybe you should sit down."

The concern in Trey's eyes made me feel even more unsteady on my feet. I looked away. "No, it looks like Alecia probably needs to be alone and I came at a bad time."

"You don't need to be driving, and believe me, Alecia could use your company. Go ahead and talk to her. I'm sure you both have a lot to catch up on. Do me a favor? Tell her I needed to go, but I will check on her later."

I didn't realize Trey had been holding my arm until he took his hand away. I grabbed my arm where he had just touched it and watched him walk out the front door. He closed the door softly behind him.

That man really hadn't changed. My cheeks were burning in a way I hadn't felt in a long time. There weren't too many men in my life who left me feeling like I was sixteen all over again. *Get it together, Rena!* I turned in the direction of the room to which Alecia had retreated. I had come here on a mission.

Now I was bit more intrigued about Marty. I wished I had had a view of the shooting from the front of the store. It seemed silly to consider it, but I wondered if what I had witnessed last night was really just an armed robbery. The boy with the red jacket had worn shades. It had been pitch black outside. He had purposely hidden his identity, whereas the other boys had not. I wondered if the boy with the hoodie had even known what was about to go down.

Something about last night's shooting had felt personal, but I hadn't been thinking in that direction, because Chris was involved. By now I realized that Marty had *anticipated* that something was going to happen.

CHAPTER NINE

Thursday, 12:45 p.m.

I stood in the doorway and looked on as Alecia wiped tears from her face with a crumpled tissue. I wasn't really good at dealing with another person's emotions. I didn't know how to deal with my own. Alecia was a true friend and family. I hadn't noticed before, but she was wearing scrubs. Alecia had always wanted to be a nurse. She must have just finished a shift at the hospital. I did know from conversations with Aunt C that Alecia had supported the household when Leon was unemployed.

It had been a bit awkward when Alecia was fifteen and was hanging around then nineteen-year-old Leon. I remembered that Aunt C hadn't approved at all. In his own way, Leon had managed to stay a gentleman, and he had asked Alecia to marry him. Chris came along a bit later, after Alecia had had at least two miscarriages that I knew of.

I owed it to her to be a friend right now, given all the years I'd been absent. So I took a deep breath and stepped into the room as if I were walking on an unsteady surface. The room looked more like a family room than a living room. Alecia was sitting on the couch with video game consoles scattered around her feet and on the wooden coffee table. A large television was across from the couch. This was definitely a teenage boy's zone.

Alecia turned toward me, and I stopped, as if I'd run into some invisible force field. "I'm sorry. If this is a bad time, I can go," I said.

"No." Alecia shook her head. "I'm sorry you have to see me when I'm a mess."

I snorted. "Girl, I've been a mess the past year. I'm starting to think maybe my whole life has been nothing but a mess."

Alecia laughed. "Girl, you're still a trip,"

I had always been good for a laugh. Laughter was indeed good for the soul, but this wasn't really the time for humor. "Alecia, what's wrong? I know I'm probably the last person you want to confide in. I left here years ago, and I kind of feel like a stranger."

"Well, you haven't changed a bit. You did the right thing for you, Rena. Nobody can blame you for wanting to leave and make something of yourself. Everybody knew you had big aspirations and you were miserable here."

"Really? Everybody knew that?" *I guess I haven't done a good job of covering up my life.*

"You were smart and funny, and always in trouble with your stepfather. Girl, Reverend Lawson just didn't see your potential."

"No, my stepfather saw me as a heathen. Oh yeah, and I was my dad's child." I changed my voice to the deep voice Reverend Lawson would use when he was really on a rampage. "That no-good Dallas Robinson's daughter." I swallowed as tears came to my eyes. They were unexpected. I drew in a sharp breath. There it was, right there. That part of me that I kept buried.

The young girl who had been treated like she was the devil herself. Why? Because I was my dad's child. I had never understood. I cleared my throat in an effort to move past the pain, which I didn't really want to deal with at the moment. "Wow! Sorry about that."

Alecia eyed me. "No need to say sorry. I bet it felt good to say that out loud."

I'm not so sure. I needed to focus on my mission. I stepped around the coffee table and sat on the other end of the couch. "Look, I came over here to pay Chris." I dug in my jeans pocket and pulled out the bills I had stuffed in it prior to leaving the house. "How much? Twenty dollars? Forty dollars . . . ?"

"Oh, Lord, no. Your aunt didn't pay Chris to do her yard work. He's been mowing her grass since he was eleven. It was her way of helping me discipline him. His freshman year has been so turbulent, I'm really surprised he volunteered. I can't get him to do anything around the house."

"Well, maybe he came over today as a way to honor his grandmother." I wasn't really sure about that, but Alecia seemed to need encouragement.

"I guess. I should be grateful, because lately I haven't recognized my son." Alecia's voice caught, and she struggled to continue. "He was an honor student all the way through middle school. After Leon's death, Chris started going downhill, and then he became more out of control after his grandmother was taken to the hospital last fall."

"When she had the stroke."

"Yes, it was the first stroke. She seemed to be doing okay. The whole time she was in the hospital, she kept asking about Chris. He was her heart. You know, losing Leon broke her heart. Having his son around meant the world to her."

I shook my head. "I know. I probably broke her heart too." I had wanted to be there for Aunt C last fall, but I had been struggling with what to do about my career and my life.

"Rena, she was so proud of you. Maybe she never told you, because, you know, Aunt C was not big on showing affection, but she talked about her Rena, the big-time city reporter, all the time. You were her brother's child, and Chris was her son's child. You both were her connection to the two men she loved so dearly and lost."

I knew Aunt C had certainly been in my corner when no one else had cared. What would she do about Chris if she were here? I was starting to get the impression that Chris was in a lot more trouble than anyone realized. "Is Chris running around with friends who may not be good for him? You know, peers can have a lot to do with changes in a young person."

Alecia started to get up off the couch, but then she sank back down and folded her arms. "There are some boys he hangs with a lot now. I've tried grounding him to keep him away, but he is hardheaded. That's why I called Trey. I feel like I need a man to help me get through to Chris, since he's not listening to me."

I felt queasy in my stomach. I wanted to blurt out what I had seen last night, but telling Alecia that her son might have been involved in a convenience store robbery gone very wrong didn't feel right. Especially with her animosity toward Marty. I tried convincing myself I had no proof yet that it had been Chris in the store. But I also couldn't deny that the boy had seemed spooked by the investigators showing up at my house earlier. Another thought haunted me. What would the investigators find on that store camera footage?

I prodded Alecia. "Do you know where I can find Chris now?"

"I told you, you don't need to pay him. He doesn't need any cash on him, Rena."

"I just want to connect with him. He is my godson. You know, in Charlotte I saw a lot as a reporter. Maybe I can talk to him."

"Well, it's spring break this week. He may be over at Joseph Jenkins's house. Joseph is actually a good kid, and they have been friends since they were little. I can't guarantee he's there, because Chris will tell me anything to get me off his back. It's a start."

Jenkins? I knew some Jenkinses. I sure hoped this wasn't someone else I didn't want to run into. "Good. Just let me know where to find Joseph's house."

Alecia stared at me.

"What? I'm not going to give him the money."

"I'm just trying to wrap my head around you doing this. It's been a long time . . . almost like old times with you, me, and Trey. I'm grateful to have you and Trey to help. Speaking of . . ." Alecia grinned. "I have always meant to ask you. Why did you marry Benny, Trey's half brother?"

Talk about being blindsided. "Where did that question come from?"

"I noticed how Trey lit up when he saw it was you at the door."

I shook my head. "I'm sure you're mistaken. You, of all people, know I have always been Trey's buddy. You know, the one who he could get in trouble with and who would usually take the blame. There has never been anything between us."

Alecia arched her right eyebrow, as if she didn't believe me. "Never?"

I wasn't about to admit I'd spent most of my teenage years smitten by Trey, always conscious whenever I saw him with another female that I was no more than a "sister" in his eyes. I had never let Alecia know my true feelings for fear that she would betray me and tell Trey. I would be horrified if that happened.

I shrugged. "Really, we're like brother and sister. Nothing more."

Alecia crossed her arms and grinned. "Well, you sure are protesting enough, and I'm wondering why. You're forgetting I remember the past, and I had the opportunity to see how both you and Trey responded to each other. Brother and sister. Yeah, right!"

Okay, it's time to go. I stood and shoved my hands in my jeans pockets. I narrowed my eyes. "How about giving me those directions to Joseph's house?"

Despite my obvious annoyance, Alecia kept the big grin plastered on her face in place as she reached for a notepad and a pen on the cluttered coffee table in front of us. After she scratched out a map, Alecia tore the paper from the notepad and handed it to me. "You should connect with Trey. He isn't with anyone now. The timing seems perfect to me."

I grabbed the paper and pointed at Alecia. "I don't need the matchmaking. Trey seems to continue to like being the savior, and I don't need to be saved."

Alecia scowled. "*Savior.* I wouldn't say that. He's a good man with a good heart. He's been through a lot over the years, but you won't find a more stable man."

Stability. I swallowed, thinking I could sure use that type of man in my life. I wasn't sure why, after all this time, Alecia's meddling would even bother me. But she was right; Trey had always been a good man. In fact, he had always been my standard. I'd been in love, or in what I had thought was love, only to have it snatched away time after time. No other man had ever measured up to the one man I could never call mine.

CHAPTER TEN

Thursday, 1:30 p.m.

Joseph's house was only a few blocks away. From the way Alecia had described Joseph, I liked him already. After last night, I certainly hoped Chris had chosen to keep his distance from his crime-chasing friends. I rang the doorbell several times. Finally, a boy opened the door.

I asked, "Is Joseph here?"

The boy appeared to be puzzled. "I'm Joseph."

"Oh." I expected Joseph to be a lot taller since he was fourteen years old. Maybe puberty was coming a bit late for him, or maybe my godson was extra tall for his age. "You're Chris's friend. His mom told me I might be able to find him here."

The boy pointed his thumb over his shoulder. "Yeah, he's here."

As we approached one of the rooms near the back of the house, the sound of crashes and explosions grew louder, and I knew the boys were watching a movie or playing a video game. I let out a sigh of relief when I saw Chris glued to a monitor, frantically pressing buttons on the black console in his hands. He wasn't wearing the baseball cap, and he looked younger than he did when I saw him earlier in the day.

I called out to him. "Chris?"

Chris glanced over at me. A look passed over his face. He jumped up and dropped the game console on the floor.

Seeing that he looked like he was going to flee, I held up my hand. "Wait. I just wanted to say thank you."

Behind me, Joseph asked, "Man, what's wrong with you? Do you know this lady?"

I stared at Chris, who seemed to be sweating.

Finally, he answered, "Yeah, I know her."

"Can I talk to you a minute?" I nodded at the television monitor. "I will let you get back to your game."

"Sure." Chris grabbed his cap, which was sitting on the table.

I peered back at Joseph, who looked unsure about whether or not he should have let me in the house. I patted him on the shoulder. "He will be right back."

Chris walked to the other side of the room, and I followed. We went through the kitchen and out a back door.

He placed the cap back on his head once we got outside and turned to look at me defiantly, his eyes hooded under the cap. He stated in a low voice, "I know why you're here."

"Do you?"

Chris glared at me. "You were there . . . last night."

My heart sank. *Oh no!* "I didn't see anything. As far as I could tell, you didn't do anything wrong, Chris."

Chris looked around. "No, I didn't. I had no idea what was going to happen. I thought we were just going to the store."

That explained why Chris had walked down the aisle. He had just gone hunting for something to buy. Still, he was in a whole lot of trouble either way.

I crossed my arms. "A man died."

Chris's hardened face crumpled as despair overtook him. His spoke hoarsely. "I know that. I didn't do it."

"But you know who else was there." I stepped closer. "Chris, who had the gun?"

Chris shook his head and looked back toward the kitchen door. "Keep your voice down. I won't tell you. I'm not a snitch."

That was a problem. I'd seen this before, while working on countless stories: when people were intimidated and fearful, they often chose not share what they had witnessed. I wasn't any better. The cops had questioned me twice. Something in me wanted to protect the godson I barely knew, but deep down the investigative reporter in me, the one hungry to seek justice, couldn't let what had happened stay locked in my mind.

Chris stared at me, looking more like a little boy. "What did you tell those cops?"

I shook my head. "Nothing. I told you I didn't see anything."

"Good! You can't say anything, or someone else will get hurt."

I was curious. "How did you know they were cops?"

Chris grimaced. "I know the black cop."

"So you saw them and ran. Why did you really come to my house?"

Suddenly the "little" boy's face hardened. Chris bit his lip, as though he was determined not to say anything else.

This was worrying me. Because he had flat out confessed that he was there, and also because he knew I had recognized him. He had come by the house to question me and to make sure I didn't get him in trouble. If Bev and the girls hadn't been at my house, I wondered if he would have even offered to mow the grass. This was a smart kid. Dumb in a way, but definitely smart.

I made a decision I hoped I would not regret. I hoped he wouldn't totally shut me out. "Look, I know how this goes, Chris. I was a reporter in Charlotte for many years. I know what's at stake here. I know you're scared. Let's just keep calm. You don't want to appear like you are about to have a nervous breakdown around people. You know what I mean?"

Chris's shoulders dropped slightly, but he still looked like he wanted to explode.

"You have to do something for me."

He narrowed his eyes. "What?"

"If you want to be clean and not draw attention to yourself, you need to act clean. That means keep your distance from these guys. Like you're doing today. You haven't spoken to them, have you?"

Chris stuttered, "I—I . . ."

Now I was a bit concerned, and I stared at him. "Who else knows I was there?"

Chris shook his head. "They don't know what I know."

He's protecting me too. That was nice, but scary. Chris knew the other two boys, especially the boy who was the shooter. That was making me really uncomfortable. I felt like we should go to the police. I also didn't like the fact that Alecia was not aware of what had happened.

I jabbed my finger at him. "Does your mother know?"

Chris looked back at me; his defiant eyes reminded me of my cousin Leon's eyes. I stared him down. I could never let anyone win a staring match.

He looked away and pushed his cap up a bit off his forehead. "I can't tell her, but she knows something is wrong. Look, I have been laying low."

"Good. The best thing is to keep your distance, but you may want to let your mom know before she finds out another way."

There was still the store camera. If the police handed images recorded during the robbery over to the media, someone else might identify Chris. His mother would be blindsided by Chris's involvement, even though she clearly wasn't a fan of the victim, Marty. Our best hope was that those camera images, if retrieved, would turn out to be grainy; and the people in them, unrecognizable. That those images wouldn't help the police catch Marty's killer.

Chris swallowed and stuffed his hands in his jeans pockets. "I feel bad about that guy, but I know a lot of people didn't like him."

Remembering what Trey had said earlier, I eyed Chris. "Marty? He was friends with your dad, right?"

He shrugged, "I think so. My mom didn't like him."

I should have asked Alecia some more questions about Marty. I didn't feel right about this connection between Marty and my cousin. It was one of those connections that could be manipulated and turned into a possible motive for murder in a court case, but I wasn't trying to let my mind go in that direction. "Don't worry. We will figure this out."

I followed Chris back inside. Joseph looked at Chris as he sat back down on the couch. Then he looked at me, curiosity in his eyes.

I winked at Joseph and said, "I will let myself out. You guys have fun."

After I got back into my car, a wave of nausea engulfed me. *What is wrong with me?* Did I think Chris could wean himself off the riffraff who had committed murder? Chris would always have threats over his head. His mother needed to know what had happened so that she could make a decision about the course of action for her own son.

What bothered me more at that moment was the image in my head of Marty lying in his own pool of blood. Alecia didn't seem to care that her husband's friend had been murdered. Why should she? Leon's murder was unsolved. Would I be concerned about Marty receiving justice if he was possibly responsible for my husband's death?

It wasn't like me to *not* stick my nose where it didn't belong, and I was becoming more convinced that there was more to last night's incident. The more I thought about it, the more I realized that the repercussions of that murder could affect my family. When I'd arrived at the store last night, I had been almost sure that Marty was expecting trouble. I wasn't buying the theory I floated past myself that Marty had been expecting a group of adolescents, one of whom had a deadly weapon in his possession.

I knew Marty didn't have to die. Probably neither did my cousin Leon.

CHAPTER ELEVEN

Thursday, 11:00 p.m.

I watched the six o'clock news and then flipped through channel after channel on cable until the eleven o'clock news came on. Even though the convenience store robbery and shooting were at the top of the news hour, no footage from the surveillance camera inside the store was shown. The police must not have been able to pull any footage from the camera. Or were they purposely not releasing the footage to the media?

The blond news anchor reported, "Three unidentified young men were said to have entered Supermart on late Sunday evening. The owner, Martin Davis, better known as Marty in the community, died from a gunshot wound to the head. Police are still seeking to identify the young men involved."

I noted that the people who were interviewed on camera seemed to love Marty. Many talked about what a loss the community had suffered with his death. There were a few flowers and candles outside the store. Where were the people who didn't like Marty? He was the victim, but I wanted to know more about the other sides to Marty. If he and Leon were such good friends, why was Marty the first one the police looked at when they were investigating Leon's shooting?

I turned in soon after the eleven o'clock news. Sleep came in fits. I finally gave up, sat up in the bed, and stared at the clock. It was three o' clock in the morning, an unnatural time to climb out of bed. So I lay back down, my thoughts on my cousin Leon. He would not want this for his son.

I remembered the day he called me to ask me to be Christopher's godmother. I was truly flattered. I was still married to Benny then, but by that time we had grown apart as a couple. Benny wanted kids, and I wasn't ready, despite already being close to thirty. It seemed almost ironic to me how quickly I accepted the godmother role over being a mother.

Now I was no longer obsessed with getting a story. For the first time in about a year, I felt like I had some purpose. *Is that possible for me?* In the quietness of the room, I called out to God, something I had done more often than I would ever admit to anyone, especially my sister. I was not the religious type, but in the past year I had yearned for something bigger than myself. I wanted to be whole again. Most of the time I wondered if I ever really had been a whole person.

My voice cracked as I spoke. "God, are you listening? It's me again. I just want you to know, I want to do what's right. Please protect Chris from harm. He is the sole male left in the family, and I know Aunt C and his mother have big dreams for him. I want justice for my cousin Leon and for this man who was his friend. Marty didn't have to die. That boy, whoever he is . . . please let the police find him."

After uttering that prayer, I fell back to sleep.

I awoke at eight o'clock on Friday morning, feeling rested, which was pretty unusual. I was feeling so good, I decided to leave the house and head out for breakfast. I found myself at the Huddle House again, which was fine, because I wanted to find out what the locals were talking about and how people really felt about Marty. I wasn't trying to find something negative about the victim, which was what a good defense lawyer would try to do, but I certainly wanted to know what events in the past could come back to haunt my godson and my family.

I was seated at the same table I had occupied two nights ago, after the shooting, but I didn't see Iris. I was served by an older woman this time. I didn't recognize her, but she seemed to know me.

"You're Claudia's niece, aren't you?"

I raised my eyebrows. "Yes. How did you know?"

"Oh, sugar, I remember you when you were this high." The stout woman held her puffy hand at her waist. "Your aunt and I used to work together on many missionary programs. She would bring you with her. I remember that sulking face sitting on the pew. Your aunt would ask you to come help pack the baskets."

I chuckled. "Wow. That's a blast from the past." I did remember enjoying going to church with Aunt C. It was a much better experience than the Sundays I had to suffer through when was my stepfather was in the pulpit.

I looked at the name tag on the older woman's blouse. "Margaret, I guess you knew my cousin Leon."

"Oh yeah. That boy was a handful, but Claudia would take up for him and defend him. I felt so awful when he got shot. Your aunt just about had a breakdown. We prayed over her. It was so sad, because she prayed and did so much for others in the community."

I shook my head. "I know." I had spent many nights on the phone with Aunt C. After Leon's death, I could tell that the joy that she had often brought to our late-night conversations had left her. She was never quite the same after that. "It's a shame they never found whoever is responsible for shooting Leon. Sounds like the cops are now having trouble identifying who shot Marty." I studied Margaret's face for her reaction to my statement.

Margaret's eyes were already large, but they seemed to widen behind her wire-framed bifocals. She opened her mouth, but no words came out. Finally, she spoke, her voice barely above a whisper. "Lots of people thought Marty killed Leon."

I leaned forward, curious as to why she felt the need to lower her voice. "Why? He wasn't arrested."

Margaret straightened her shoulders and tapped the pencil on the order pad she had in her hand. "Let me get these customers over here. I will come back with some more coffee. I really shouldn't be talking right now."

"Sure. I will be here." I had no intention of leaving now.

After downing a few cups of coffee and eating a hearty plate of scrambled eggs, toast, and grits, I waited until Margaret returned to my table and sat down.

She plopped down in the seat across for me. "I have a bit of a break now."

"Good." I leaned forward in the seat. "I get the sense that something happened between Leon and Marty."

"Yes. They had an argument. It was loud, and I believe they fought, like, physically . . . exchanged punches. A lot of people saw it."

"When? And what was the fight about?"

Margaret shrugged. "Well, I didn't see it, but I know the fight happened over at Leon's house. Marty showed up, accusing him of something. I heard it could have been about a woman, but I never believed that. Alecia had always been Leon's girl. Some people think Leon took something from Marty. The police broke them up. While they were taking them away, Marty said he would kill Leon. Everybody heard him."

I frowned. "So, there were many witnesses who heard Marty threaten Leon?"

"Oh yeah. There was some kind of party going on. It might have been Chris's birthday party. Such a shame.

You know, a few days later they found Leon, shot in the chest."

"The cops talked to Marty?"

"Oh yeah, but he had an alibi. Claudia was so upset. I had never seen your aunt that angry before. She just knew Marty had something to do with Leon's death. She had never liked the man."

This wasn't good, another member of the family who didn't like Marty. I wondered out loud. "What about the gun? Maybe the crime couldn't be traced back to Marty, because the cops never found the gun."

Margaret shook her head. "I don't know about all that, honey. I guess you're right. If they did find something to connect Marty to the crime, he would have been arrested. Look, I need to get back. My break is about over, and my boss is giving me the eye now."

"Sure. Thanks for sitting down to talk to me."

Margaret patted my hand. "No problem, sugar. Don't be a stranger. I look forward to talking to you again, you hear?"

"Yes, ma'am." I grinned, thinking how easy it was to slip back into the habits I'd had as a young girl. I didn't remember the last time I referred to someone as "ma'am" instead of using their name.

I gulped down the rest of my coffee, which had grown cold, but I needed the caffeine. The little bit of rest I had had seemed short-lived now. I paid my bill and left a large tip on the table for Margaret. She deserved it because she had got my juices flowing.

As I headed out to my car, something made me turn around to stare back into the restaurant. A deep chocolate, bald man was sitting in the corner, about two tables behind where I had sat. He was looking out the window at me. I turned away and opened my car door. How long had he been there? Was he listening to my conversation with Margaret? I wondered.

I climbed inside the car and closed the door. I glanced back up at the man. He was no longer looking at me. Maybe I was just being paranoid. Still, I noted his facial features. I wasn't taking any chances, even if I didn't understand why I was feeling alarmed. Just two days ago I had experienced a similar sense of foreboding, and a man was shot less than ten minutes later.

CHAPTER TWELVE

Friday, 5:00 p.m.

After a much-needed nap, I'd shaken off the strange feelings that I had about the man I had seen earlier at the Huddle House. It was Good Friday, and I was supposed to be at Bev's house an hour ago. Since I was running late, she told me to meet her and the girls at the church. I hadn't known that was part of the plan. I had thought all the festivities would be at Bev's house. If this was Bev's subtle way of getting me to church, I was not amused. Both Brittany and Tiffany had texted me reminders about helping with the Easter eggs, so I couldn't back out. Besides, I was excited about hanging out with my nieces, so if I needed to hang out at church, I would survive.

I had checked on Chris and he was laying low, as promised. I still felt bad about not letting his mother know what had happened, but I wanted Chris to be the one to tell her. There were some days when I regretted not being a mother. But I had seen so much in my line of work, I didn't know how much good I would be to a kid. Chris was a good kid, and I had decided that if there was some way to help him out this mess, I would do whatever was necessary.

I was grateful, but a bit suspicious, that neither of the investigators had called me back with more questions about the convenience store shooting. I'd passed by the store's parking lot a few times since that night. The store was open each time I'd gone by, but no one was in the parking lot. It'd been two days, and still no images from the store's camera were being displayed by the media. I wondered if Marty hadn't cared about keeping his surveillance camera in working condition. Then I remembered his nervousness before the shooting. Marty had struck me as a cautious man.

Didn't Chris say he knew Moses? Surely, the investigator would have recognized Chris at the scene. I shut my thoughts down, because thinking about that man elevated my blood pressure. Besides, I felt like today I just needed to breathe and enjoy my nieces on Good Friday.

I arrived at the Zion Baptist Church and maneuvered my car into an open parking space. I heard children running and shouting nearby as I walked up to the church's side entrance. Bev didn't exactly tell me where to meet up, so I wandered down the hallway, following the sound of voices. One of the voices sounded familiar. I decided to poke my head in an office. There in the flesh was Trey, and he was standing next to a woman. The woman was standing with her hand on her hip and was looking up adoringly at Trey, while he seemed to be explaining whatever they were looking at on the desk.

I went from feeling pretty good to grumpy in, like, two seconds and decided I would interrupt their conversation. I spoke louder than I had intended. "Hey, Trey. Can you help a sister out?"

The woman cringed and turned toward me, not looking too pleased. I tried to hide the smirk that I knew had appeared on my face. Too late. The woman glared at me like I was an intruder. Here, I thought the church was open to anyone.

She reminded me of how I used to maintain my appearance. A year ago I wouldn't have had any problems wearing that silky mane with honey-blond highlights. I would've rocked that red lipstick too. Her eyelashes were a bit much, though. I mean, we were in church. I thought churchwomen were supposed to be more modest looking.

"Hey, Rena." Trey smiled like he hadn't seen me in a while, when in fact this was the third time in one week. I was truly delighted to see those pearly whites flashing at me.

To be polite—although, I didn't really feel like it—I said, "Sorry to interrupt. I was looking for Bev."

The woman spoke up. "You mean Beverly Lawson. She's probably down in a classroom. I can take you."

"Queen, I need to head down that way, anyway. I will show Rena." Trey stepped out into the hallway.

I looked back at the woman whose name was Queen. Ooh, I recognized that look. Queen Bee had just been dismissed, and she was not too happy.

"Your sister should be in the classroom next to the sanctuary." Trey moved his long legs and headed down the hall.

I matched his stride and scolded him. "You could say thank you. I just did you a favor."

He grinned. "You did me a favor?"

"You're running from the *queen* as fast as you can."

"It's not like that at all, Rena. Queen and I were working on the pastor's upcoming appreciation. I'm helping you find your sister."

"Hmm. Yeah, I know you like helping out damsels in distress."

Trey stopped mid-stride and blinked. "What?"

"You like being the hero, especially if a woman is involved."

He cocked his head to the side. "I like to help *people*." Trey refused to admit that he was a ladies' man.

"I'm just making an observation."

"Well, you need to rethink your observations and not make assumptions. People do change," Trey responded. "It's good you're here to help your sister. We always have a huge turnout for the Easter egg hunt."

Well, he didn't have a problem changing the subject. "Who said that's what I am here to do?"

Trey narrowed his eyes at me. "You certainly are the same old Rena. I hope you will stay to help. It will be good for you to be around others."

We arrived at a classroom, where groups of women sat talking. My sister sat at a circular table by herself, surrounded by piles of bags and colorful eggs. She looked up, and for the first time in a while, she had a smile on her face. I guessed she was in her element. I stepped into the room and looked at the other women. They turned and looked at me, or probably at Trey.

I addressed my sister. "Well, I made it. What do you want me to do?"

Instead of answering me, Bev came from around the table and approached Trey. "Hello, Trey. Can you stay and help too?"

I frowned at my sister and then looked back at Trey.

He shook his head. "I will be happy to help when it's time to hide the eggs. Right now I need to take care of a few things."

"Sure. Thanks for bringing my sister. She didn't need to get lost accidentally."

Trey glanced over at me. "I agree. Glad to be of assistance." He pointed. "Rena, try staying out of trouble."

Trouble. I watched him leave, and a surge of anger rose up in me. Then I remembered where I was, but being in church didn't calm me down. I knew Trey had meant no harm, but his words had elicited a very vivid memory of my stepdad. Reverend Lawson was standing in my face, telling me that trouble was right there with me wherever I went. Funny thing was that old man had prophesied over me and my life, because I knew how to stay in trouble quite well.

I turned around to ask my sister once again what she wanted me to do. She was staring at me with the craziest grin on her face. I held out my arms. "What? I'm here."

She shook her head and walked back to the table and opened a bag of chocolates. "Just help me open these bags first." She sat down in a chair and looked up at me. "Almost like old times, seeing you and Trey together."

Following her lead, I sat down in a chair and grabbed a bag of chocolates. "Trey showed me where the classroom was, Bev. How does that bring back memories for you?"

"You two used to get into trouble all the time in the choir. I know you haven't forgotten."

It wasn't that I'd forgotten. Memories like that had been wiped clean for various reasons. There was that one time my stepdad had come upon Trey and me as we sat together and laughed innocently. I was having a good time, but you would have thought we were making out in church the way Reverend Lawson berated me in front of Trey.

As I tried to rid my mind of that memory, Bev started talking. The only thing I caught was, "He was good for you."

I stopped and eyed my sister. "Who?"

"Trey, silly! Aren't you listening?"

I finally split the bag open, spilling the chocolate eggs on the table. "Have you and Alecia been talking?"

Bev frowned. "Alecia? No, I haven't talked to her in a while. Why?"

I shook my head. "This conversation sounds like something she said yesterday." I pushed the chocolate eggs together into a pile and then grabbed one for myself. "I have no idea where people are getting these ideas about me and Trey. We were buddies. Always have been." I popped the chocolate in my mouth, savoring the buttery flavor. My mind strayed to Trey's handsome face. Now I kind of wished he'd stuck around.

Bev slapped my hand. "Stop eating the chocolate. This is for the kids." After scolding me, Bev's half smiled. "It could have been different between you two if . . ."

"If what . . . ?"

Bev's phone rang. She picked the phone up off the table and looked at the screen. I waited while she answered, wondering what in the world she was trying to tell me.

"Mama, are you okay?" Bev said into the phone.

I stared at my younger sister, as she seemed to be trying to console our mama about something. "No. Look, Serena is here. We will come right over. It will be okay. I promise."

Bev hung up the phone. The smile on her face had disappeared, and now her expression reminded me of the times when we were younger and she was ready to burst into tears.

"Bev, what's wrong with Mama?"

"You need to come with me."

Bev ran over to talk to a group of women on the other side of the room. One of them nodded and looked back at me. Bev marched back over and grabbed her purse.

"Let's go," she said.

I grabbed another chocolate egg on the table. I had no idea what was going on and what was about to go down. I just knew that I was heading to the one house I had sworn to myself I would not step foot in ever again.

CHAPTER THIRTEEN

Friday, 6:00 p.m.

Bev probably wasn't a speedster, but she was pushing the speed limit and making me nervous. I hadn't been to the house where we grew up in five years. After my stepdad's funeral, I managed not to walk in that house at all. I stood outside the whole time and watched people I barely remembered or knew enter the house to give their respects to and console Mama and Bev. I just didn't want to go in there for fear that I would hyperventilate. Even after the Reverend Lawson's body had been buried, his presence clung to the house.

A month after his burial, I asked Mama if she wanted to move. I had even looked into houses for her in Georgetown, as well as in Charlotte, but she wouldn't budge. At one point she yelled at me and accused me of trying to destroy her life by taking her away from the home she'd always known. I found that interesting, because I'd left that house, and despite my issues, I'd been living life just fine.

As Bev pulled the car in front of the house, I was struck by how unkempt the yard looked. It was spring, so tall green and brown grass, along with patches of weeds, had taken over the front yard. I needed to talk to Bev about either having her husband, Clay, come over or hiring a crew to help Mama get the yard looking decent again.

Bev turned off the ignition and jumped out of the car. I climbed out of the passenger side and immediately noticed the cracked sidewalk in front of the house. As Bev sprinted to the door, I moved like a turtle, observing the houses on either side of Mama's house. This neighborhood looked nothing like I remembered. Everything seemed beaten down and weathered. Several houses, most with small porches and carports, lined the street. At the house next door, a pit bull strained against his chain as he scolded me with his barking. The dog jumped from side to side like a boxer ready to deliver his knockout punch.

I hurried up the walkway to join Bev, who was banging on the front door. I stepped up on the porch and felt one of the floorboards bend underneath my weight.

This house is falling apart. We need to get Mama out of here.

Finally, the front door opened, and Mama stuck her head out. She peered at Bev, and then her eyes connected with mine.

Bev said, "Are you okay, Mama? You sounded worried on the phone. Let us in."

Mama shook her head. "You can go. I'm fine."

No, she wasn't fine. Mama looked so much older. The times I had seen her since my return, she'd worn hats and scarves. Her head was bare now, and I noticed that her hair was completely silver. Her hair was cut short like mine, but her Afro didn't seem well groomed. I knew she wasn't more than sixty-five, but she seemed so much older.

I didn't want to go into that house, but now that I was here, I felt compelled to walk through that door. I walked closer to Mama. "We haven't talked in a while. It's time for us all to spend some time together. Don't you want to spend time with both your daughters, Mama?"

Bev choked back some kind of whimper. She was scaring the crap out of me, and I could picture a dark cloud hovering above us.

Mama opened her door a little wider and disappeared inside the house.

Bev didn't look back at me and just walked through the door. Or, I should say, she squeezed through the door opening.

That should have been my first clue.

I tried to push the door back, but it wouldn't budge. So I squeezed through the door opening too.

Then I stopped.

The first thing that hit me was the smell. There was something rotten in here. I wasn't referring to the spirit of my stepdad. It was dark in here too. I placed my hand over my nose, but then my eyes started to water as I tried to adjust to what I was seeing.

Time could have stopped for all I knew, because I felt like someone had punched me in my chest. I didn't know whether to gag, run, or scream.

There was stuff everywhere. Piles of stuff. Boxes stacked up high. Mounds of what might have been clothes or Lord knows what. I couldn't see the living room furniture at all. I turned my head and observed how narrow the hallway was now. There were bags and more boxes stacked against the walls in the hallway. I didn't know where Bev and Mama had gone, and I didn't care. I wasn't going any farther into the house. I could no longer stand the sight and smell of this place, which used to be a decent small house.

As I turned, something caught my eye. A gold frame glimmered from the top of a box. From where I stood, I knew it was a photo I hadn't seen in many, many years. I inched toward the box and grabbed the framed photo.

How odd that in all this mess, Mama had this photo of my dad and me just sitting out here. In the photo I might have been three or four years old. My hair was in two Afro puffs, and I was wearing a yellow-striped sundress.

My arms were wrapped around my dad as he held me up high. It occurred to me that a year or two after that photo was taken, my dad left our home. After he left, I occasionally saw him, but it was never the same.

"Rena."

I turned to see Bev staring at me.

I croaked, "This is what you were trying to tell me."

She nodded. "You haven't seen the backyard. Clay and I usually try to get out here to help her, but he's been busy with the law firm caseload, and I started back working at the school. I really didn't know how overgrown the yard had become. The neighbor behind her has been asking her to get it cleaned up back there for months, but I didn't know. They finally reported her to the county. Mama could be summoned to court, and none of us have money to pay any fines."

I said under my breath, "Does she have good insurance still? Maybe light a match to the place."

"Serena, that was cruel to say, and that's illegal. It's a lot more complicated than cleaning this up. There are memories in this stuff." She pointed to the framed photo I held in my hand.

I bit my lip. "I was just kidding. I wouldn't know where to start. Is she okay?"

"She's upset and is not really aware there is a problem. She doesn't want anyone to touch or take her things. Go talk to her."

"And say what?"

"I don't know, but she's your mama too. Whatever you have been angry about, you need to let it go, because she needs you now."

Up until a week ago, I had just wanted my own sanity back. Instead, I had witnessed firsthand my godson's involvement with a very violent individual. Now the childhood home I couldn't stand was falling apart around my estranged mother. I thought I was dysfunctional, but it had been confirmed now. I heard shuffling behind Bev. My sister stepped to the side as best she could in the narrow space as Mama approached.

Mama looked at me. She looked hurt, even though I hadn't said a word to her. I guessed my expression said it all. Suddenly I wanted to break down and cry, but that wouldn't do much good. I knew brokenness when I saw it. I felt so guilty. All those years I had stayed away, angry with her for marrying a man I hated. She was still recovering from the way my dad left her all those years ago. Whatever my thoughts about Reverend Lawson, he had provided a stable environment for a brokenhearted woman and her young child, while my dad had continued to run the street.

The enormity of that revelation, the junk around me, and the framed photo in my hand made the tears that I'd been holding back run down my cheeks. I wiped at my face as soon as the tears started to fall. I tried to talk as if I wasn't about to break down and cry. "I haven't seen this in a long time."

Mama shuffled over to me. "Dallas was a fine man."

But that was all my dad was, a good-looking man. Looks weren't enough. "He hurt you. Us."

Mama squeezed her shirt with one hand, as if she wanted to rip it. Then she grabbed the framed photo from my hand. "He left. Thomas left. Everyone leaves."

Bev touched Mama's arm. "Serena and I are here, Mama."

I was here now, but I felt like I had just stepped in sinking sand. I looked at my younger sister as she wrapped her arms around Mama, thinking that in so many ways she was more mature than me, and I was the oldest.

I took a deep breath, feeling the pounding in my chest and the swell of more tears. I offered all that I could: I stretched my arms and hugged both Mama and Bev. I also prayed, because I had no clue how to deal with this situation. It truly called for a miracle.

CHAPTER FOURTEEN

Friday, 7:00 p.m.

I rode back in the car with Bev after we consoled Mama. The silence between us felt accusatory. Bev didn't say one word. I wished she would yell or say something to me, but the fact was that Mama's hoarding wasn't either her fault or mine. We both had our lives to live, and even with Bev's proximity to our childhood home and her visits, Mama still felt some need to gather what had appeared to me to be a lot of unopened packages. It was like she spent a lot of time just shopping online or via some television shopping network.

Right now I was suffocating under a pound of emotion, and I simply didn't know what to do with it. I was once again questioning why I had decided to stay here in town. I could have easily sold Aunt C's house, but instead I had broken my apartment lease and had put my belongings in storage in Charlotte. My belongings were meager compared to the piles of stuff in Mama's house. When I was growing up, Mama hadn't kept the most pristine house, but she hadn't been a shopper, either, at least as far I could recall.

Bev parked the car in the church parking lot, slammed the door after getting out, and kept walking without looking back. I climbed out of her car. My instincts told me to run to my car, but I didn't feel right leaving my sister like this, and I hadn't been the best person when it came to keeping promises. I trailed behind her and entered the church.

There were more women and children bustling around in the classroom now. Colorful eggs in bags were piled up in a corner of the room. Bev's daughters ran over to her, and both of them embraced her, as if she'd been gone for days.

A memory flashed in my mind of me and Bev embracing a younger version of my mother. Then I pictured my sister and me hugging my aged mother a little less than an hour ago. Mama had been a very pretty woman, but she had always had a serious expression. I remembered coloring eggs, the real kind, which were boiled and then placed in colored water. Mama was smiling in that memory. It was like in this one week, God was opening my eyes to my life in ways I hadn't seen it before. It wasn't pretty, and I didn't think that hiding my head in the sand or feeling sorry for myself would work anymore.

I walked over to Bev. "If you don't need me here, I'm going to head home."

Bev looked up. Her eyes couldn't hide the emotions she was feeling, but she smiled at me, anyway. "I understand. We have plenty of help now, and most of the eggs have been filled. The girls will see you tomorrow morning, right?"

I looked down at Brittany and Tiffany. "Sure. I will be back and will make sure I help hide those eggs really good, so you two can't find them."

Tiffany squealed, "I will find every one of them."

I stretched out my arms. "Give me a hug before I go."

Both girls extracted their arms from around their mama and wrapped their arms around me. I placed my arms around their shoulders and kissed them both on the forehead. "I will see you two tomorrow."

I turned and walked away, feeling a bit of relief just to be out of the room. I needed to lie down. The sleep that wouldn't come to me at night seemed to want to take over now. I was ready for the fetal position.

"Hey, Rena. You're still here."

Oh no! Not now! I took a deep breath and turned around to face Trey. He was walking toward me, grinning. I couldn't help but grin back. Something about that man lifted my mood.

He stopped in front of me. "So, you're heading home so soon?"

I nodded toward the room. "They have plenty of help in there. I told Bev and the girls I will be back in the morning to help hide the eggs."

"Good. It's a great weekend for connecting with family."

Trey didn't know I had just left my mama's home and had seen the condition it was currently in. "Yes, I guess."

"You guess? Don't sound so enthusiastic, Rena. It's a beautiful celebration ahead of us on Sunday morning."

Maybe I was overly sensitive because I was in church, but I felt like Trey was about to deliver a sermon. I turned and started walking away. "I'm aware of what Easter is all about, Trey. I'm not a total heathen."

Trey caught up with me with his long legs. "I know that, and I wasn't trying to insult you. I was just hoping that the good news of Jesus's resurrection would put a smile on your face. You have been looking pretty glum lately, more so than usual." He grabbed my arm to stop me from walking. "What's going on?"

For a brief minute, I felt touched that my old buddy would even ask me about my well-being. Then I realized I didn't really need to open up to Trey that way. "Nothing. Just tired. All this church stuff isn't my thing."

Trey raised an eyebrow. "You used to be a church girl."

I put my hand on my hip and glared at him. "That wasn't by choice. Thank you. I was the stepdaughter of a preacher." I didn't consider myself a PK, but I guessed I was in that category all the same. I freed my arm from Trey's grasp, made my way to the exit, and shoved the door open.

"You're still angry," Trey noted, walking right behind me.

I whirled around once Trey and I were outside. "Why in the world are you following me, Trey?"

"I'm concerned. You don't seem well."

"Really? Well, guess what, Trey. A crazy man almost killed me this time last year. I stayed in the hospital for a while with a head injury. When I finally was able to get back to 'normal,' I realized I couldn't function in the career that had been my thing for twenty years. I came back to this small, crummy town, which before I couldn't wait to leave, only because my dad's sister, my most favorite person, died. In her odd loving way, she thought I should have her house. And then there's my mama and . . ."

Chris getting caught up in a gang. Alecia being close to losing her son. Marty's shooting. Leon's unsolved death.

I stepped back, heaving. "I'm just trying to keep my sanity at the moment. I'm feeling overwhelmed. So I'm sorry if I don't seem to be my old bubbly self."

Trey held up his hands, as if offering a truce. "I'm sorry, Rena. I know that for you to be back here, life has to have turned difficult for you. Just remember, I'm still your friend. I want you to know I'm here if you need me. I would never push you. Take your time. Drive safely, okay?"

Before I could respond, Trey turned and walked back inside the church.

"Well, thanks a lot," I said under my breath as I headed to my car. I opened the car door and then slammed it shut. Now I felt worse. I quite frankly didn't know how to react to Trey's concern. If I was in one of those crappy romance movies, I would have run behind him and hugged him so tight, he would have had to pry me off of him.

Instead, I stuck my key in the ignition, and this time I didn't stop the tears from running down my face. As the tears ran down my neck and onto my shirt, I felt like I needed them to flow and take my angst with them.

CHAPTER FIFTEEN

Saturday, April 18, 1:45 p.m.

I giggled with my nieces as they ran around, grabbing eggs to put in their baskets. Last night wasn't a great night, but I got some sleep and woke up this morning with more anticipation than I had expected. Hours later, after helping to hide the Easter eggs, I stood and watched children of all ages run around the church grounds. It was a beautiful afternoon, and I wanted—no, I needed—to enjoy the day. My mind was still trying to grasp all the events from the past few days, and I needed a break.

I looked up from the street and noticed that Alecia had arrived, with Chris behind her. So far today I hadn't given too much thought to Chris's predicament, but when I caught sight of him, my concern returned.

"Are you doing better today?"

I jumped, startled by the voice behind me. I tried to look annoyed when Trey walked up beside me. I was touched by his concern yesterday, and I felt ashamed about my response. But I couldn't bring myself to let him know.

"Trey, you really need to stop sneaking up on people."

He shook his head. "I can't seem to win with you. What happened to us?"

Us. What exactly did he mean? I didn't recall there ever being an "us." At least not like that.

I stared into his eyes. I had forgotten how intense and luminous those brown eyes could be when he was all serious. The moment oddly reminded me of the many times I had stood around him like some puppy dog, hanging on his every word, just happy I had his attention. I was starting to feel really warm, and it had nothing to do with the sun rays beating down on my head.

I cleared my throat. "Sorry. I didn't mean to spill my life story on you yesterday."

"Not a problem. Sounds like you may need to talk to someone and get more of those pent-up emotions out."

I raised an eyebrow. "What are you? A therapist or something now?"

Trey stepped closer to me. "I do counseling from time to time."

Really? "What kind of counseling? Are you serious or just pulling my leg?"

I didn't get my answer, because an older woman came up behind us. She walked right up to Trey, passing me like I was invisible. "Minister Evans, I'm so glad I found you. Could you come help us out in the kitchen? We need another table, and we can't seem to find anyone else to help."

Minister? Did she just say Minister Evans?

"Sure, Ms. Durant. I will be happy to help." He turned to look at me. "I will hopefully catch up with you later. That counseling session is still open." He winked and then followed the older woman back toward the church.

"Rena, why is your mouth hanging open? Girl, you are going to catch a fly."

I shut my mouth and spun around to look at Alecia.

Alecia grabbed my arm. "Are you okay?"

"No," I answered. "Trey's a minister?"

"Yes. Wow, Rena. I see you have been out of the loop for a long time. Trey's been a minister for about seven or eight years. He went to Dallas Theological Seminary while he was in Texas. He facilitates the men's Bible study and fills in for Pastor Larry Walker on some Sundays, but mainly, he's the minister of music."

The entire time Alecia was talking, I felt like the world was spinning. Trey was a minister, like Reverend Lawson.

"Rena, are you okay?"

"Yes. No." I waved at her. "It's the sun. I'm not used to standing out in the sun." That wasn't exactly true. I had just been punched in the gut. I had nothing against ministers. They just weren't my type. But Trey was my type of man.

Oblivious to my inner turmoil caused by her cousin, Alecia answered, "Well, we can go inside. It looks like the Easter egg hunt is wrapping up now. They will be serving refreshments soon." Alecia looked around. "Now, where did my son go?"

"I thought I just saw Chris behind you."

Alecia held her hand above her eyes to block the sun's glare as she gazed about her. "I told that boy to stay close today."

While Alecia looked in one direction, I turned in the opposite direction to see if I could locate Chris. The lawn was clearing now, as many of the children were heading toward the church's fellowship hall. I squinted and then spotted Chris.

Two young men were standing on either side of Chris. Their stances seemed a bit threatening to me. What alarmed me more was the fact that I thought I recognized one of those jackets from the back. Surely, that boy wouldn't be out in the middle of the day, with the same red jacket he'd worn during the robbery. Then again, Chris was wearing the same baseball cap. The two boys flanking Chris obviously thought they were invincible, and Chris was terribly naive.

I tapped Alecia on the shoulder. "Alecia, who are the boys standing over there, next to Chris?"

Alecia swung around and then hissed, "Those boys have no business being here."

Before I could ask my next question, Alecia marched across the church lawn, toward the boys. I followed behind her, wondering if she knew more than I had thought about the convenience store robbery. Had Chris confess to his mother that he had been involved in the robbery? That might explain why she'd told him to stay close to her.

Alecia yelled, "Chris, what are you doing?"

I thought she was going to backhand him the way her arm swung toward Chris. Instead, Alecia turned around and pointed at the boys. "You need to leave."

I approached slowly, my eyes on the boy with the skull on the back of his jacket. Now that I could examine the jacket up close, I saw that there were actually two snakes curled around the skull. The snakes were pointing toward each other above the skull. Something like a dagger was sticking out of one of the skull's eye sockets.

The taller boy wore a black jersey with the Oakland Raiders logo. He sneered at Alecia. "We just stopped by to talk to Chris. This is a church. You trying to say we're not good enough to be here?"

Alecia was a tall woman, so she faced the boy without a problem. "I want you away from my son."

I applauded Alecia's boldness, but at the same time I was getting nervous. I whirled around, hoping to find someone who could help if the need arose. When I turned back around, the boy with the red jacket was staring at me.

Now I was really nervous. I'd never seen this boy's face before. Or had I seen a partial view of his face? The boy who did the shooting had purposely worn shades today.

This boy was looking at me like he'd seen me before. Did this boy know I was there in the store on Wednesday night? Since he had shades on, I couldn't tell if he was the same boy or not, although he appeared to have the same complexion.

What if he had seen me being questioned by the investigators that night? Would he have pushed Chris into coming to see me Thursday morning? Even though Chris told me he had seen me at the store, I still found it odd that he would come to my house for the surprise yard work. Unless he was expecting me to seek him out.

I glanced over at Chris, who had his head down, like he wanted the ground to swallow him whole. Alecia wasn't helping the situation. I called out to Alecia and Chris. "Hey, let's go. Everyone else is going back inside now." It was better to be in a crowd. I locked eyes with the boy who was staring at me, and then I turned toward the other boy. "You guys want to come in for hot dogs and punch too? I'm sure there's plenty."

I heard Alecia say something that I was sure shouldn't be said on church grounds, but I had a method to my madness. I needed a way for these boys to get caught. I envisioned calling the investigators while the boys were preoccupied by refreshments.

"Naw. We're good. Catch you later, C," said the taller boy.

The two boys slowly moved backward and then sauntered down the street, like they had all the time in the world. I assumed C was Chris.

I should have known that would be too easy.

I monitored Chris. He was definitely not looking well. "Have you lost your mind?" I scold Alecia.

She glared at me. "Do you have kids, Rena?"

"No, but . . ."

"If you did, you would do everything in your power to protect them." Alecia looked at her son. "Go inside, Chris."

Chris looked at his mother and then at me. He shook his head. "You shouldn't have done that, Mom. I don't need you in my business."

Alecia raised her hand. "Boy, you're fourteen years old. You don't tell me what I should . . ."

Chris took off and sprinted in the opposite direction down the street, away from the other boys, but also away from the church.

Alecia shouted, "Chris, you come back here!"

The people who were outside the church were staring at us now.

I stood in front of Alecia. "Chris is right. Those boys are going to bother him again, especially since Mommy came to the rescue." I hated to say it, but I had to. "You may not be around to protect him next time. Why were you so agitated by them? What have they done?"

I needed to know what Alecia knew. She might need a lot more protection for Chris than she could physically provide.

"Oh, please, Rena. I don't need you being a busybody."

I frowned. "You didn't mind me stepping in to help just a few days ago." I observed Alecia closely. Her face showed that she was experiencing a range of emotions. "What's going on? Is Chris in trouble?"

Alecia bit her lip and sucked in a sharp breath. "Investigators came by the house today, before we left. They were asking questions. Chris wouldn't tell them anything. I know he knows something, and those boys had something to do with it. He's been hanging around them for months. They were probably here to threaten him to keep his mouth shut."

The hair on my arms stood up. "What were the investigators asking about?"

Alecia turned away.

I moved around her and looked her in the eye. "If Chris is in trouble, you need to let people help you."

Alecia let out a deep sigh that was almost a yelp. "They have him on camera. He was running out of Marty's store Wednesday night. They think he has something to do with killing Marty." Alecia started heaving. "My boy is not a killer. That man might have had something to do with Leon's death, but Chris wouldn't have touched him. He doesn't have it in him to harm someone else. He's a good boy."

I looked down the street, in the direction in which both boys had disappeared. No, Chris hadn't gone anywhere near Marty. The killer could have been here just minutes ago. Now, if only I could find out his identity without getting Chris into any more trouble.

CHAPTER SIXTEEN

Resurrection Sunday, April 19, 11:40 a.m.

"He arose. He arose today. Praise the Lord. Jesus has risen."

I clapped as Tiffany finished saying the remainder of her Easter speech. She did a curtsy in her pale blue dress and then ran over to sit down with the other children on the front pew. Both girls were dressed in the usual pastel colors and patent leather shoes for Easter. Their twists were piled up high on top of their heads. My nieces reminded me so much of Bev and myself long ago at Reverend Lawson's church, reciting Easter speeches and dressed in similar attire.

I had listened to both girls practice their Easter speeches so much yesterday afternoon, I had memorized their lines with them. My goal was to mouth the words if either of them forgot, but they didn't need me. I was a proud aunt today.

My eyes strayed from where my nieces sat to where Chris sat behind the drums at the front of the church. He was not only a good boy, but also a church boy. That was an odd picture compared to the boy I saw with the baseball cap slung to the side, obviously trying to be something he was not. How did Chris wind up running around with two young men who now had him in serious trouble?

Alecia had gone after Chris yesterday, and I had wanted to help her find him. He really shouldn't have run off alone like that, with the boys bothering him. Since I had managed to get roped into family time, I had alerted Trey about the Robinson family's troubles without telling him too much information.

I observed Alecia, who was sitting on the opposite side of the church. I imagined she was keeping her eyes on her son. I didn't know how the conversation had gone between mother and son about his involvement in the store robbery gone wrong. It occurred to me that though he had not been the best influence, it would have helped Alecia to have Leon alive and around to help raise Chris. Both of them had seemed to be doing a good job. I had no hands-on experience, but it seemed to me that parenting was the world's hardest job.

I turned my head the other way and glanced down the pew. My sister and her husband sat on that side of me. Bev's husband, Clay, had his arm stretched across the top of the pew and around his wife's shoulder. That must be nice. I was happy for my sister. Clay was a good guy and a good father. I wondered how Clay and Bev would cope once the girls grew older. Bev turned her head and smiled at me. I knew Bev was glad I was attending church this morning with the family, but we still had unspoken words between us.

Mama sat in between Bev and me. She wasn't agitated, like she'd been on Friday, and she seemed to be enjoying the service. Mama wore a peach, silk wide-brimmed hat that matched her peach suit. She looked pretty today. In her appearance there was not a hint of the condition of her home. I was her eldest daughter, and I knew the routine. I had been on television for years. You had to look the part always, never let anyone know the real deal, never let your real emotions show, and present the facts.

I tried to focus on the service, but I found my eyes wandering to Trey as he began to lead the mass choir in another musical selection. In all my observing this morning, I probably lingered on him the most, as I was still processing the news that he was a minister. I had to admit I enjoyed seeing him sway to the music as he played an up-tempo song on the piano and then close his eyes when he sang a worship song.

I hadn't been in church much, but I did recall that Trey had been just as good in the choir as he'd been on the football field. I couldn't stand being in church all the time, but Trey seemed to thrive at church, singing solos on Sundays.

Right now his face was peaceful as the emotions in his voice swelled, setting off an energetic current in the sanctuary. "*Here I am to worship. Here I am to bow down. Here I am to say that you're my God,*" he sang. I closed my eyes and focused on Trey's voice. "*You're my God.*"

After Trey finished the last note of the song, Pastor Walker stood to preach. I felt a bit guilty, because I only half listened to his words as I peered at Trey. He must have felt my eyes on him, because Trey looked in my direction, or at least it seemed like he was looking right at me. I turned away and faced the pastor. Today was the only time I'd been to church since my aunt's funeral in January, and I was already acting up.

I felt a bit sad because Trey was out of reach for me. Again. Maybe we weren't meant to be more than friends. *Lord, forgive me for asking, but I need to know. Am I ever going to have a relationship that isn't dysfunctional?*

Now it seemed like Pastor Walker was looking at me as he said, "We need that authentic relationship with God. That comes through His son, Jesus. He made the ultimate sacrifice."

Relationship. I couldn't say that I'd ever had a relationship in which I felt completely okay with being myself.

Lately, I hadn't been okay with me, so why did I expect anyone else to be? This pastor didn't make me feel like I was some heathen, though. In fact, I sat up a bit and tuned in to his sermon.

Pastor Walker must have heard the rant in my head. "God accepts us as we are. He knows every hair on our head. How many of you know that about yourself? I'm happy to have some hair God can count." The pastor reached up and patted the top of his bald spot, and the congregation erupted in laughter. I had to admit, the older preacher was pretty funny.

After the service we headed back to Bev's house. When I walked into the kitchen, I stopped and stared. Glass dishes and aluminum pans were lined up on the kitchen counter. I went over and pulled up the aluminum foil on a corner of each one so I could peek inside. There was macaroni and cheese, yams, green beans, and collard greens. I gazed at my sister.

"You cooked all this. When did you have time?" I said. I knew my sister was a wonder girl, but this was a nice spread of food. "I don't think I have seen this much food in a long time."

Bev pulled a big pan holding a glazed ham out of the oven and sat it down on the kitchen counter. "I don't cook like this often, but it's Easter, and I wanted to make it special. You and Mama could probably use a really good meal. Neither one of you eats well."

My sister was right about that. I had never been much of a cook. I looked over my shoulder to where Mama sat in the living room with the girls. "So how do you think Mama's doing? She looks very pretty today."

Bev grabbed a knife and started carving the ham. She laid the slices nice and neat on a long serving dish. "It's a good day for her, but we still need to deal with the house. Let's not talk about that today."

That was fine with me.

Bev opened one of the cabinets above her head and handed me a stack of plates. "Can you put these out on the table?"

"Sure thing, sis." I couldn't remember the last time I had set a table. When we were young, Bev and I took turns setting the table and clearing it after the meal, a chore we much preferred over washing dishes in the sink. After I set the table, I helped Bev carry out dishes from the kitchen. The baked spiral ham made my mouth water as I inhaled the pineapple and molasses glaze.

When we were all sitting at the table, Clay said grace. As we passed the dishes around, I looked over at Mama to see how she was doing. She was strangely quiet, almost agitated.

I asked, "Mama, you doing okay?"

Bev glanced at me. Mama didn't look up, but she nodded as she passed the macaroni and cheese to me. I reached for the dish. It was good to be around Bev and her family, but I wasn't sure how to handle the suddenly withdrawn person who sat across from me.

In the distance I heard my phone ringing. *Who would be calling me?* I felt like it was rude to get up from the table, so I ignored it. I hadn't talked much to my brother-in-law, who was the strong, silent type except when he was presenting a case in court, so I gazed at him and said, "Clay, I guess you're looking forward to some vacation time. I imagine your court caseload is always heavy."

Clay grinned. "Yes, I am. I have had some interesting cases lately." He winked at Bev. "Some time away would be great. You know, I don't know if Bev mentioned this to you, but I can always use an investigator on staff."

I looked at my sister and then back to Clay. "Well, I'm doing okay, but I guess if I decide to stay here, I will need a job eventually. I will consider your offer, Clay."

Bev didn't look at me, but I imagined that job offer was something she had talked over with Clay quite a few times. I wasn't sure whether to be touched or not. Working at a law firm could prove to be interesting. That is, if I planned to stay in Georgetown.

My cell phone began ringing again.

Brittany, who was sitting beside me, said, "Aunt Rena, is that your phone?"

I sighed. "Yes. Unfortunately. Bev, I'm sorry. I don't know who would be calling me now."

Bev waved her hand. "See who's calling you. It sounds like they really want to get in touch with you."

I pushed my chair back, rose from the table, and went into the living room. I retrieved my phone from my bag, which lay on a chair. It had stopped ringing. I peered at the screen on the phone, but I didn't recognize the number. It appeared to be local. I quickly hit the CALLBACK button and waited. The call was picked up on the second ring.

I said, "Hello. Someone there has been calling this number."

"Yes, Rena. It's me, Trey. Sorry. Your sister gave me your cell phone number."

Did she now? I thought. I could see the dining room table from where I stood, and I glanced at my sister. "Hey, Trey. What's going on?"

"Thank God I reached you. I need you to come meet me at the hospital."

"What happened? Are you all right?"

"It's not me. It's Alecia." Trey seemed to be trying to catch his breath. "We need to be there for Alecia. Chris has been shot."

No! I gripped the back of the chair. "What? When did this happen?"

"Apparently, an hour ago. The details are sketchy right now, but I thought you being Chris's family, you should know. Alecia could probably use the support. You know she doesn't have much family."

I turned around to see Bev and her family watching me. "Sure. I will be there as soon as possible."

"Thanks, Rena."

I stared down at my phone and then reached for my bag. All kinds of emotions and thoughts were bombarding me now. *The store. The shooting. The boys. Alecia yelling at them yesterday. Chris's innocent face.* This was starting to be too much.

"Rena, what's wrong?" Bev asked from the dining room.

I stuffed my phone inside my bag. "I'm going to need to leave, and I'm going to ask that you pray." That sounded pretty odd coming out of my mouth, but I knew that was what Chris needed. I glanced at the girls, who looked wide eyed and scared.

"Chris has been . . . hurt. He's in the hospital, and Trey asked me to sit with Alecia."

Bev jumped up. "Oh no. No. We can all come."

I looked over at Mama, who was looking down at her plate. I wondered if she had heard anything I'd said. "There probably doesn't need to be too many people at the hospital. If you can let others know . . ."

Bev stepped around the table. "Yes, I can call the prayer team." She came up to me and touched my shoulder. "Let Alecia know we're praying for Chris and for her."

I looked at my sister and then at her family. I motioned for her to meet me in the hallway. When Bev stepped into the hallway, I pulled her to the side.

"I didn't want to say this in front of the girls, but it's a lot more serious than Chris being just hurt. Somebody shot him."

Bev grabbed her shirt. "Oh, my Lord. I will definitely get the prayer team together right now. Who would hurt him? He's such a good boy."

Good boy! How many times had I heard that in the past five days?

I headed out the door. I hoped that God would grant my godson a second chance and would save his life.

CHAPTER SEVENTEEN

Sunday, 5:55 p.m.

I arrived at Georgetown Memorial Hospital and found Trey sitting in the waiting room. There were young people and old people, some sicker than others and some with injuries, waiting to be seen by the emergency room staff. I wasn't a fan of hospitals after spending months as a patient last year.

When Trey saw me, he stood. "Thanks for coming, Rena."

I waved at him so that he would sit back down and then took the chair next to him. The plastic chair was hard, but I ignored my discomfort and asked Trey, "How's Chris doing? Where was he shot?"

Trey leaned toward me. "I really don't know the details. Alecia called in a panic. I told her to call an ambulance and get him to the hospital as quickly as possible. He's in surgery right now. They are trying to stop the bleeding from the gunshot wound."

If this were any other scenario, Trey's closeness would have set my nerves on fire, but I was too shaken by Chris's shooting to give it much thought. I found Trey's presence comforting, because I wasn't used to violence being quite this close to home. It was almost like old times, when we leaned on each other in times of trouble, except this was a very different situation than those we faced back then. *What if we lose Chris?* That thought was unbearable. I cleared my throat.

"Where were Alecia and Chris when he was shot?" I asked.

"They were at home, or at least they had just arrived home. They were walking up the driveway, toward the front door. Alecia mentioned seeing a car drive by. Someone must have shot him from a car window."

I sucked in a breath. *Gangs. A drive-by shooting.* This was a dinky little Southern town. Evil and violence could show their faces anywhere and at any time, but this didn't feel right. "I just saw Chris at church a few hours ago. He's not a bad kid, just a bit lost without his dad. I have to say, seeing him play the drums was a bit of a contrast to the other times I have seen him. He's a really good musician."

Trey sat back in his chair. "Well, Chris has always been interested in music. When Leon was alive, he made sure Chris had money for lessons. Alecia used to say that Leon was really proud of his son's talent. Unfortunately, Chris started to slack off after Leon's death. He would show up sporadically for choir practices, which was understandable. I guess around the time your Aunt C's health started to decline, he stopped showing up for choir practice all together. This morning was the first time he has played the drums for a church service in months. Believe me, that was after a lot of convincing yesterday."

I shook my head. "I'm glad you were able to get through to him. Where did you find him yesterday?"

Trey responded, "It wasn't too hard to find him. Usually, he ends up at his childhood friend's house. That's the one good thing about Chris having a friend and, well . . . a cousin like Joseph."

Cousin? I hadn't realized the boys were cousins. "I met Joseph last week. He does seem like a good kid. Why doesn't Chris just stick to being friends with him? Unless he is really trying to be with the cool kids. Not that Joseph isn't cool."

Trey hesitated for a moment. "Joseph has his challenges. I agree, it would be a good idea if Chris would be more conscious of his friends. Joseph is kind of sickly sometimes. He's in and out of the hospital a lot. The other kids don't understand Joseph's condition. I guess Chris felt like he had to find some other friends to hang with during those times when Joseph isn't doing well."

"I see. That's a shame about Joseph." I wanted to figure out how the boys were cousins, but I was more anxious about Chris's condition at the moment. I looked around the waiting room. "Where is Alecia?"

"She went for a walk." Trey looked around. "There she is now. Maybe Chris is out of surgery."

I turned around and observed Alecia as she moved through the waiting room. Her arms were crossed, as if she was freezing. Alecia looked like she had aged ten years. When she approached us, I stood and swallowed back the guilt riding up my throat.

"I'm so sorry, Alecia. Any word from the doctor?" I said.

Alecia shook her head and started rubbing her arms up and down, as if she was reliving the event all over again. "Not yet." Her voice wavered. "There was so much blood. He's going to be okay?" She looked at Trey for confirmation.

He stood and guided her to a chair. "I'm praying for him, and a lot of other people are praying for him too. Don't lose hope, Alecia."

Trey was definitely more than Alecia's cousin at that moment. I could clearly see the man of God he had become. Like he had earlier at church, he touched the soft spot inside of me when he comforted Alecia, and he reminded me of his consistency and his friendship.

I glanced down at Alecia's shirt, which was covered with speckles of blood. I had always thought of myself as an "I can handle anything" chick, but lately, I didn't know. I looked at Trey and said, "We should get her some clean clothes."

Alecia waved her hand. "I'm fine." She stood, turned away from us, and paced the waiting room floor. "I just need the doctor to tell me something. My boy was in such pain. I rode over with him in the ambulance. They were trying to stop the bleeding."

Trey came over and placed his arm around Alecia's shoulders.

Guilt crept in my mind at the thought that I could have stopped all this from happening. It broke my heart that someone had tried to take Chris's life. *But why?* Chris wasn't going to say anything. He wouldn't have admitted anything or revealed either of the boys' identities to the investigators, his mom, or even me. I had already asked him, and he had refused to talk.

I suddenly became obsessed with getting Alecia a change of clothes. She was about the same size as Bev, so I grabbed my phone from my pocket and called my sister. After Bev said she would bring some clothes over to the hospital and we hung up, I returned to Alecia's side. Trey still had his arm around her shoulders. I didn't bother to look at him, although I could tell he was observing me.

I asked Alecia, "Did you see who did this? Have the cops been by to talk to you yet?"

Trey removed his arm from around Alecia's shoulders. "I think the investigators are here now."

I turned to see both Baldwin and Moses coming toward us.

Baldwin nodded at Trey and then at me before turning his attention to Alecia. "Ms. Robinson, I'm sorry about your son's shooting. Can we go over here so we can take your statement?"

Alecia let the investigator lead her away from the curious onlookers in the waiting room. I followed behind, not really caring if I hadn't been invited. From behind, I heard Alecia say, "It happened so fast. I heard a loud bang, like a gunshot, and then I heard Chris cry out. I turned, and he was on the ground. There was blood soaking the side of his shirt. I looked up and thought I saw a car drive away."

Moses had been eyeing me, basically to let me know I had no business listening to them question Alecia. I gave him a look that let him know I was not moving.

Moses must have received my message, because he turned away from me and asked, "What can you tell us about the car, Alecia?"

First-name basis. Now, that made one of my eyebrows arch for sure. Did Moses know Alecia well enough to call her by her first name? Chris had said that he knew Moses. I crossed my arms, because I definitely wasn't moving now.

Alecia yelped, "I don't know. I was trying to help my son."

"It's okay." Moses stepped toward Alecia, lowered his voice, and placed his hand on her shoulder. He had turned into the good cop right before my eyes, appearing almost gentle now, which was quite a change from the gruffness I had experienced. I leaned forward, straining to hear what else he was saying to Alecia.

Alecia didn't seem to mind having Moses's hand on her shoulder. I watched as she shook her head, rejecting whatever Moses had just suggested. Then she said softly, "No. I need to be here when the doctor comes out."

Baldwin, who had been scribbling away in his notebook, stepped up to join his partner and Alecia. "Do you remember seeing anyone around the house when you got home? A vehicle maybe?"

Alecia closed her eyes, as if trying to remember. "I think I saw a car. It was dark, but not black. Or maybe it was black."

"Make and model?" Moses asked.

Alecia shook her head. "I'm not good with cars."

I couldn't stand this. I marched over and faced Alecia. "What about people in the car? A man? A woman? Boys? Could you see anyone?" Both the investigators and Trey looked at me. I shrugged. "What? I have questions too."

Moses glared at me. "How about you let *us* do our job, Ms. Manchester?" He turned his back to me. "Well, did you see a person in the car? If so, can you identify the gender?"

I tried not to smirk as I stared at the back of Moses's head. As I started to roll my eyes, I noticed that Trey was watching me with amusement. That changed my tune a bit. I certainly didn't need to be acting up in front of Minister Evans.

I respected his calling, but he was still Trey to me. That man knew me like no one else did, even if it had been over twenty years since we'd hung out. I hadn't changed much, and he should understand that. I gave him a quick smile and turned my attention back to Alecia, who was twisting her hands like she was ready to tear them off her arms.

She finally said, "I think there were young men in the car."

I narrowed my eyes. Did she really see boys in the car? I wondered. "The same boys who were at the Easter egg hunt yesterday?" I asked.

This time Baldwin raised his eyebrows at me. The slim older guy never seemed to show any emotion on his face. Instead of berating me like his partner had, Baldwin asked, "What happened on Saturday, Ms. Robinson?"

Alecia seemed like she was in another world. She was staring at the floor.

Is she going into shock? I decided I would step in whether anyone wanted me to or not. "I'll tell you what happened. Two young men came up to Chris at church yesterday. They seemed to be threatening him. So Alecia and I walked over to see what was going on. Alecia, being a good mother, told them to leave her son alone and get off church property."

Moses inquired, "How did they respond to that? What did Chris say about them?"

I continued, "I'm sure they were not too pleased to have us walk up, but Chris seemed relieved to me when they walked away. No. I take that back. He was nervous. He wasn't quite comfortable with them being there or with having his mother approach them."

Baldwin asked, "Can either of you identify these boys?"

I remembered Alecia had said that the investigators had seen Chris on the surveillance camera footage. Hadn't they seen the other two boys too? If so, why were those boys out on the streets? That wasn't right. I answered, "There was something about one of their jackets that I remember seeing before."

Moses turned his intense eyes on me. "You mean you saw this jacket prior to yesterday?"

I sucked in a breath. I looked at Alecia, who was no longer looking at the floor. Her gaze went past us. She rushed over to a gray-haired man who was balding on top. The scrubs indicated to me that this could be the doctor who had operated on Chris.

My body became stiff, and I prayed that Chris had made it through the surgery just fine.

Alecia had her hands clasped together, and she was looking at the doctor. Trey had walked up to stand beside her. Suddenly Alecia turned toward Trey. When his arms went around her, I didn't know how to feel or what to think.

I just knew I had to make it right. Somehow.

CHAPTER EIGHTEEN

Sunday, 7:00 p.m.

Thankfully, Chris had made it through the surgery, but he was in critical condition. The bullet had impacted his abdomen, and extensive repair work had to be done. Now the doctors needed to make sure that Chris's body healed and that no infections interfered with his recovery. Chris was sedated and was in the intensive care unit, with Alecia by his bedside. Bev had arrived with a change of clothing, but neither one of us could get Alecia to change her shirt. She was prepared to spend the night by her son's side.

I briefly caught a glimpse of the young man, whom I had just seen play the drums during the Easter service at church. How had he got to this place? Had the boys come back to hurt him, and why? Chris was too scared to be a snitch.

I didn't have long to think about this, because Moses was waiting for me when I walked back into the waiting room.

I sighed and folded my arms. "So, are you going to go after those boys in car?"

Moses stated, "Alecia can't confirm she saw those boys, and you"—he pointed a finger at me—"have been with-holding valuable information."

I saw that somebody was back to playing the bad cop. I really was not in the mood, so against my better judgment, I raised my voice when I said, "I told you every-thing I saw."

Moses lowered his voice. "You're sure you don't re-member anything else you forgot to mention?"

Lord, help me. That was a really pitiful prayer, but I needed to brace myself as I dealt with Moses. "Okay. I thought I recognized Chris during the convenience store robbery, but I wasn't sure."

Moses stared me down. "You *thought* you recognized him? Or you *did* recognize him?"

I wanted to hit him, but I didn't need to be hauled off to jail for assault and battery of a law enforcement officer. I figured I was in enough trouble, but I stepped closer, so that I was toe to toe with Moses, liking the fact that I could look him in the eye. In some strange way, he'd lit a fire under me. I'd been in a funk the past few months. I had been really depressed and had not been sure about what was next for me.

I was feeling like my old self again.

"Moses, I said, 'I *thought* I recognized Chris.' I am a reporter. I know about collecting the facts. I know about getting the story right. I wasn't going to incriminate a boy who I knew was good and who had a solid family. No, I wasn't taking that chance."

Moses's eyes bulged. "Our investigative work is helped when you tell us everything you saw. With that informa-tion, we can put together the clues. We could have picked up the suspects sooner if you'd told us everything. If I had gotten to Chris, he would've talked to me."

"You think so. Chris was in the wrong place at the wrong time. There are folks in the Georgetown Police De-partment who remember his dad, Leon Robinson. They may not realize that Chris is nothing like his dad. He's a boy who is trying to fit in, and he got caught up with the wrong so-called friends. I can tell you that Chris was not about to snitch on his friends to you."

Moses growled, "I know Chris, and I know that I could have helped him."

"So why didn't he go to you?" I didn't tell Moses that his very presence at my house had sent Chris running last Thursday.

Baldwin had come from out of nowhere and placed an arm between Moses and me. "All right, you two are making a scene in here. Step back and calm down. Both of you."

I hadn't realized how close we were to each other's face. I stepped back and blew out a breath. My arms were trembling, so I crossed them.

Moses reached out and tried to grab my arm. "Come with me."

I snatched my arm back. "Why?" I looked at his eyes, and that fighting spirit I had had a minute ago started to escalate again. I glanced over at his partner, who was also staring at Moses, with concern in his eyes.

Baldwin looked around and quietly said, "Why don't you two take this discussion outside?"

Moses snapped, "Fine. Let's go."

I wasn't really sure I wanted to go anywhere with Moses. I looked behind me and saw that most of people in the waiting room were watching us.

Great! Now I was looking and feeling like I was a criminal.

I followed Moses as he headed outside. Before we walked through the sliding doors, I turned to see Baldwin watching us and noticed that Trey had entered the waiting room. Our eyes met. I had no idea what Moses wanted to talk to me about outside, but the concern in Trey's eyes reminded me that Trey had my back.

Moses walked over to a well-lit area lined with benches. The sun was starting to descend in the sky, and the streetlamps were starting to glow. I lagged behind Moses, mainly because I wanted to keep my distance. I was still rattled by the fact that I had practically lost my temper with a police officer. *That isn't too smart, Serena.* Maybe I needed to take my sister up on that offer to get my head examined again while I was here.

I didn't understand where Moses's animosity was coming from. Moses had mentioned that he had lived in Charlotte. I did have a reputation with the Charlotte-Mecklenburg Police Department as a hard-nosed reporter, but that was ancient history. Plus, my work on the case last year that had almost killed me was a huge shocker to the city. I had brought down big city government people, including the mayor of Charlotte. But I had no ego right now. That cocky reporter who used to be me was long gone. I didn't want to start off on the wrong foot here in Georgetown. I was acting as a concerned relative right now, not as a reporter.

As I came up behind Moses, he seemed to be taking a deep breath. I watched the back of his shoulders rise and slowly fall. He turned around and looked like a totally different man. Almost the way he had when he was comforting Alecia a while ago. *A regular old Dr. Jekyll and Mr. Hyde, I see.*

I walked closer to him, feeling some of the tension between us subsiding. We stood next to each other, not saying anything.

Moses finally broke the silence. "I'm sorry. I didn't mean to take my frustration out on you. I know Alecia and Chris very well. This is all upsetting to me. It's not my intention to be unprofessional."

I nodded my head. I observed the side of his face. At that moment I realized that the look in his eyes was familiar to me, and this startled me. It was the look a person had when talking about someone he or she cared deeply for and even loved.

"I can tell you and Alecia must know each other. You grew up around here, Moses?"

"Yeah, my family lived here until I was in middle school. Alecia and I grew up in the same neighborhood. My family moved to Charlotte while I was in high school. I lived there until about two years ago. My mother had grown ill, so I decided it was a good time to be closer to home."

"Oh, well, I can relate. I came back here because my aunt Claudia had died and had left me her house. I haven't figured out my next step."

Moses nodded. "I'm familiar with Claudia Robinson. I'm sorry for your loss. Your aunt was well loved around here. Chris is family to you, so I see why you were hesitant to say you saw him in the convenience store that night."

"Chris is my cousin and godson. I'm supposed to look out for him. How did you know my aunt?"

Moses hesitated. "I met her not under the best circumstances. Baldwin and I were assigned to her son's homicide case."

I sensed tension sneaking back between us. "Leon's case is still open, since it's unsolved, right?"

"Ms. Manchester, you should know from your career that homicide never sleeps. There is always another case. When opportunity allows, we try out best to review the evidence and follow new leads. I have to say that when I was called to the scene of Marty's shooting, I had a bad feeling. Then I saw Chris on the surveillance camera footage."

My respect for Moses rose a notch, but I still had some questions. "I hope you don't mind me asking, but Alecia said you questioned Chris about being at the store during the robbery. You didn't see the other two boys on that surveillance camera footage?"

Investigator Moses stared across the parking lot. Finally he spoke. "We have the boys."

I frowned. "You have them?"

When he turned to look at me, the gruffness had returned. "We picked up both young men last night. One was wearing the jacket that you described. It was hard to miss such a distinctive jacket. The only problem is neither of them had a weapon on them. We have a search warrant to search their residences. Whoever shot Chris today, it wasn't either of the two assailants from the store robbery."

I closed my mouth, which had fallen open. Voicing my first thought out loud, I said, "You're sure you have the same boys on the camera footage? Who else would have a motive to shoot Chris?"

"That's a good question. We will be on the lookout for the dark car Alecia described, and we'll see what we can nail down. That's going to be a needle in the haystack without the make and model of the vehicle. Maybe Alecia saw more than she remembers right now. Some other eyewitnesses seemed to remember more a bit later." He cut his eyes at her. "We'll talk later, Ms. Manchester. I want to check on Alecia."

I watched him walk away, thinking that maybe he wasn't so bad, after all. He really seemed to care for Alecia and Chris, so that lifted some of the guilt that had been clinging to me. I wasn't their only protector. The problem was, neither I nor Moses had actually protected Chris. There had been another threat out there that neither one of us had seen coming.

I let out a sigh and placed my hands on my head. I should have remembered that no matter how hard Aunt C had tried to protect them, the men in the family had still got into hot water and had had to face the consequences of their actions. I just hoped that Chris could be saved and turned around.

"Rena, are you all right? What was that about?"

I took my hands off my head. I should have known Trey was going to come find me. "Nothing."

"Nothing. Serena, I saw you two at each other. You do know that guy could have put handcuffs on you and hauled you off to jail, right?"

That had occurred to me. "I didn't assault the investigator, Trey. I just had a . . . healthy discussion with him."

"A discussion about . . . ?" Trey cocked his head at me, waiting for my answer.

Great. He wasn't going to leave me alone. "I was at the convenience store when the robbery went down. I . . . heard Marty get shot."

Trey grabbed my shoulders. "Why didn't you say anything? You could have been hurt or killed too!"

I looked down at Trey's hands on my shoulders. I wasn't sure if I liked this or not, so I gently removed his hands. "The boys in question didn't know I was there, or at least I don't think so." I recalled that yesterday the boy with the red jacket seemed to be looking at me like he'd seen me before.

Trey stared at me like he was trying to comprehend. "Boys? I don't understand. What does this have to do with Chris? Why did someone shoot him?"

"Chris has been hanging out with a certain group of boys who could be a part of a gang. I don't think Chris knew what they were planning to do, but he entered the convenience store with them. The investigators have him on camera too."

"Chris? You mean he was there the night Marty was shot?"

"Yes. The other two boys—I assume they have the shooter—are in custody already."

Trey nodded his head. "That's good. Does Alecia know this?"

"She doesn't know that. . . . I don't think. Look, earlier, she was telling the investigators that she thought these boys shot Chris. But it couldn't have been them."

Trey thick eyebrows furrowed together. "So you're saying someone else is out there, trying to harm Chris. Why?"

"I don't know, but Chris could still be in danger."

I needed to identify Chris's shooter, because I was sure there was something I had missed about last Wednesday. It was probably irrational that I thought there was some clue that I had not relayed to Moses and Baldwin in their investigation, but Chris's shooting didn't make sense at all. I had a feeling that neither of those boys in custody would reveal anything or lead the investigators to any answers.

I might have been pretty slack over the years when it came to keeping up with family, but no one messed with my family. Aunt C had died of a broken heart over her son, Leon. I couldn't let Alecia lose Chris too. Justice had to be found for both of them. I could almost hear Aunt C saying, "Go get them, girl!"

CHAPTER NINETEEN

Monday, April 20, 11:00 a.m.

I found myself back at the Huddle House once more. It must have been the coffee, which wasn't bad at all. I really missed the coffee shop in Charlotte where I would sit for hours, researching and composing notes for my stories. It had been a great alternative to sitting in the office while producers ran all over the place, rounding up stories for the next broadcast.

As usual, I wanted to hear any town chatter. Chris's shooting had been reported on the eleven o'clock news last night, but only sketchy details had been given. The news anchor had said more about Marty's funeral arrangements than about whether or not his alleged murderer was in police custody. I guess the investigators wanted to keep things quiet, since Chris's shooting probably complicated matters.

Baldwin and especially Moses might not appreciate me interfering in their investigation, but I had an advantage. I wasn't a cop, and I could do some snooping without raising people's suspicions. That was definitely on my agenda today. The boys in custody had to be somebody's son, grandson, or cousin. Somebody had to know the boys had been picked up. Despite the fact that the investigators had used camera footage to identify the boys, I wanted to know for sure that those boys were the same ones who were at the convenience store last Wednesday night.

Since I never saw their faces at the convenience store that night, it wasn't like I could do a police lineup. I could be sure that the boys who had shown up at the church were the perpetrators of the crime. Still, that red jacket was so identifiable. It seemed like the boy wearing it would be the same guy. I thought back to the brief moment when I saw the boy in the jacket turn around in the store. *Ugh!* That was when it occurred to me that I had never mentioned to the investigators that the boy had been wearing shades. And if he was wearing shades, how could they really identify him on the surveillance camera footage?

I picked up the carafe and noticed I had drained the coffee already. The half-eaten omelet in front of me had long since grown cold. People walked in and out of the restaurant, but none of them interested me enough to start a conversation. I looked around for my waitress and noticed that Iris was behind the counter. I hadn't noticed earlier that she was here. I remembered that when I came here last Wednesday night, she and Trey had seemed cozy with one another. That could have been my imagination too.

She must have noticed I was staring, because she waved. I smiled and waved back. A moment later Iris came over.

"Do you need anything else? You've been here awhile," she said.

"Is it okay if I monopolize this booth? I was just trying to get out of the house for a while, until I could check on my godson."

"Your godson? You mean Chris Robinson?"

"Yes, that's right."

"That is a shame about him getting shot. You know, I forgot he was related to you. I remember how your aunt loved that boy. He clung to her, I guess, until he got too big. I remember his clinginess used to get on Alecia's nerves."

Well, I didn't have to look any farther for someone willing to chatter. Iris was just bursting with energy. I responded, "I can imagine that wasn't a big deal. Alecia and Aunt C always got along. I remember that Alecia appreciated Aunt C looking after Chris while she worked."

Iris raised her eyebrows. "I don't know. . . . I don't think they got along all the time. I mean who does, right? You know, Alecia can be a bit of a . . . Well, she can have her moments."

I looked at Iris as I thought about how, the other day, Alecia had walked up to the two boys at church. She hadn't been scared and had had no intention of backing down. "She's a tough cookie. With her height and her athleticism, Alecia was one of those girls who could hold her own in school."

Iris grabbed the carafe on my table. "You mean she was a bully. Let me get you some more coffee, since you will be here awhile."

I watched Iris walk away to fill up the carafe with more coffee. Iris's observations and opinions were a bit odd to me. Alecia and I had been pretty close at one point in time. But it appeared that there had been more animosity going around, and I didn't quite understand it.

When Iris returned with the coffee, she poured some of the hot liquid in my coffee mug.

"Iris, Alecia and I were pretty tight at one time. She said what was on her mind." I thought, *Of course, I do the same thing.* "I never got the impression she was a bully. It sounds like you two didn't get along."

Iris put her hands on her hips. "You got along with everyone, Rena. And you're right. We didn't get along. I guess Alecia just didn't like me. But that's not the point here. I feel bad for her because I love Chris. He's such an intelligent and good boy."

"Yes. I agree." My mind was still hung up on the animosity between Alecia and Iris. The more I thought about it, the more it seemed like it had to do with Trey. Alecia could be pretty protective of her cousin, so Iris must have done something to Trey that Alecia didn't like. Trey and Iris had broken up years ago for some reason. Although, the other night they had appeared to be on friendly terms.

"Iris, I know you're working right now. Do you mind if we talk later? I have some questions."

"Sure. What about, though?"

"I'm not sure yet. I'm trying to piece together a few things, and you've been here in town all this time, so you know most people, right?"

Iris twisted her mouth like she was thinking. "I've never left this place, so yeah, I guess I know most people around here, but a lot has changed too."

"Cool. I'd like to catch up with you. If that's okay with you."

"I get off at six o'clock. I have to pick up my baby from the sitter's house. If you don't mind hanging with us for dinner, you can come by later tonight."

"Sounds like a plan."

Iris wrote down her address on a napkin. After she walked away, I had second thoughts about agreeing to dinner, but stuffed the napkin in my bag.

I reached for the check and then stopped myself, feeling a bit creeped out again, like someone was watching me.

Is this my imagination, or is my brain doing odd things?

No, I knew this feeling. I sensed danger. I peered around the restaurant. Most of the patrons were eating or were engaged in conversation. I looked out the window and tried to appear like I was just casually looking around and not searching for someone.

There appeared to be someone sitting outside in car, but I couldn't really be sure, because the car windows were dark. What really struck me in my gut was the vehicle's shape and color. It was a dark blue Crown Victoria.

Was this the car Alecia had seen driving by the house yesterday, when Chris got shot? If it was, she wouldn't have been able to see anyone clearly through the tinted windows.

Then another memory stirred in my mind. I had completely forgotten that when I arrived at the convenience store last Wednesday night, there was a similar car in the parking lot. I had a feeling Moses would throw a fit when I told him this tidbit. Could I blame him? My unreliable memory was starting to drive me up the wall.

The investigators had focused on asking me questions about Marty's shooting. Now I asked myself a few. Was the car in the parking lot when I came out of the convenience store? No, it wasn't. That car wasn't there when I drove off. Perhaps those boys were in that car, plotting their next moves, when I pulled up to the convenience store. But if Chris was with them, he would have heard what they were about to do. Not if they had their plan in place *before* Chris got in the car.

My head was full of so many questions. It was time for answers, because now I was wondering if my being in that store that night meant I was more in a danger than I had realized.

CHAPTER TWENTY

Monday, 12:00 noon

I slowly rose from my booth, then walked over to the counter and paid for my food. In an effort to appear normal, I waved good-bye to Iris, but she seemed preoccupied with a customer and didn't wave back. So I headed out the restaurant door and casually glanced over my shoulder. The dark Crown Victoria was still there. Since the windows were tinted, so I couldn't be sure if someone was sitting in the driver's seat, watching me. I locked the door as soon as I climbed in my car and stuck the key in the ignition. If I only I could peer inside that car without being obvious.

Before I could decide what to do, I heard the car's engine start up. Maybe I was being silly or maybe I really needed to make better use of my time, but as the car pulled out of the space, I started my Honda and backed out. I swerved out of the parking lot just as the other car stopped at the red light at the intersection ahead. Seeing this car was no coincidence, I decided. And what if it was the same car Alecia had described? I stopped at the light and tried to commit to memory the car's features. The license plate wasn't a South Carolina one, but a North Carolina one. I made a mental note that the license plate number ended with MHW.

When the light changed, the car took off. My gut said to keep following the vehicle, but at a distance. So I hung as far back as I could without losing sight of the car. I had no idea what I was going to do if the person stopped and got out of the car.

I trailed the car for a few miles, until we turned onto Highway 17. At that point I checked my gas gauge in a halfhearted way to convince myself that following this car was not a good idea. Fortunately, I had half a tank of gas, so my half-baked plan was to continue following the car and, if necessary, stop the madness, turn around, and go home. This would be my adventure for the day. I just hoped it would be worth the craziness.

I didn't have many more miles to go before the driver turned on his or her right turn signal. I decided to wait before turning on my turn signal until I could gauge where the car was heading. Up ahead I noticed a sign that read NEW BETHEL CHURCH. As I slowed my speed, a small church came into view, and I watched the car make a right into the church parking lot. There were many cars in the parking lot, as many as would be expected before service on Sunday, except that it was currently the lunch hour on Monday. I turned in and parked near the back of the parking lot.

My eyes were focused on the hearse and the limousine in front of the church, and I missed where the Crown Victoria went. Then I remembered last night's news broadcast, and it suddenly dawned on me what was happening.

This was Marty Davis's funeral service.

Did I just follow a person who was planning to pay his respects to a dead man? Had I really become this paranoid? If the person had noticed me peeling out of the parking lot of the Huddle House, he or she must have thought I was crazy. I was certainly feeling really foolish, but that had never stopped me before. I still wanted to know who was driving that car.

I looked down at my attire. I wasn't dressed for a funeral, as I had grabbed a sundress this morning. It was pale blue, not exactly the right color for blending in with the mourners. I had talked to Marty minutes before his death, so the least I could do was pay my respects to him. I climbed out of my car, cupped my hands over my eyes to reduce the glare, and looked for the car I followed here. It occurred to me that the car could have circled the parking lot and exited by now.

Wait! There it is. The Crown Victoria was on the other side of the parking lot, but I didn't know if the driver had left the vehicle yet. I reached into my car and grabbed my bag. I pulled out my shades and placed them on my face. I secured my car and walked through the parking lot. As I approached the entrance to the church, I saw the door to the Crown Victoria open and a man get out. I squinted behind my shades.

I'd seen him before. He was at the Huddle House last week, when I was talking to Margaret. Goodness, the man could have been eating breakfast there this morning, and I just didn't notice him. *Have I really become this paranoid?* I came to a stop among the parked cars and watched him approach the church's entrance. There was no indication that he knew I had followed him here. He didn't look around for me before he entered the church.

I wasn't satisfied about not knowing his identity, so I moved quickly across the parking lot and followed him inside. Once I stepped into the vestibule, an usher handed me a funeral program. I took it and looked for the man. He had sat down on the second-to-last pew. I slid in behind him on the last pew. I was thankful to be able to be sit, because I had just noticed my knees were shaking. I probably could have taken my shades off, but it dawned on me that this occasion was perfect for hiding my eyes behind glasses.

The funeral hadn't started yet. I peeked through the open doors behind me and could see that people were getting out of another limousine that had arrived. Marty's family would be entering the church soon. I tried to decide if I wanted to stay through the whole funeral service. I decided I would stay. I had this crazy notion that I would somehow be able to determine the identity of the man in front of me if I just stayed put.

I might just introduce myself. The old Serena had no problem staking out and nailing people for information. It was what had made me a good reporter for so many years. The rush of adrenaline I felt at the thought of this was making me giddy.

I knew I couldn't exactly tap him on the shoulder and say, "Hey. How are you doing?" I needed an angle, so I studied his back side. The top of his head was bald, and he had closely shaved gray hair on the sides and the back of his head. I assumed he was in the same age range as Marty, between forty-five and fifty. He was driving a car with North Carolina plates, so whether he was a Georgetown native was still up in the air. His white shirt fit pretty tightly across his broad shoulders. It was probably a size too small.

Someone from the other side of church walked over and sat down beside the man. This man was slim, and the brown suit he wore seemed rumpled, hanging on him like he was a coatrack. He looked back at me, but I bent my head and pretended to read the obituary.

The slim man whispered loudly, "This feels wrong. Leon. Now Marty. What's going on?"

The other man turned and glared. "Man, sit tight. This is not the time or the place to be talking."

The slim man sighed deeply and sank down in the pew like a sulky child. "It feels like we're being punished. I'm probably going to be next."

Him next? What was going on to make this man think he was going to be killed too?

The organist at the front of the church changed to another hymn, which I immediately recognized. "Be Still, My Soul." As I observed the family make their way through the door down the church aisle, I realized I was staying for Marty's home-going service. I needed to know what Marty, and Leon, for that matter, supposedly did that led to their murders.

CHAPTER TWENTY-ONE

Monday, 1:00 p.m.

I didn't know how well the minister knew Marty, but he painted a beautiful portrait of the man lying in the coffin. Marty was an upstanding citizen, husband, father, uncle, businessman, and even grandfather. Nothing about threatening to kill my cousin. Of course, this wasn't the time or the place for that. He could say anything derogatory in front of the man's family.

As it turned out, neither of the men in front of me said another word during the funeral. I would have liked to have learned their names at least. But it wasn't over yet. Since the man I had followed might be suspicious of me, I devised a plan to talk to the slim man after the service.

After a beautiful rendition of "What a Friend We Have in Jesus" by the New Bethel choir, the funeral home director asked us to pay our respects so the family could have their time. I had had my shades off for a while, but I decided to put them back on as the usher guided us toward the front of the church. When my turn came, I looked down at Marty's face, recognizing the man whom I'd spoken to only a few times since I'd come back to Georgetown. He had seemed so friendly, and yet it appeared that he had left a lot of turmoil in the wake of his death.

I moved quickly down the aisle to see if I could catch the slim man. When I stepped outside, I stood on the steps and looked around. I saw both men standing together by a tree near the Crown Victoria. That messed up my plan to have a word with the slim man once he was alone. I looked around some more and decided to walk up to them casually and start a conversation.

I took a few steps toward them before a large hand clamped down on my shoulder. I whipped around to find Moses eyeing me with a smile. Moses showing up and grabbing me from behind was totally weird, but that smile just about scared me. This man hadn't smiled once since I met him over a week ago.

"What are you doing here, Moses?"

His smile disappeared. "I should be asking you that question, Ms. Manchester."

I shrugged. "I came to pay my respects." No, I had actually followed someone here in my car and had forgotten that this was Marty's funeral, but Moses didn't need to know that. I kind of suspected he didn't believe my story for being at the funeral. I glanced back at the two men and decided to walk back toward my car. I didn't need law enforcement trailing behind me.

Moses followed behind me. "You sure that's all? What's with the shades? It's been overcast all day."

This time I turned and grinned. "I'm not exactly dressed for a funeral."

Moses looked down at my body. For a moment, I kind of liked the way his eyes lingered on me, but then he must have come to his senses, because the usual gruffness returned. "No, that's not normal funeral attire. So why are *you* really here?"

I sighed. I thought Moses and I had made peace yesterday, after he humbled himself a bit. Now he was starting to get on my nerves again. He was also holding me up. I tried to peer around him. "It was a last-minute decision, Moses. Okay. I wasn't sure if I should go or not."

He seemed to buy that for the moment. I watched as the guy I'd followed to the church opened the door to the Crown Victoria and the man with the brown suit opened the passenger door. I felt perspiration starting to form. I really wished Moses was not here.

"What has your attention right now?" Moses inquired and turned around.

I touched his arm, which was a solid mass of muscle under the suit. "Nothing. Marty seems to be well loved. I was just looking at the people who came out for his funeral." I watched as the Crown Victoria turned out of the parking lot, and snatched my hand away from Moses's arm. I screamed inside my head, because I still had no idea who those guys were and how I could find them.

I must have displayed my frustration on my face, because Moses asked me, "Are you all right?"

I tried to smile. "Yes. No. Look, you said you had a funny feeling about Marty getting shot. Before I mentioned the boys or you saw the camera footage, did you think anyone else was responsible for shooting Marty?"

The investigator stared at me for a moment. By the look in his eyes, I knew the wheels in his head were turning. I wish I could have pulled out his thoughts, because he wasn't sharing.

Moses rubbed his hand across his head. "Does it really matter? We have the shooter."

I wasn't so sure Moses had the shooter, since I knew the boy who shot Marty was wearing shades. I said, "So you clearly identified the shooter from the camera footage? He didn't have anything on his face blocking his features?"

Moses gave me a look that made me want to run. He threw up his hands, as though he were surrendering. "You know, I get that you probably miss being a reporter. You were really good at what you did, and you took down some pretty powerful people in your time. Right now this investigating thing you got going needs to stop. I really wish you weren't at the convenience store that night, because you haven't been straight with us."

"Who said I was investigating anything? I'm just asking questions. It's great that you possibly have Marty's shooter, but who shot Chris?"

"I agree with you, there is something off about Chris's shooting. But we will find his shooter too. Go home, Ms. Manchester, or better yet, go be with Alecia and Chris. You're their family, and they need you."

I narrowed my eyes. "You're right. I'm their family, so I have a right to ask questions, Moses. I'm telling you, there is more going on here than some gangsta wannabe boy coming into the store to shoot Marty. I mean, the fact that he shot Marty after he had already opened the cash register doesn't make sense. Did Marty have anything to defend himself with behind the counter? Did the boy feel threatened?"

Moses's shoulders seemed to wilt. "No, Marty didn't have a weapon behind the counter."

"So what provoked the shooter to shoot him, anyway?"

Moses shook his head. "I don't know. He is a trigger-happy, immature, violent young man."

Now my shoulders wilted. I felt like I had spent my day running around in circles. Moses was right. I needed to go support my family, but really the only way I knew how to be helpful was to do what I did best. I dug deep to find the truth.

I looked around the church parking lot and saw that most of the funeral attendees had left. Many had probably gone to the graveside for Marty's burial. I was really tired all of a sudden, but I wanted Moses to hear me out on one more thing.

"Can you do me a favor? If you can do this, I promise I won't meddle in your investigation," I said.

He peered at me. "What?"

"Are there cameras outside the store that point at the parking lot? Can you check for cars that entered and exited the store's parking lot on the night of the shooting?" I stepped forward. "Specifically a dark car."

Moses stared at me for a long moment. He finally responded, "A car like the one that Alecia tried to describe at the hospital yesterday?"

"Here's a theory, if you want to hear me out. The boys arrived at the convenience store and got away pretty quick. Suppose someone else was at the store that night during that time? Usually with these robberies, someone is the driver and lookout person, right? Suppose there's a fourth person, someone I never saw, because he didn't enter the store?"

Moses shook his head. For the first time, he didn't dismiss me as a crazy former reporter. "This fourth person could be Chris's shooter. Not bad thinking. I will see what we can find, Ms. Manchester."

I watched Moses's back as he walked away. If he could find out that one piece of information, it might answer a few of my questions about Chris's shooter, but it certainly wouldn't answer all my questions.

My request that Moses examine the camera footage from the parking lot as a way to track down the other car in the lot that night had a dual purpose. I needed to know who owned the car and who the possible drivers were. Moses didn't know that my other mission was to find any connection between Marty's and Leon's shootings. In my opinion, Chris would have never gotten involved with these boys if his dad hadn't been taken away from him. I was pretty sure Leon would have done everything possible to keep Chris from the life that he, Leon, had chosen.

CHAPTER TWENTY-TWO

Monday, 4:00 p.m.

I walked into the hospital after going home and taking a much-needed nap. If I didn't find time to rest, my short-term memory would become worse. I still felt tired and worn out, but I wanted to make it to the hospital to check on Chris. When I arrived at Chris's hospital room, I was grateful to see that Alecia had changed into the clothes Bev had brought her yesterday. Chris still was sleeping.

"How's he doing?" I whispered.

Alecia turned to me; her eyes looked bloodshot, probably from crying. Her voice was hoarse when she spoke. "Hey, Rena." She got up from the chair and stretched. "Chris woke up earlier today in a lot of pain. They gave him some meds so he could sleep."

I nodded. "That's good. He needs the meds so he can heal. Can I talk to you in the hallway for a minute?"

Alecia turned her attention toward her son.

I touched her arm. "We'll be right outside the room," I assured her.

She followed me into the hallway. "What is it, Rena?"

"Did Moses talk to you?"

Alecia frowned. "Malcolm?"

Investigator Malcolm Moses. I had been calling him Moses. "Yeah, Moses. You do know they arrested the boys, don't you?"

Alecia clutched my arm. "No, he didn't tell me. When did they get them?"

I realized that maybe I shouldn't have said anything. It also occurred to me that I had just got Alecia's hopes up and I was about to squelch them. I wasn't going to do that yet, so I asked her a question I had posed before. "Are you really sure about what you saw on Sunday?"

I watched Alecia's face contort, as if she was trying to remember. She put her hand on her head and leaned against the wall. "I know I saw a dark car drive by the front of the house. I heard a loud noise, like a gunshot. Then I saw Chris on the ground, with blood soaking through his white shirt." Alecia threw up her other hand in her grief and grabbed her head. "Why is this happening to my family? I've been here before. I lost my husband this way. I didn't get to say good-bye to Leon. He was just gone."

I stated my thoughts out loud. "We need the whole story. Who was in the store? Who else knew about the shooting?"

Alecia glared at me. "You want Chris to talk to the police? Jeez, Rena, they have the camera footage. They should have been able to identify those boys the same way they identified Chris. You said they arrested the boys already. They need to leave Chris out of this now."

I agreed with Alecia, but what she didn't know was that Chris's shooting had thrown a monkey wrench into the whole ordeal. The killer was still out there, or at least someone who thought he had a good reason to shut Chris up. What bothered me was the boy who had worn *that* jacket. He had had shades on his face in the convenience store that night, which made me think the investigators wouldn't be able to identify him with any accuracy, unless the police department had some fancy face-recognition software. I had no idea about the level of sophistication of the police equipment in this town.

I knew that on Saturday I couldn't tell if the boy who confronted Chris at the church was the shooter I saw briefly last Wednesday night. It was time to inform Alecia of that reality. "Moses possibly identified the other boys who were in the convenience store with Chris that night. I'm sorry that no one has told you this yet, but the boys were arrested Saturday night, which is *before* Chris was shot."

Alecia stared at me and then bent down, gulping for air. Concerned, I rubbed her arm and her back, telling myself that I should have kept my mouth closed. But she was Chris's mother, and she needed to know.

Alecia lifted her head and then leaned against the wall. I wasn't a mother, but I knew and understood the fear in her eyes. She finally spoke. "This means the person who shot Chris is still out there. They could try to hurt him again, Rena."

"Alecia, I don't like that someone tried to hurt Chris, but it may be to Chris's benefit not to keep quiet about the robbery and shooting. We need to locate this person before he strikes out at Chris again or at anyone else."

Alecia pushed herself away from the wall and got up in my face. "Why didn't you tell me that you were at the store that night? You didn't see any way to help Chris?"

I stepped back and took a deep breath. I hadn't shared my eyewitness account with Alecia, so I assumed that Trey must have told her. I held up my hands in surrender. "I'm sorry, Alecia. I was in the back of the store, watching events unfold through the corner mirror. I just wanted to get out of there. The only face I thought I saw was Chris's, but I was hoping he wasn't involved. I didn't say anything to the police at first, because I knew Chris was a good kid and there's no way he would've been there if he had known what the other boys were planning."

Alecia glared at me like she wanted to hit me.

Is she going to blame me for what happened to Chris?

She walked away from me and started to pace the floor with her arms crossed. "This is my fault."

My shoulders sank from the relief I felt when she walked away and from my despair over the fact that she was now playing the blame game. "What are you talking about?"

"Since his dad was killed, I haven't been there for Chris like I should. I've been angry, and I don't treat Chris nice all the time." She stopped pacing. "He looks so much like Leon. Now he's getting into trouble like his dad too. He's only fourteen years old. He never used to get into trouble. This is a boy who made straight As easily. He loved making music. I don't recognize him now. That's on me."

"Come on, Alecia. You probably have done the best you can under the circumstances. Chris is at an impressionable age. He lost his dad, and he wants to fit in at school. Being the brainy, good kid was okay probably until puberty hit. We've been there, and we know how peer pressure works. It's ten times worse these days."

Alecia looked absently at the floor. "Leon wasn't the most ideal father, but he tried. He was there for Chris. He pushed Chris to be more than he was himself."

We stayed silent for a few moments. Something occurred to me that had been mentioned to me earlier. "Did Chris witness Leon's shooting?"

Alecia shook her head. "Chris said he didn't see anything, but he did find his dad. He heard the gunshot from inside the house and went running."

"So he didn't notice anyone running away or any cars around?"

"He was too traumatized. Kind of like I was when I saw Chris on the ground. Rena, I know I saw a car, but my world closed in on Chris and the fact that he was bleeding and in pain."

This might not be the right time, but I had to inquire. "I just asked because . . . well, there's some history here. I've heard various rumors swirling around Marty. Do you think he had something to do with Leon's death?"

Alecia's eyes flashed. "Why would you ask me that? Chris didn't know what he was walking into when he went into that store. My son wouldn't hurt a fly."

I held up my hands. "Hold on, Alecia. I'm not accusing Chris of anything. I think there's more going on here. I just want to know what happened between Leon and Marty."

Alecia stepped back, as if she was trying to collect her thoughts. She finally spoke. "I wouldn't wish what happened to Marty on anybody, but I've seen firsthand the damage inflicted by some of his plans. Marty deceived people."

"Just like Leon."

Alecia swallowed and took a breath. "Sometimes Leon could be so trusting of the wrong people. He tried doing normal, honest jobs, like construction, and he even worked at the beach. I know he wanted to provide for his family and make his mother proud. Still, he didn't think about all the consequences of his choices."

That I knew about my cousin. I had had countless conversations with Aunt C about her son's escapades.

Alecia continued, "I'm afraid that Chris inherited that part of his dad. My boy doesn't think about consequences, either. If he hadn't been around those boys . . ."

I reached out to Alecia and patted her arm. "Hey, it's going to be okay. Chris is going to make it through this. It's a hard lesson to learn, but I believe God is watching over him. Aunt C has to be standing right there next to God, pleading for Him to protect her grandson."

It wasn't like me to offer encouragement in this way, but even I knew that God had His hands on Chris. That young man had had a brush with death, and evil could have easily prevailed. But it hadn't.

Alecia tried to smile, but the curve of her mouth didn't reach her eyes, which were sad. She looked weary. "Thanks, Rena. I appreciate you being here."

"Get some rest, girl. I will check on you and Chris later."

I watched as Alecia returned to Chris's room.

When Chris woke up, I hoped Alecia would question him. If he could just share some names, that would certainly narrow down the list of individuals who could have pulled the trigger that night in the convenience store.

I was pretty sure there was something else the investigators were looking into, but I doubted that Moses would share that information with me. It could take weeks to confirm this, but I wondered if the gun used to shoot Marty was the same one fired at Chris. It seemed possible to me that the shooter in both incidents was the same person and that he was trying to keep Chris quiet permanently.

I also knew from my past experience working on criminal cases that even if Chris didn't say a word, the identity of his shooter might become known. The shooter would likely do damage to himself if he had a big ego and was immature. Driven by testosterone, he might have a strong desire to brag. And he might brag to the "wrong" person, somebody willing to come forward.

That could have been wishful thinking on my part. It would certainly take the burden off Chris, eliminate his sense that if he talked candidly to the police, he was a snitch. I had a sneaky suspicion that this situation had not been resolved and that it would escalate into something more. My mind went back to the second time the boy pressed the trigger in that convenience store. He had had every intention of killing Marty. That made him a very dangerous person to set off.

CHAPTER TWENTY-THREE

Monday, 6:15 p.m.

It wasn't until I looked through my bag and saw the napkin that I remembered that I was supposed to meet Iris Jenkins tonight at her house. As I studied the napkin, I recognized the address. I left the hospital and turned down a few streets, until I arrived at the house I had visited for the first time last week, when I was looking for Chris.

When I rang the doorbell, Joseph opened the door. I saw the recognition in his face. Joseph's eyes grew wide behind his glasses. "Hey, you're not looking for Chris, right? You do know what happened to him, don't you?"

I assured him that I did. "Yes. I just saw him at the hospital and talked to his mom."

From behind Joseph, I heard a female voice. "Joseph, who is at the door?"

"Um, the lady who came by the other day to see Chris." He peered back at me. "Sorry. I forgot your name."

I smiled. "No problem. Tell your mom, Rena is here."

"Sure. Come in." I stepped inside and cringed when Joseph shouted, "Mom, Rena is here."

Iris came around the corner, holding a boy who appeared to be about two years old in her arms. "Rena, hey, I almost forgot you were coming. Welcome to my house."

"I remembered on the way over that I have been here before, looking for Chris. He was playing games with Joseph."

"Oh yeah. I didn't know that. I must have been on my shift." Iris gave her son the eye and then turned around to explain. "Sometimes I take James to the sitter, but Joseph is old enough to take care of himself."

"Not a problem." I wasn't sure why Iris felt the need to explain this to me, although I did remember that Trey had mentioned that Joseph was sickly sometimes. I looked over at Joseph, who was looking back and forth between us. I figured that he wanted to know how I knew his mom. I grinned and explained, "I went to school with your mom, so we go way back."

I made it seem like Iris and I were friends, but we weren't that close. In fact, if it wasn't for Trey dating Iris, I probably never would have talked to her. I was certainly not the cheerleader type, which probably would surprise the people who used to see me on television.

"Oh, so you know my dad!" Joseph exclaimed.

I started to ask who his dad was, but Iris interrupted. "Rena, the boys and I are having hot dogs and chips. Not that fancy, but you can certainly join us for dinner."

I had had a long day, and the last time I had eaten was before I chased behind a car that drove to a funeral and a lot more questions. I was starving, so I would take whatever was on the menu.

"I appreciate the offer."

I followed Iris and her boys into the small kitchen. Joseph fixed his plate and took his food to the other room, and I sat at the small kitchen table with Iris and her younger son. As we munched, Iris and I caught up on what both of us had been up to since high school. I was really surprised that Iris had never left this town.

I asked, "Do you take vacations and take the boys to other places?"

Iris shook her head. "I can't afford to go anywhere. Plus, we live close to all these beaches. We visit Myrtle

Beach sometimes. I would love to take the boys to Disney World one day." Iris fed her son another piece of the hot dog that she had cut into little pieces. "You wouldn't believe me, but being employed at the Huddle House has been the longest job I've had in a while. That all may change soon, though."

"Oh? Why the change?"

An uncomfortable silence nestled between us. Joseph, who had been sitting quietly in the other room, appeared in the doorway and then took his paper plate over to the trash can. There was a brief exchange of looks between Iris and her oldest son. I honed in on the unhappy look Joseph directed at his mother. He walked back out of the room, and Iris stared at him as he went. She was oblivious to the fact that the younger boy in her lap had grabbed the ketchup bottle.

"Uh, Iris . . ." I pointed at the little boy just as he squeezed ketchup onto the table.

"Oh no, no." Iris got up from the table, with James in her arms, though he had seemed perfectly content with painting the table with his ketchup-covered fingers. She brought the wiggly boy over to the kitchen sink and grabbed a towel and began rubbing the ketchup off his hands.

I waited to speak until she sat back down with the toddler, who had grown increasingly upset. I imagined it was time for the little guy to go to bed. Iris wrapped her arms around him and began to rock him.

"Iris, I'm sorry. I didn't mean to pry into your business, and if this is a bad time, I can come back."

"No. You're fine. I appreciate the company."

I didn't know how long Iris would feel that way, because I was about to make our conversation a bit uncomfortable. "You know, this morning we talked about Alecia and how you two didn't get along. You said she didn't get along with Aunt C, either. I had no idea."

Iris blew out a breath and tried bouncing the boy on her lap. "Your aunt was really protective of Leon. She kind of stuck her head in the sand about him sometimes. It's what moms do with their sons, I guess. Alecia would get mad and would accuse Leon of being a mama's boy. They argued."

"How did you hear all this if you and Alecia weren't close?"

"I would hear her talking to Trey. Those two talked about everything with each other. Sometimes I wish he wouldn't have shared some things about me with Alecia."

Trey. That explained why Alecia didn't care for Iris. "What happened to you and Trey, anyway?"

Iris looked at me as if she was surprised I'd asked. "I messed up things with Trey. I guess I just took him for granted."

I was equally surprised by her confession. I'd heard Trey had proposed marriage to Iris, but that was back when I had married his half brother. I conveniently remembered being on a story for the television station and not really being interested in attending the wedding. Later on, Benny said the wedding never happened. I never asked why.

Maybe I was secretly glad the wedding never happened.

The doorbell rang. Joseph, who had positioned himself in front of the television in the living room, sprinted to answer the door. Iris stopped rocking the baby and stood, propping him on her hip. She held the baby with one arm and used her free hand to smooth her hair.

I was so impressed with Iris's multitasking that I didn't notice that a man had appeared in the kitchen doorway. I glanced over and then did a double take. I wasn't about to say the cliché "Well, speak of the devil," because this was a godly man who had just entered the house.

Trey stood in the kitchen doorway with his arm slung around Joseph's shoulders. I looked at Joseph's eyes behind his big round glasses, and then I looked at Trey's eyes. If someone could have peered inside my head, I was sure he or she would see there was something like fireworks going off. Of all the revelations today, this one topped them all for me.

At the hospital I'd been puzzled about the fact that Trey had referred to Chris and Joseph as cousins. Now I understood. The fact that Iris had seemed nervous about her appearance all of sudden also made more sense now. The two high school sweethearts might not have ever married, but Joseph was definitely Trey's offspring.

Life was just full of surprises.

CHAPTER TWENTY-FOUR

Monday, 7:30 p.m.

I was not sure how I'd missed the memo, or rather, the baby announcement. All this time, I'd thought Trey was childless like me. I didn't know why I'd assumed that about him, since we'd barely kept in touch since high school. Right now I felt tension between Trey and Iris, and it wasn't that love tension. I sensed animosity under Trey's calm demeanor. He had never been one of those people who would explode and thus give people reasons to want to send him to anger management class.

That was my issue. I had a fuse, and if you lit it, I had no problem catching fire. I had attended some anger management classes in my life.

I observed Iris as she held the toddler on her hip. She said quietly, "Hey, Trey. I need to put James to bed. We can talk later. Besides, I have company now."

I raised an eyebrow. "Oh, don't let me hold you up."

Trey turned toward me. I could see the anger set in his jaw, but he seemed to take a breath and let whatever was bothering him go. "We can't seem to stop running into each other, Rena."

I smiled. I wasn't complaining. In fact, right now I was very interested in this story.

Iris looked pretty uncomfortable. "I'm going to take James in the other room to get him ready for bed."

"I will come with you," Trey responded.

It appeared Trey had come over for a reason, and he was determined to prevent Iris from backing out of the conversation. I wanted to follow them down the hallway and put my ear to the door, but then I saw Joseph's face.

The young boy was barely fourteen, but I declared he looked like he was ten years old. Puberty was really dragging its feet for this boy. Then I remembered Trey had been kind of like that too. He had had a baby face for so long., By the end of our freshman year, he had grown at least four inches and had acquired muscles.. Anyone who had picked on him the year before had been shocked to find him trying out for quarterback of the junior varsity football team. It hadn't taken him long to impress the coaches. He made varsity by his sophomore year.

Joseph seemed to be more studious than Trey had been. Behind those Harry Potter–looking glasses was an intellectual. I was enchanted with him when I met him for the first time a week ago. I felt like he was a good influence on Chris. So while Iris and Trey were in the other room, I took the liberty to sit down next to Joseph on the living room couch.

He didn't seem to mind, although I could tell from his furtive glances down the hallway that he was worried about his parents.

"Parents can get into it sometimes. No need to worry," I said.

Joseph nodded. "I know. They don't argue that much. My dad is really cool. But . . . this time, I don't know if my dad likes my mom's plan."

"What's going on?"

Joseph grabbed the game console, but he didn't turn on the game. He just sat there and held it. "She wants us to move and live with James's dad."

"Where does James's dad live?"

"Charlotte, North Carolina."

"Really? I just moved from Charlotte. Pretty nice Southern city. Definitely a lot more going on than in this little town."

Joseph shrugged. "Yeah, Charlotte sounds cool, but I won't be around my friends, and I won't be able to see my dad as much."

Oh! Now I was starting to understand. It was funny that lately I'd been talking to Iris, who'd never left this place, and now she wanted to move away. That was tough. I couldn't blame her, because I was out of this place before I'd barely taken off my graduation robe. I felt really bad for Trey.

"Have you seen Chris?" Joseph asked me. "Is he going to be okay?"

"He's still being watched carefully by the doctors, but it sounds like he should be. Are you worried?"

Joseph looked at me. "Do you think they will try again?"

That caught my attention. Chris couldn't or wouldn't say anything to the authorities, but, I wondered, how much did he share with Joseph? I didn't feel very comfortable having this conversation with Joseph, but nonetheless I casually asked, "You think there are some people trying to hurt Chris?"

Joseph shook his head. "I was just asking."

I moved an inch closer to Joseph on the couch. "Do you know the guys that Chris hangs around with?"

Joseph remained quiet. He finally answered, "Yeah, I know them, but my dad wants me to stay away from them."

Trey must be a great dad for Joseph to have so much respect for him. I had feared my stepdad, Reverend Lawson, and at the same time I had rebelled against him because of the way he made me feel. My biological dad was just a fun guy who was in and out of my life until he died. I hadn't known whether to take Dallas Robinson seriously most of the time. So I was impressed by Joseph's willingness to listen to Trey. I wondered how long that would last, since at some point all adolescents go through a rebellious stage. Maybe Joseph would skip that stage. It certainly might save his life if he did.

Joseph rambled on, and I found it endearing that he would talk to me. "I told Chris those guys were trouble, especially the ones wearing the jackets."

I knew my mouth fell open. I quickly shut it, because Joseph was taking me into territory that I had been on my mind most of the day. "What kind of jackets?"

"They're red, with a skull on the back. All kinds of creepy stuff around it, like snakes. Ugh. I can't stand snakes. You?"

My eyes widened. We were having a casual conversation, but I was ready to explode with the information. "No, I'm not a fan of snakes, either. So there is more than one person who wears this type of jacket?"

"Oh yeah." Joseph picked up the console and started the game.

Joseph had confirmed something that had been brewing in my mind for a while now. I wanted to ask him more, and actually get real names, but just then Trey walked in from the other room. While my mind was trying to process what Joseph had confirmed for me, I noticed that Trey appeared to be disturbed. He had this look of longing and hurt on his face as he stared at his son.

"Well, I need to call it a night." I grabbed my bag and nodded at Joseph. "Trey, quite a boy you have here. It was great getting to know him better."

Trey beamed with pride at Joseph, and then his eyes focused on me. "You're leaving? I will walk you out."

Although I really did want to get him out of the house, I waved at him and said, "You don't have to do that. I'm sure Iris needs your help."

He responded, "She's giving James a bath."

"Okay."

I waved at Joseph and noticed how he was looking at his dad. Iris might want to rethink this move. It looked like she was tearing a father and a son apart. I didn't know the circumstances of Joseph's birth, or anything about Trey and Iris's broken relationship and how they got to this place, but it was clear that Trey and Joseph had a close bond.

Trey closed the front door behind us after we stepped out onto the porch. He looked really pensive.

I appreciated the cool breeze and stopped at the edge of the porch. I reached for Trey's arm to get his attention. "Are you worried about Chris? You look like something is really bothering you."

He shook his head. "Chris will pull through fine. He has a fight ahead of him, but he's young and strong. Alecia has always been a strong woman. She's pretty worried, and rightfully so. I believe whoever is responsible will be found."

"You sound pretty confident, so why the worried look on your face?"

Instead of answering right away, Trey trotted down the steps.

I followed behind him. "You are free to talk to me, you know. Remember, you extended that invitation to me a few days ago."

He turned and glanced back at the house. "Iris and I have a serious conversation ahead, and she does not want to have it with me. I'm not too happy about the situation, because she's made up her mind. That's all."

"I didn't know you had a son with Iris."

He looked at me. "I didn't know he was my son until two years ago."

I stepped back. "What?" I turned and looked back at the house. The window curtains seemed to have moved. Was Iris peeking out at us?

I reached in my bag for my keys. "Look, whatever is going on between you two, I don't want to be involved." I never had. I had hated when they got into arguments in high school. He would always talk to me. If he couldn't find me, he'd find Alecia. But then, as fast as I said that, I got angry about what Iris had done. I questioned Trey about it. "So, how come you didn't know your son until two years ago? What was going on after his birth and while Joseph was growing up all this time?"

Trey shook his head. "I thought you didn't want to get involved."

"I don't. I just want to know. It's obvious you're an awesome dad and he's a great kid."

He had that crooked smile going on. I could tell Trey was really proud of Joseph.

Here I was, getting involved, anyway, because now I was really feeling angry with Iris. How could I not be? This was my old buddy Trey here. "Joseph told me about the upcoming move to North Carolina. He's in high school, and these are pretty critical years for him as he becomes a man. I imagine that's not good for him or you."

The smile faded on Trey's face. "No, it's not, but there's a lot more to the story." A muscle in Trey's jaw twitched. "I'm trying to seek a solution prayerfully that works for all of us, but the man Iris is involved with now, James's dad . . . I just don't want him around Joseph."

We had stopped at my car, and I clicked my key fob to unlock the doors. I really didn't want to leave now, but I could feel my adventures from the day starting to wear on me. I touched Trey's arm. "Hey, let's save the whole story for another time. I need to go. It's been a long day."

"Sure. We will make a date of it." He winked and opened my car door for me.

A date? I was sure Trey didn't mean anything by that statement. Or did he? Why was I asking myself these questions? Nothing was going to happen between me and Minister Evans. We were two buddies getting reacquainted with each other, so I wasn't even going to take myself down that road.

I climbed in my car and let Trey close the door. I looked up at him. My body felt so tired, and a deep sadness seemed to swallow me in the car. I looked away from him and started the engine. My feelings for Trey and my inability to be in a relationship with him would have to be filed under the heading "yet another lost opportunity."

I definitely didn't want to get involved in his situation. I had other things on my plate, like the questions swirling around Leon's death, Chris's shooting, and Mama. I didn't need to be distracted by a relationship that was never going to develop beyond a friendship.

As I drove off, I began to think back over all that I had discovered today. My head was jumbling everything together, but there was one solid question that stood out from my brief conversation with Joseph. Which boys did Moses have in custody? I sure hoped the investigator could locate the other car in the parking lot that night at the convenience store. A suspect was still out there . . . and maybe more than one. And that person was responsible for shooting Chris.

CHAPTER TWENTY-FIVE

Tuesday, April 22, 10:00 a.m.

I checked out the news before going to sleep, but there was no mention of names in the news story about Chris's shooting, since the boys were minors. I felt like the actual shooter was older, smarter, and he had slipped past the police's radar. As I drifted off to sleep, the red jacket drifted into my dreams, along with snakes.

I slept and slept. I probably had the best sleep I'd had in a long time, because Monday had been such a full day. I would've kept on sleeping if the doorbell hadn't rung. I stumbled out of bed and nearly stepped on Callie. The feline took off in the other direction, hissing. I had given up on the idea of throwing her out of my bedroom, which used to be Aunt C's bedroom.

For some reason, Bev standing at my front door was not that much of a surprise to me. I opened the door and glared at her. "I sure hope this is good, because I was sleeping. In fact, I would say that's the best sleep I've had since I got here."

Bev walked past me like she couldn't care less that for once I had had a full night's sleep. She was dressed in jeans and a T-shirt. I looked at her attire.

"Aren't you supposed to be back at work this week?" I asked.

Bev sat down on the couch. "I had to take the day off and get Mama to the doctor."

I grimaced. "Is she okay?"

"Yes, it was her annual checkup. She was okay, but very stressed. She didn't tell me until we got back to the house that she received a notice from the county code inspector. Mama is going to get a heavy-duty fine by the end of the month if she doesn't clean up her place."

Well, that shut down my rant about losing sleep. Bev had warned me. I sat down in the chair across from the couch. "What are we going to do?"

Bev threw her hands up in the air. "We need to get her place cleaned up."

"How are we going to manage that feat? I didn't get past all the mess that should have been the living room. The furniture was buried in that room."

Bev crossed her arms. "I hired an organizer and a professional cleaning crew to come by and help us on Thursday."

"Thursday?"

"This is serious, Serena."

"I know that, but that's two days away." I sank down on the chair. I'd seen hoarding incidents before, but this was my own family, the woman who gave birth to me. "Is Mama going to cooperate?"

"She says she wants help, but she could change her mind. She has before."

I raised my eyebrows. "You tried this before? Great!"

"I tried to do this last fall, but she backed out after the organizer showed up at the house. She needs help, Serena. She has for a long time. I believe my dad was holding her together. When he died, she just let things go."

I was about to disagree that Reverend Lawson had had any part in doing something good for my mother, but I had to admit that the man had loved Mama. I still wasn't too sure he had cared to have me as part of a package deal. I was sure he'd got more than he'd bargained for with me as his stepdaughter.

"Where have you been? I was trying to get you all yesterday," Bev said, changing the subject.

Well, there was no way I was going to share all my activities on Monday with my sister, but I decided I would mention one thing. "I went to Marty Davis's funeral."

Bev frowned. "The man who was shot at the corner store."

I sighed. "I talked to him a few times." I wasn't sure I should tell my sister the whole story.

Bev shrugged. "That's reasonable. I guess the store is close to the house. Have you checked on Alecia and Chris? I'm still trying to figure out what to tell my girls."

"I guess just tell them the truth. Someone shot Chris. You know the girls are going to hear about it at school, if they haven't already. Kids talk." As I stretched my arms above my head, my statement hit home. My conversation with Joseph last night had been pretty informative, but I wondered what else I could find out.

"Serena?"

I focused on my sister. "Yeah?"

"What's going on? You're distracted, and I know it's not just because I woke you up. You just went off somewhere in your thoughts just now."

I held up a finger. "Yeah, I'm missing something this morning. Let me get some coffee." I walked into the kitchen and first grabbed a can of cat food from the cabinet. Callie sat there, looking rather diva-like, waiting on her food. This cat had me trained. I was feeding her before making my cup of java. As I fed the cat, my sister traipsed into the kitchen, still looking worried.

I threw out the empty can, washed my hands, and grabbed some K-Cups from the counter. As I waited for the first cup of coffee to brew, I turned to my sister. I didn't know if it was a sudden case of guilt or the fact that she'd probably find out, anyway, but I decided to spill all that was going on with me, starting with walking into the convenience store and being an eyewitness to the shooting. By the time I was finished, Bev looked really troubled.

I grabbed the coffee mug off the Keurig and sipped while I waited for a response from Bev. "Well, say something."

"I don't know what to say, Serena. I was scared about Mama, and now I'm thinking you are a walking time bomb. Don't you think you should let the police investigate?"

I drank the rest of my coffee and slammed the cup a little too hard on the table. "I investigated criminal cases for most of my career as a reporter. No big deal. Besides, I haven't found out anything helpful. I just keep digging up more questions."

"You're starting to get back to yourself again, I guess," Bev stated.

"I guess." I was feeling more alive than I had in months.

"Does this mean you are going to leave here and return to Charlotte?"

I observed my sister. "I haven't thought about returning to Charlotte. I've been preoccupied with everything going on here in Georgetown. Why would you ask me if I'm leaving?"

"I just think it's been good for you to be home. The girls have enjoyed getting to know you."

I wasn't going to agree with calling this place home, but I smiled, anyway. "Is that all? The girls like me being here. Or are you really saying you like having your big sister in town too?"

Bev smirked. "I'm not admitting anything to you."

I laughed. I had to admit, I wasn't missing my old life. I didn't know whether my brain was up to its old tricks of distracting me from the conversation, but an image of

Trey's face came to mind. I couldn't say it out loud, but I suddenly had a lot of reasons to stay in Georgetown a little while longer. In fact, I was wondering if Aunt C was in cahoots with God, planning out this journey that I had been on the past few months.

CHAPTER TWENTY-SIX

Tuesday, 2:00 p.m.

After Bev left, I decided to make myself more useful. I wasn't sure how things were going to go down at Mama's house on Thursday. I couldn't stand that house, and now I was going to have to spend a whole day there, trying to clear the junk my mama had hoarded for whatever reason. Maybe I should have been more involved in her life, especially after Reverend Lawson died. I'd always sensed the damage my father did to her when he left. Here I was, thinking I was mental from a bump on the head, and Mama had been struggling through her feelings by hoarding stuff.

Maybe I wasn't all that different. I had certainly had my share of men. Never the right one. I had a collection of stuff that no one could see. I was still contemplating Trey's statement last night about a date. The man was a minister, and he was a father. There were quite a few things about Trey I didn't know. My goodness, there was no way I would share some of my past choices with Trey. I would be, well, embarrassed.

Date. Yeah, I need to pull myself together.

I had spent all those years behind a desktop computer or a laptop, typing up notes for a story, and yet I'd barely turned on a computer since arriving here in January. I had no need to keep up with e-mail now that I was no longer employed. It was a pleasure to stay away from social media. In the old days I would frequent those sites, always keeping an eye out for hints of a possible story.

I had been enjoying my freedom from information overload so much, I actually had to look for my laptop. I finally found my laptop bag in the hall closet. Aunt C had DSL from the local phone company, and although I hadn't been using it, I'd kept paying the bill. The computer she had in her office was practically ancient—it had Windows XP—so I made room on the desk for my laptop. I plugged the network cable into my laptop and then plugged the power cable into the wall. In a few minutes, I was connected to the Internet.

I figure in it wouldn't hurt to peek into the lives of the boys involved in the convenience store robbery and shooting. I decided to start by finding out more about the red jacket. Was it sold in town, or would it have to be ordered? I wasn't trying to engage in stereotyping, but the jacket reminded me of a clothing line I had seen before. I typed "urban clothing" in the Google search box and looked through the resulting images. I scrolled through the images for a long time before I decided to narrow the search by adding "jackets" to the search box.

There were all the usual name brands: Timberland, Rocawear, Sean John, and so on. I was starting to get really frustrated, because I hadn't run across anything that was even close to the red jacket. I stopped scrolling and decided to do another search by changing "jackets" to "red jacket."

It seemed liked I scrolled forever before I ran across a similar jacket. I clicked on the image so I could view it up close. It was the exact shape, but the symbol wasn't the same. I clicked to view the Web site and realized the image was a part of a blog post. The blog seemed to be some fashion blog. As I scanned the blog post, I saw that that particular jacket was being sold in ten exclusive designs for a limited time. I looked at the blog date. The post was written last fall, which meant that these exclusive jackets went on sale around October.

As I read more, I learned that the jackets were designed based on a popular hip-hop artist's newly released album. I opened a new window and did a search of his name, Maverick. I had heard of Maverick before, but I certainly didn't listen to his music. I would never admit that I had indeed grown old and preferred the music I'd grown up with in the 1970s and 1980s.

I had to read about Maverick. I discovered he had his own style but was often compared to the popular artist Drake, mainly because they looked like they could be brothers. Maverick opted to wear his hair in long dread-locks, like Lil Wayne. He kept the sides shaved close and the rest of his hair pulled back. He didn't mind being bare-chested. His exquisite six-pack, or possibly eight-pack, was not what grabbed my attention as I scrolled through photos of him.

It was the gold skull hanging from a chain around his neck.

The more I read, the more I was struck by this guy's interest in death. Most hip-hop artists had distinct run-ins with death on the streets, but Maverick had an unhealthy obsession with skulls. His music bordered more on hard rock and heavy metal, versus the hypnotic beats and the pulsating bass found in most hip-hop.

I clicked back over to the blog post to see if there were any more hints about the other designs on the jacket. I finally scrolled to the bottom of the blog post and read this sentence: "The designs are all very eclectic, with one being a representation of the symbol Maverick was known for on his debut album." When I clicked over to Maverick's Web site to look at his discography, sure enough the cover art on his debut album was a perfect match for the design on the back of the jacket. There were definitely snakes coiled around the skull.

Those jackets were exclusive, though. The blog post mentioned that they started at around three hundred dollars. I knew kids walked around in hundred-dollar sneakers and other hundred-dollar clothing, but three hundred dollars for this fancy jacket was a bit much for me. Joseph had said that more than one person had this jacket. I wondered how many had one and how they got it. Given that it was a limited edition, I doubted the jacket was sold at a local store. I bookmarked the page to check it out later.

I decided to take a different angle in my search. Privacy didn't seem to bother teens, and they would post anything online without really understanding the consequences. I imagined, like I told Bev, that kids did talk. Unfortunately, some liked to talk out in public on social networks.

I logged on to Facebook for the first time in months. I had many the friend requests and notifications awaiting my attention. I sighed and decided to ignore those for now. They would only disrupt my focus, and I didn't want to be reminded of my old life. I had too much going on now.

I started by searching for Chris's profile page. Interestingly enough, I was friends with my younger cousin. When did that happen? I wondered. I just accepted his request, and that was it. I was supposed to be on a mission, but it didn't take long for me to get sidetracked. I scrolled through Chris's list of friends and clicked on people we had in common. I was amazed. I had friended Alecia, Bev, Trey, and even Iris on Facebook.

Funny how I accepted friend requests, but I had started to get reacquainted with some of these people only in the past few weeks. As I looked over Trey's and Alecia's pages, I noticed that they weren't on Facebook much.

They had probably signed up for it just because everyone else had. Now, Iris lived on Facebook when she wasn't at work. She had tons of posts.

Okay, I didn't have time to be nosy and peruse Iris's page, so I clicked back until I was back on Chris's page. The last time he had posted was last Wednesday afternoon, before the robbery went down. In the selfie posted on his time line he was wearing the same clothes from that night, including the cap. I couldn't tell where he was, but I knew he was outside. I checked out the rest of his photos and noticed that Joseph had tagged Chris in two photos. In one of the tagged photos, Chris and Joseph were clowning around in front of the camera.

I stared at Joseph for a while. That boy certainly looked like Trey. I wasn't sure why I hadn't caught the resemblance at first. There was an instant likability with Joseph, just like with his dad. I felt bad that Trey had missed out on so much of his son's life. Boys needed their fathers. It probably would help Chris if Leon were still alive.

On the second tagged photo of the boys, it appeared that they were outside, in the backyard, and a barbecue was going on behind them. I looked carefully at the photo and decided that it was taken about two Saturdays ago. There were people behind the boys. I clicked on the photo so I could enlarge it and get a better look.

What I saw caused me to grab both sides of the laptop, as if to prevent myself from jumping into the photo. Unless I was seeing things, Marty and the same man who had driven that dark Crown Victoria were behind the boys. Neither of the men looked happy. In fact, I would dare say they were exchanging words. At the moment they took this selfie together, neither Chris or Joseph probably knew that the two men were in the background.

Where was this photo taken? I wondered. I knew Alecia wasn't a fan of Marty. Would she allow Chris to be around him? Who was this other guy? Once again, in my search for something in particular, I had gotten off track. Why did these older guys keep showing up in what had started out as a gang of boys robbing a store, one of them shooting Marty?

I didn't know why, but the fact that Joseph was in this photo made think of his mother. So I decided to return to Iris's Facebook page. I clicked immediately to her photos, because there was one thing I knew for sure about social media. Some people just didn't know when sharing too much was, well, too much. And it didn't matter the person's age: every age group had its culprits. It took me a few minutes, but I found the photo I was seeking.

Like someone twenty years younger, Iris stood with her arms wrapped around the same man who I'd seen driving the Crown Victoria. What was it that Trey had said last night? He didn't want Joseph around this man.

Now I just needed to figure out who he was and why I felt so suspicious of him. I knew who to call, and he was going to be surprised that I was calling to ask *him* out on a date.

CHAPTER TWENTY-SEVEN

Wednesday, April 23, 11:00 a.m.

Trey kind of took away my joy when I asked him out on a date, mainly because he didn't sound too surprised when I called him. I knew that in this day and age, men expected a woman to make the first move, but I remembered that Trey had always been the gentleman. Maybe he just figured it was me and it was no big deal. But then he surprised me when he requested that we drive up to Murrells Inlet together on Wednesday. That made me think Trey had been planning something all along.

My gut was about to kill me from nerves as I sat outside my house and waited for him to arrive. This was technically not a real date; at least that was what I had convinced myself. I was just hanging out with an old buddy today so I could get some information. Trey soon arrived and pulled his car into my driveway. He jumped out and opened the passenger door for me. I raised my eyebrows at him as I climbed in his car. The perfect gentleman, as usual.

As I sat inside Trey's Audi, which was a couple years old but smelled new and looked pretty polished, I couldn't help but examine his profile. He had aged rather nicely. Some men just had it like that—a few gray hairs, a little bit of extra weight, but they still looked like a million bucks. I, on the other hand, was kind of wishing for my old look.

As Trey drove, I looked down at my nails and curled my fingers up into fists. I used to have no problem making hair salon and manicure appointments. I had to appear a certain way on television, and if I didn't show up looking great, the cameras would make me look positively awful. Plus, I was always running after someone or something for a story, and I was always being asked to emcee some event, so I had to look good. Now I couldn't even remember the last time I had pampered myself with a bubble bath.

I rubbed my hand over my natural curls, which were growing pretty fast. I had tried twisting my hair last night, so I had a bit of a spiking thing going on. I had decided to wrap a golden-yellow headband around my head. It matched my sundress. Trey had seen my natural look the last few times we talked, so I figured it wouldn't hurt to add some mascara and lip gloss. My silver hoops brought my ensemble together.

This was me. The work-in-progress Serena.

"Didn't take you long to want that therapy session, I see," Trey teased.

I spun around in the passenger seat and stared at Trey. I liked looking at this man, but he could be annoying. "I didn't ask you out to talk . . . well, at least not about me."

Trey glanced at me. "No?"

"No. I want the rest of the story."

Trey leaned his head back and laughed. "For someone who doesn't want to get involved, you just can't seem to stop your curiosity."

"Are you kidding? Your story had my imagination on fire last night."

The smile on Trey's face disappeared. "Well, don't get too excited. The story has been bittersweet."

"Because you have a son?"

"Yeah. I missed out on most of his life because . . ."

I waited for him to finish, but he seemed hesitant and said no more. An uncomfortable silence crept between us. Since he was driving, I thought maybe it was best for us to arrive at our destination before I bothered him again. I sensed in him that same simmering anger that I had witnessed last night. It appeared that I was the one acting as the therapist today.

It was fairly quiet as we traveled down Highway 17. There was some traffic flowing around us. In about a month, when Memorial Day arrived, the traffic would increase as tourists started to trickle in from various places around the country. These were some of the best waters on the East Coast. I missed coming down to the beach. I didn't know what my plan was as far as staying around here, but I needed to find a swimsuit and enjoy the water one day. Over the years, I'd forgotten how to just relax and have fun.

Trey had his sunroof open, so I threw my head back and slipped my shades on while he drove. Many of the things I had examined on the computer yesterday came to my mind. I wanted to dissect all the details, but the sun was making me sleepy. I must have dozed off, because the next thing I knew, a hand was shaking my shoulder and someone was calling my name. I sat up suddenly.

Trey said, "We're here, sleepyhead."

"Wow. Sorry. I didn't know I was going to take a nap." It was weird that I just fell into an easy sleep around Trey. I opened my bag and checked my face in my mirror before exiting the car. I looked up and noticed we were in the parking lot of a restaurant. I smiled. "I remember this place. It's still here."

Trey grinned. "Still the best seafood around."

Seafood by the Sea had opened when I was a teenager. I remembered I didn't care for seafood, or at least I thought I didn't, until Trey's family let me and Alecia tag along to a family dinner at this restaurant one Sunday afternoon. Whenever I ate seafood, this place always came to mind because it was my first real taste of good seafood. The shrimp were legendary. They were so fresh and were fried to a golden brown.

I had always liked being around Trey's mom and dad. They were two beautiful people. With the one exception that Trey's dad had a brief affair early on in the marriage, and it resulted in my second ex-husband, Benny. I learned later that Trey's mom forgave his dad and they remained together. Both were still around town, but I hadn't gone to visit with them. I wondered what they would think of me and Trey together today.

Stop it, Serena. I needed to stop getting caught up in the fact that Trey and I were out together. *No big deal.*

When we entered the restaurant, I noticed the place seemed a bit modernized, but it still had the same feel it had about twenty-five years ago. The furniture was different, and the place was more expansive. The hostess seated us pretty quickly and handed us menus. The menu had also expanded since the last time I had visited. "Wow. They are big-time. How do you choose what's good to eat?"

"I usually get the sampler. You get a little taste of clams, lobster, flounder, and more," Trey commented.

"Sounds good to me." The smells in the restaurant were tantalizing and reminded me that I was living off a cup of coffee from earlier this morning.

Once the waiter took our orders and returned with our drinks, I waited patiently for Trey to continue the conversation that had gone nowhere in the car.

He caught my stare and held up his hand. "Okay, I know, I know. You want the story. I'm going to tell you pretty quickly, so hang on for the ride."

I sat back and crossed my arms.

Trey practically drained his iced tea before he began talking. "You may remember Iris and I were supposed to get married. It didn't happen. Mainly because she came to me and told me she couldn't go through with the wedding. She had become involved with someone else."

I started to open my mouth to say something that was not very nice, but then I realized that if I did, Trey might just stop talking. So I played the good girl and squeezed my hands together under the table.

He sighed and leaned forward. "You know, Iris had been my world for years. I never imagined when we started dating our junior year in high school that we would be together so long afterward. I went off to the University of South Carolina and came to visit on the weekends. We managed to keep it going, even though we were on and off a few times."

The waiter interrupted Trey when he arrived at our table, carrying a large round tray above his shoulders. I could see the steam rising up from the food as the waiter sat our plates down in front of us. Once the waiter walked away, I watched Trey bow his head, and I quickly followed suit. Trey said grace, and I said, "Amen."

We ate in silence, though it wasn't as awkward as in the car earlier. The food was delicious. It was hard to believe, but the popcorn shrimp tasted just like I remembered.

"Is it good?" Trey asked.

I nodded. My mouth was full, and my stomach was incredibly happy. I didn't want Trey to stop talking, though. We hadn't gotten to the part of the story that I interested me. "So you and Iris went your separate ways. When I talked to her, she said she has never left Georgetown."

"No, but I did. After our wedding was called off, I went to Dallas, Texas, for a while, and then I went to Maryland, and finally I decided to come back here. I had a friend who was looking for someone to play music, and by that time I had started getting noticed a bit from playing at conferences and other events."

"So you're an actual minister?"

Trey shook his head. "Yes. I was a bit lost after the wedding was called off. I can't say I was very productive in my life for a few years. I decided to go to Dallas Theological Seminary after attending a Bible study for a while. I just started to get new direction in my life from God."

I was feeling kind of lost myself at the moment, but I wanted him to get back to the good part of the story. "Cool. So you found out about Joseph . . . when?"

Trey stared at me.

"What?" I said when he remained silent.

"You know, I'm not surprised you became a reporter. You always have been the person who wanted to get to the bottom of everything. You know, it was your constant questions and your drive to get answers that got you in trouble sometimes."

I opened my mouth and closed it. What was there to say? I wanted to know what I wanted to know. I wasn't trying to let anyone pull the wool over my eyes. Right now Trey was dragging this story out.

Trey pulled his napkin off his lap and placed it on the table. "I probably would have never known that Joseph was my son. It just happens that the guy that Iris decided she wanted left her when he found out she was pregnant. She kind of failed to tell him that there was a possibility the child wasn't his. He may have gotten wind of it, anyway, or maybe he was one of those guys who wasn't trying to get tied down by a pregnant woman. I don't know. I just know she chose not to tell me."

"So all this time, she knew Joseph was your son, but she never contacted you. Well, how did you find out?"

"Remember, I said this was bittersweet. Joseph, you may have noticed, is not quite where he could be at his age. He's been sickly most of his life. He has sickle cell anemia."

"Oh no. I didn't realize."

"Yeah, well, I knew that I had that trait. It was something my mom asked me to get tested for early on. With me having the sick cell trait, it's pretty important to make sure the woman I have children with doesn't have it too. If we both have it, the chances that a child could be born with sickle cell anemia increase.

"Well, when I returned to Georgetown, Alecia would come over with Chris, and he had a friend named Joseph. He and Chris were tight friends, but I noticed one day that Chris was down about his friend. Chris thought something had happened to Joseph, because he hadn't seen him in a while. So I looked up Joseph's address and went to check on him. I never made the connection about his last name, but when I rang the doorbell, Iris opened the door."

"Let me guess. Iris saw you and decided to confess."

"No. It was a few months later, after Joseph had been hospitalized again. She finally mentioned his disease. Before then she would say things like 'He is sickly,' but she never quite revealed that he had sickle cell anemia. So it got me thinking. I even started calculating the years after I found out Joseph's age. I finally asked her if she knew whether she had the trait. She said she didn't know. Then the conversation went downhill, because she didn't want to admit that Joseph was my son. You see at the time, she was pregnant with her other son, James."

Okay, this was starting to get more interesting to me. "So, she was with the same guy that she's with now? I assume he's the dad."

"Yeah. She finally admitted to me that Joseph was my son, but she didn't want me messing with her life now. Apparently, this guy takes care of them. He understands

Joseph's condition, and we have since met. Like I said, I can't say I like him around Joseph. Iris and I have worked out when Joseph can spend time at my house, but I have considered—or at least Alecia has asked that I consider—trying to get custody of him."

"I agree with Alecia."

"It's not that easy. Joseph and I get along great, but he does love his mother. He's a good kid, small for his age, but he's more mature than other kids because of struggling with being sick. His condition alone is a big stressor on Iris. She's struggled with other issues, but she's gotten back on track."

I remember Iris saying her job at the Huddle House was the longest she'd ever worked anywhere. I wondered what Joseph's life was like with his mother. "Why don't you like the man Iris is with, and what's his name?"

"Kenyon. Kenyon Cooper."

I finally had a name. I was definitely going to try to decipher Kenyon's connection to Marty.

The waiter came around and asked us if we wanted dessert. I was tempted, but I was pretty stuffed. Trey paid the bill and left a tip on the table.

We walked out of the restaurant, but instead of returning to the car, we strolled down the sidewalk a bit.

"So how are you going to stop Iris from moving away with this Kenyon guy?"

"I don't know," Trey replied. "He's not from around here. I think he might be from Florida. It sounds like he's lived in a couple of places. I'm not really sure how he ended up in Georgetown, of all places. He just is one of those guys. . . . I don't know. There are rumors. I try not to get caught up in what people are saying."

"But your son is around him. He's basically a father figure in Joseph's life, and now he wants to take him to Charlotte."

Trey wilted right before my eyes after I mentioned the move. "I know Iris wants to leave and start something new. Me and you have been away from this place and have come back. Iris has been here since high school."

"Charlotte isn't that far."

"No, but it's not an ideal situation. Although he never says anything, I get the feeling that Joseph is uncomfortable around Kenyon. He's a huge, intimidating guy."

I didn't think it was wise as that moment to let Trey know why I was really interested in Kenyon Cooper. Now I was starting to wonder if I was being overly silly. I mean, what had I caught the man doing besides going to the place where his girlfriend worked. Maybe I was suspicious of Kenyon for the wrong reasons, but I knew what I heard at Marty's funeral.

The slim man had been upset about both Marty's and Leon's death, and he clearly thought he was next. That photo I found on Joseph's Facebook page showed that there had been obvious tension between Marty and Kenyon. And by Wednesday, approximately four days later, Marty was dead. Something about that scenario felt oddly similar to how Leon died. A disagreement. And then Leon was shot to death a few days later in his own yard.

But Kenyon didn't shoot Marty.

Still, I agreed with Trey. Kenyon didn't sound like the type of man to have around your son. Iris might have to rethink this move, or Trey might need to prepare to fight for custody of Joseph.

CHAPTER TWENTY-EIGHT

Wednesday, 3:00 p.m.

On our way back from Murrells Inlet, Trey said he wanted to stop by the hospital to visit Chris and Alecia. I decided I would tag along. Plus, I wasn't quite ready to leave his presence just yet. I was still trying to soak in his story and was wondering why in the world Iris hadn't contacted Trey earlier in Joseph's life. I imagined her son had been diagnosed with sickle cell when he was younger, and that had to be hard.

We arrived at the hospital and walked in together. Trey was quiet, and I guessed I couldn't blame him. His son was about to move away, and his young cousin, Chris, was in the hospital after being shot. I was feeling pretty downcast myself, especially because I was still looking for some connections that probably had nothing to do with Chris's shooting. I was just going with my gut, and I wasn't sure if my gut instinct had been affected by my "accident" last year.

When we arrived on the floor on which Chris's new hospital room was located, Alecia was standing outside the room, talking to the investigators on her son's case. I wondered if Moses and Baldwin had any news about the actual shooter. I sped up, walking a bit ahead of Trey, to catch the rest of the conversation.

As soon as Moses saw me, he had this look on his face that said, "Oh no. Here she comes." As I got closer, the look on his face didn't change. I got the impression Moses really didn't like me, but I couldn't figure out why. I'd known this guy for all of a week. I certainly didn't remember every running into him in Charlotte, so we had no past history.

Moses turned his attention away from me and nodded at Trey in that way males did to acknowledge each other. I wondered if Trey was aware of Moses's feelings for Alecia. He certainly was standing close to Alecia, like he was in protection mode.

I ignored him and walked up to Alecia. "Any news?"

Alecia shook her head. "No. This isn't really a good time. Chris is awake." She looked up at Moses and said, "I need to check on him. Keep me posted." Alecia headed back into the room.

Trey glanced back at me and followed Alecia into Chris's hospital room. I wasn't buying that Moses and Baldwin had nothing to share. Both men had started walking down the hallway. I caught up to them.

"You don't have anything yet?" I asked.

Moses offered, "We tried talking to Chris, he didn't say anything, and he didn't offer any names."

"Of course not. He's scared. You need to find the boys who purchased that jacket. It's not a jacket that's found in stores. It's very exclusive."

Moses stopped in front of the elevator and punched the DOWN button. He turned to me. "How do you know that?"

"Um, Google. The symbol on the back of the jacket happens to be associated with a very popular hip-hop artist by the name of Maverick. He had only a hundred jackets made, so it's pretty exclusive. Since this is a small town and only a few kids own this jacket, you should be able to narrow down who purchased it and where, don't you think?"

Baldwin looked at me, then at Moses. "Well, Ms. Manchester, I'm impressed. We need to get you through the police academy and then have you work your way up to investigator."

I gave Baldwin a look I usually reserved for Moses. I expected sarcasm from Moses, but not from Baldwin. I wasn't trying to do anything but help these guys by doing what I knew how to do best.

The elevator door opened. Both men stepped in the elevator, but I wasn't finished. So I jumped in the elevator too.

"Moses, are you sure you didn't see anything else on the surveillance camera footage?" I asked.

Moses sighed.

Baldwin looked from me to Moses. "Moses, what is she talking about? You're not sharing information with this woman, are you? She's a civilian and a reporter."

I corrected him. "A *former* reporter. No, he's not sharing anything with me. But I did ask him to check the camera footage to see if anyone else was around the store that night."

Baldwin and Moses stared at each other.

"There was a group of boys hanging outside the store prior to the shooting," Moses revealed. "They probably arrived in a car. That's all I'm giving you now, Manchester."

I thought back to the scene at the convenience store when I drove up that night. Moses didn't need to say anything else. That confirmed it for me. All three boys *were* inside that Crown Victoria.

The elevator arrived at the lobby. Baldwin shook his head. "We could use real witnesses. Right now your eyewitness account, as well as that of Chris Robinson's mother, just isn't helping us develop any solid leads. We need Chris to talk. He is the main person who could clear up a lot of issues, but he's not talking, because his mother won't let him now."

I responded, "The boy was shot and almost died. It's understandable that they're scared."

As both investigators stepped off the elevator, Moses remarked, "You need to stop meddling in the investigation. We're looking at the facts and the evidence. Let us worry about catching Chris's shooter."

Both investigators walked away, making me feel deflated. I stayed on the elevator and punched the button to go back upstairs.

Maybe I was being annoying and was in the way of the investigation. I had left my career a few months ago, because I couldn't handle the stress and the deadlines anymore. Who was I kidding? I'd done nothing but bombard the investigators with all these questions, and I had been going off on tangents that didn't make a whole lot of sense. When the elevator opened on Chris's floor, I got off and walked back down to the room. I found Chris in bed, propped up by pillows. Both Alecia and Trey were still in the room.

Chris looked fragile now. He was no longer the young boy who had tried to exhibit a bit of swagger last week, when I confronted him about his involvement in the convenience store robbery gone bad.

I walked up to the head of his bed. "Hey, you. You're looking much better."

Chris grimaced. "I don't feel any better."

"Glad to have you back with us." I looked at Alecia, who was observing me from her seat on the other side of the room. Since Chris was awake and the investigators were gone, I wanted him to talk to me. He had talked to me before. "So the investigators were here. Is there anything we can do to help them out?"

Alecia stood. "Serena, please. We're not going there again. Chris answered the investigators' questions the best he could, and he needs to rest now."

"I have just one question." In my peripheral vision, I could see Trey motioning to me. I looked over at him, and he was shaking his head. I probably should have complied and kept my mouth closed. But I really wasn't good with warnings sometimes, so I asked, "The jacket that your friend was wearing . . . do you know where it came from?"

Chris frowned. "No. I don't think it came from around here."

"How many boys have the jacket?"

"I've only seen two guys."

"And those guys—"

Alecia exploded before I could finish my question. "Serena, what are you doing? Get out! He's not answering questions from you or anyone else! You're not a cop, and if you want to get a story so bad, maybe you need to leave and go back to Charlotte."

I stood still for a second, reeling from the fact that Alecia had told me I should go back to Charlotte. "What is it with all the animosity here? I'm trying to help."

Alecia walked over to me. "Are you really? You don't care about anyone here. You just came back here because Aunt C died and she left you her house. Why would you care about Chris? You haven't been around him for most of his life."

"Alecia, come on. That's not fair," Trey said from the other side of the room.

I knew he was trying to defend me, but it was too late at that point. I turned around and left the room. For some reason, the investigators thought I was meddling in their case. Then Alecia flat out accused of me of what I already knew. Okay, so I'd been selfish. I'd been living my own life. But that didn't give her any right to question my intentions. I walked down the hall as fast as I could and jabbed at the elevator button.

Behind me I heard someone call my name. The elevator door opened, and I waited for the people inside the elevator to come out before I entered. Just as the elevator door was about to close, Trey showed up and leaped in.

"What?" I cried out.

He sighed. "I'm your ride home."

That's just great! His cousin had just blasted me for trying to help, and now I was going to be stuck in a car with him. I crossed my arms and leaned against the elevator door. So much for the time I spent with Trey earlier today. At this rate, I might just start packing my bags tonight.

CHAPTER TWENTY-NINE

Wednesday, 5:00 p.m.

It was a pretty awkward drive back to my house. I sat with my face to the passenger window the entire way back. I knew Alecia was trying to protect her son, but I was really confused about her lashing out at me. This was my family, and I was trying to help.

"She didn't mean it," Trey said finally, trying to smooth my feathers as he drove.

I turned my face from the passenger window. "Well, it's interesting that she wants me to head back to Charlotte. Yesterday my sister said it was great having me back home. So I don't know whether to pack my bags or just hide in the house, like I have for most of the time I've been here."

"I don't think you should make any rash decisions. For the record, I agree with your sister. Being back here for the long term may be good for you. God has His reasons for the timing of things. Sometimes it's good to connect with family and your roots."

I wiggled around in the seat and sighed. "Alecia and I were good friends. We connected last week like we had been hanging out together this whole time. I thought she knew I was trying to help. I don't get her reaction just now."

"Serena, it's been hard on her. You got to know that losing Leon in their front yard was pretty devastating.

Now someone tried to shoot her son in front of their house. That's, like, the biggest and craziest coincidence. She doesn't know who to blame, so she lashed out at you. Believe me, I've borne the brunt of her anger too. She wants to protect her son."

I did remember Alecia confessing that she was angry all the time and that sometimes it affected Chris. "You're right. I appreciate you reminding me of that, Trey. I guess I don't need to be all supersensitive." I looked over at him. His smile almost made me forget my hurt.

Trey turned into my driveway. He left the engine running, but I didn't jump out of the car. I felt like Trey was on my side. I needed someone to know I did care about my family. Leon. Chris. Alecia. Most importantly, I knew how Aunt C had operated. She had made a way for me to come back home.

"You said that you think I'm back home for a reason. What's the reason? I mean, this thing with Chris is kind of driving me up the wall. I want to do something."

Trey turned off the car. "I can't answer that. I don't know why God has you here. You will need to do some soul-searching and have a heart-to-heart talk with God about what your purpose is. I can say that He's using your tenacity to seek the truth and thus to help your family. I have no doubt Moses and Baldwin are excellent investigators, but they have all kinds of cases they're dealing with, and you have the luxury of focusing on just one."

Maybe more than one case. What Trey was trying to explain to me made sense. God had made me the way I was for a reason. I had been depressed a few months ago, when I thought my twenty-plus-year career was gone forever. Now I wasn't thinking about career advancement. This was the one time when I really had only one objective or motive: I wanted the truth, plain and simple.

Trey continued, "You don't talk about it, but I read about your story last year. You were responsible for helping to bring some pretty powerful people to justice. I hate that you got hurt in the process."

"Yeah, me too, but I've always been good at getting into trouble."

"I wouldn't call it trouble. You've always wanted honesty and to know why things happened and what could be done to make it better."

I laughed. "Yeah, that's me. So, what do I do about me?"

Trey raised his eyebrows. "Be careful. Promise me that you will be cautious."

I looked over at him. "I promise I will do my best. You know, you are a good therapist."

We both laughed.

Trey stopped laughing first. "I wish I could get Alecia to open up more and talk like this. Maybe she wouldn't stay so angry."

Something occurred to me, and I didn't know why, but I asked Trey about it. "Did you talk to Leon before his shooting? I mean, was there anything different about him?"

Trey raised his eyebrows at me again. "You know, it's interesting that you ask, because he *was* different."

I leaned forward. "How so?"

"He was nervous about something. I mean, Leon was not one to be in church on Sundays, but he started coming with Alecia and Chris. One Sunday, actually the Sunday before he was shot, he wanted to talk to me after the service."

"Really? What did he want to talk about?"

"He wasn't specific. He asked questions about forgiveness and what God thought about people who did bad things." Trey rubbed his face. "It was like he was looking for a way to be redeemed for something. I remember Alecia saying that he was always jumpy."

I shook my head. "Wow. That's so weird."

"Why?"

"The night I walked into the convenience store, Marty was nervous about something. It was like he knew something was going to happen. I tell you, less than five minutes later those boys walked in. I didn't see them outside when I entered the store."

"It could be a coincidence."

"Trey, I don't believe in coincidences. I don't know who shot Chris, or who shot Leon, for that matter, but in my gut, this is all connected." I put my hand on the car door. I didn't want to reel Trey into my thought process. Right now, my mind was all over the place as I tried to connect dots that might never be connected. I opened the car door and climbed out.

Before I could close the door, Trey shouted, "Serena?"

I bent down and looked into his eyes. I saw the concern, and it took my breath away. I swallowed and said, "Don't worry. I can be hardheaded sometimes, but I will be careful. I promise."

I closed his car door and walked up to my porch. I knew he wasn't going to leave until I opened my front door. So I unlocked the door and turned to wave good-bye. As I watched his car pull out of the driveway and then disappear down the road, I felt a renewed sense of determination. I headed inside the house.

No, I wasn't planning on packing my bags anytime soon. No matter if Moses, Baldwin, or Alecia wanted me to or not, I would find the truth.

As I changed into more comfortable clothes, my promise to Trey hung in the air. I couldn't guarantee that seeking the truth wouldn't put me in harm's way. After dressing, I sat down in Aunt C's favorite chair and prayed aloud. "God, this is old stubborn Serena. You made me this way, and I don't know what's ahead for me. The one thing I do know is I need you to help me find the truth. I'm not that same crazy person who thinks she can do this all by herself."

CHAPTER THIRTY

Thursday, April 24, 11:00 a.m.

Bev had stopped by my house early this morning. I had had sense enough to have my coffee before we headed to Mama's house. When the organizer, who was a sweet, patient woman, arrived, Mama put a bit of a fuss, but Bev, the organizer, and I did not cave. We started slowly going through the living room. The organizer had assigned members of a professional clean crew the job of cleaning up outside and going through Mama's kitchen. I was grateful, because when I made my way back to the kitchen, I thought I would lose everything I had eaten yesterday.

When I checked the time hours later, I realized that half the day was gone, but I could see some progress. Most of the magazines, books, and boxes had been moved out of the living room, but not without a constant battle with Mama. At one point, when I was throwing what seemed like unimportant items into a trash bag, Mama had a fit.

"Serena, I want those. Take them back out of the bag," she ordered.

I looked at Bev, who was purposely not looking in my direction. I blew out my breath for, like, the tenth time and wiped my hands on my T-shirt, which had become pretty grimy. I wanted to leave and call it a day, but it wasn't noon yet and we had a long way to go. "Mama, those trinkets are filthy. There's no way you can clean those properly. They would only catch dust again even if you could clean them."

"You still have no right, Serena. They belong to me, and I don't want to throw them away."

Mama stalked off. I looked at the organizer, who was trying to appear calm. Her blond hair was pushed back and held in place by a red headband. She looked from me to Mama. She finally darted after Mama, I guess to make her feel better. I, on the other hand, dropped the garbage bag on the floor and started walking.

"Serena." I heard my sister call my name, but I kept walking. I needed to get out of this house. I couldn't care less whether I ever walked across that threshold again. Besides, how in the world could we clean the house when *that* woman wouldn't let anything go? I marched down the steps and out into the yard, which was full of more stuff. There were people all over the yard, some carrying items to a truck with JUNK-TO-GO on both sides and others trying to sort things for whatever reason.

One of the guys carrying a bag of stuff to the truck caught my attention. He looked really familiar to me, for some reason. Then it dawned on me. He was the slim guy I had seen at Marty's funeral. This was just what I needed.

I walked over to the man while he stuffed the bag into the back of the truck. "I appreciate you helping. You do this a lot?"

The slim man swung around. I hadn't really seen his face up close before, and it reminded me a bit of bird. His eyes were small, and he had a large nose.

He squinted. "It's good, decent money."

I looked back at the house and gave an overly exaggerated sigh. "Hmm. Well, I don't know how much progress we're going to make. My mama is having a hard time letting some of this stuff go. Why? I don't even know."

The man's face turned sympathetic. He shook his head. "Yeah, it's tough. I know people like her. They just get attached to stuff." He leaned his head to the side and looked me up and down. "I didn't know Mrs. Lawson had more than one daughter."

Well, that's what I get for staying away. I guessed most people around here had probably forgot about my existence. "Yes. I'm her oldest daughter. I've been away. I left after high school to live in Charlotte."

"Oh, I see. Can't nobody blame you. Not a whole lot going on here, you know, other than the tourist season. I used to be a bit better about going to church. Reverend Lawson would give me work to do at the church and here at his house. I sure do miss him. He was a real nice man. So, Reverend Lawson is your dad?"

"No!" I said. I was a bit thrown off by the man's assertion that Reverend Lawson was nice. That wasn't how I had perceived him at all. I shook my head. "He was my stepdad. Dallas Robinson was my dad."

The man looked startled. "Oh, really? You're Dallas's daughter? You know what? Now I remember you. You're a lot taller now, but you used to hang around Leon, or at least be at his house. I remember a little girl who was with his mom. So y'all cousins?"

"Yep, first cousins. His mom was Aunt C to me. Their house was like a second home to me. I spent more time there sometimes than at this house." I turned and looked at the people who were sorting and bagging stuff. It was hard to believe that all the stuff on the lawn had come out of that small house. I turned my attention back to the man and held out my hand. "I'm Serena. And you are?"

He looked down at my hand. "I don't know if you want to shake hands with me. My hands stay pretty dirty since I work on cars all the time. My name is Tone. Tone Davis."

Davis. I folded my arms. Tone seemed friendly enough. I figured it was my turn to ask the questions now. "Nice to meet you, Tone. Are you related to Marty Davis?"

Something flickered in Tone's eyes. I wasn't sure whether to call it grief or fear.

I continued talking before he could answer. "I was at Marty's funeral a few days ago. Such a shame, you know, the way those boys just killed the man while he's trying to make a living."

Tone dropped his head, as if he was trying to remember something. "Yeah, the whole thing is messed up." He peered at me now, almost cautiously, and asked, "I don't remember seeing you at the funeral. How did you know Marty?"

"I used to go to the convenience store all the time. Not far from the house. We always talked for a bit. Marty seemed like a really nice guy."

"I guess he was nice when he wanted to be."

"Everyone has their moments. By the way, you didn't say if you're related. I just assumed that with the last name Davis, you—"

Tone cut me off. "He's my brother . . . half brother, but we grew up together."

"I can relate. My sister and I are pretty close, even though we live our own lives. It's been good to be back here to be around my sister and her family. I love my nieces."

I was rambling in the hopes that Tone would continue to talk to me, but I had sensed ever since I mentioned Marty's name that he wanted me to go away. I wasn't ready to give up. I wanted more information about Marty. It was like Marty had been a catalyst for attracting trouble. My cousin Leon had been associated with him and had lost his life. While Chris had innocently followed some boys into the convenience store, that whole incident had seemed to have "danger" written on it from the time I entered Marty's store that night.

Tone walked away from me to grab some lamps that were sitting on the lawn. He then walked past me and placed them in the truck. It was like he had gone back to work and was ignoring my chatter as if it was background noise. I'd almost given up on the conversation when Tone stated, "Now your cousin Leon was good people."

His back was turned to me, and I was surprised that Tone would mention Leon out of the blue. We had been talking about Marty, but Tone had decided to switch the topic of conversation back to Leon, which I found strange. Maybe Tone and Marty hadn't had the best relationship.

In keeping with the conversation's new direction, I commented, "I miss Leon. We grew apart when I left here, but I have gotten to know his son. Chris really needs to have Leon around now. That little boy has become a bit lost."

Tone cleared his throat. "I bet. Boys need their fathers. Sorry to hear about Leon's boy getting shot. Hanging around the wrong people can get you into trouble. I know."

It could have been my imagination, but I sensed a nervousness in Tone that was similar to Chris's. Which "wrong people" had Tone gotten himself involved with, and did he know the boys Chris had been hanging out with? I hated that I had eavesdropped on that conversation between Tone and the other man, who, I now knew, was Kenyon Cooper. It just created more questions.

Tone crossed his arms, seeming preoccupied by a memory of something, just as I was trying to organize my scrambled thoughts. Suddenly he looked at me and attempted to smile, as if we were having the best conversation ever. "Look, it was nice talking to you, but I need to get the rest of this stuff off the lawn and into the truck."

"Sure. Thanks again for helping out today." I moved out of Tone's way, but I wasn't finished. I waited until Tone had picked up what used to be part of a table and had heaved it into the truck before I said, "I heard Marty and Leon didn't get along."

Tone turned around and eyed me. "They were friends. Sometimes friends argue and get mad at each other. Why are you asking?"

Since we weren't beating around the bush, I replied, "Did Marty have something to do with Leon's death?"

He shrugged. "Why does it matter? Marty's dead. Nothing can be done now."

Tone had a point about Marty's death, but he hadn't answered my question. In fact, his reply sounded like a confirmation of my premise. "Do you know something?"

Tone shook his head. "I know what you're trying to do. Don't. That's all old rumors. Marty and Leon were more brothers in the spirit than Marty and I were by blood."

"I'm sorry. It's just that Marty will get justice for his murder. What about Leon? Will he get justice? What peace do his wife and son get to have after losing their husband and father in their front yard?"

Tone said nothing. He simply walked back over to the pile of stuff, grabbed a box, and then shoved the box in the truck.

I didn't know what I was expecting from this conversation. I had always gone with my instincts. That trait had led me to some unsavory places and to people I didn't need to be around, but I was usually right on target.

Tone turned around and looked at me. He looked more weary than angry about my questions. "You shouldn't worry your pretty self about these things. What we consider justice may turn out differently than what we think."

I had no idea what Tone meant by that statement. I caught his eye and nodded good-bye, then walked back toward the house, thinking the main battle I needed to deal with today was helping Mama clean up her house. Then I would go after the answers I wanted, no matter where they led me.

One thing was for sure: after meeting Tone Davis today, I was closer to the truth. He had changed the subject on me, but I sensed that Tone believed his own half brother had something to do with Leon's death too. Family never betrayed family; after all, blood was thicker than water. I wondered if, after a period of time, Tone's fears would propel him to reveal more of the truth.

Somebody around here needed to start talking.

CHAPTER THIRTY-ONE

Friday, April 25, 3:00 p.m.

After I left Mama's house yesterday, I slept pretty well. I was starting to enjoy getting a full night's sleep again. Of course, I realized my insomnia was cured only because I had worn myself out physically and mentally this week. But I wasn't focused on myself and my circumstances, because I had a mission and a purpose. *Isn't that what Trey told me?* I wanted to believe that I was of some use to God. I had certainly caused enough trouble in my lifetime.

Despite my numerous run-ins with Mama yesterday, I was happy about the progress that had been made at her house. Her backyard was now presentable. Hopefully, the neighbor who had reported her would see the improvement and would back off.

While we had made a dent at Mama's house, there were at least two rooms that no one had touched. One of those rooms was my childhood bedroom. When I had opened the door and had seen the piles of clothes and boxes hiding my twin bed, I couldn't help but think of all the stuff and baggage I had inside me. Mama's house wasn't the only residence that needed purging.

Now that I was more rested, I decided it was time to continue my quests. I drove to the City of Georgetown Police Department. One thing I knew from working with law enforcement was that there were times when investigative work was conducted at a desk and paperwork was required. I wanted to be respectful, but I needed to know where the investigators were with Chris's case. So I checked in at the front desk to see if Moses was available. I waited in a chair for what seemed like well over twenty minutes. When Moses finally came out, I was prepared for him to send me away, but he waved me back.

"What can I do for you, Ms. Manchester?" he asked over his shoulder as I trailed behind him.

"You could start by calling me Serena. No need for the formalities." I figured that taking a friendly approach wouldn't hurt.

Moses didn't turn to look at me or respond as I followed him back to his desk. His partner's desk was across from Moses's. Baldwin cut his eye in my direction as he talked on the phone. Moses pointed to a chair next to his desk.

"Have a seat, Manchester."

Manchester. All right. Whatever. I didn't mind if he dropped the "Ms." deal as long as he was listening to me. I sat down, but I wasn't sure where to start, since I seemed to have caught Moses in a good mood. I casually glanced at his desk, and my eyes fell on a photo of the jacket. I pointed at the photo. "Did you find out anything?"

Moses sat down behind the desk and leaned back in his chair. "I should have known you were going to come around. Alecia is still pretty upset with you."

I frowned. "You talked to her?"

"As friends. She did mention that you sounded like you were investigating the case."

I hadn't bothered to contact Alecia, even though Trey had tried to console me. I understood where she was coming from, but her anger was unwarranted, since I was trying to help.

Moses must have read my mind. "We can handle this case without your help, Manchester."

I raised my eyebrows. "Really? I brought you the information about the jacket."

Moses's face turned grim. He picked up the photo. "It was a good catch, but this police department does excellent work."

"I don't doubt that you do." I beamed.

Moses grunted. "We were able to trace the purchases to a specialty urban clothing store out of Atlanta, where the jackets were sold exclusively. Apparently, the first ten were available at the brick-and-mortar store for one day only, and the others were available online. We are working out the details with the Atlanta Police Department to help us access any store records or camera footage, if they're still available."

"So you think you can trace the credit card records to the people who made the purchases?"

"That's the idea."

I was really curious about how the boys had acquired those jackets. "It's my understanding that these jackets are all pretty different."

Moses nodded. "There are ten designs, and ten jackets were made with each design, which gives us a hundred jackets. The jacket that we have on our camera footage, and the one that you saw, helped us narrow down the list to the ten people who purchased this particular design."

"And we know at least two or more of those jackets were purchased for some boys here in town," I noted.

Moses frowned at me. "Two or more? And you know this because . . . ?"

"Old habits don't die, Moses. I can't reveal my source." My source happened to be another young boy, and I was already in guilt mode about Chris.

"Are there any other reasons why you're here, other than to give me a headache?"

"I'm so glad you asked." I felt pretty confident that the investigators would eventually run across Chris's shooter, but I needed to find out what I could about Leon. I focused on Moses's face. "Did you question Marty about my cousin's shooting?"

Moses sighed. "The man was just laid to rest. Do you really want to go into this now?"

"Yes. I want to find out what led up to Leon's shooting. I know Marty and Leon argued. I also know Leon was nervous about something before his shooting. And as it turns out, Marty was really nervous when I arrived at the convenience store last Wednesday."

Moses crossed his arms. "These are two different homicides, Manchester. Why are you trying to connect them?"

"Look, I have a hunch. You know about those, don't you? I know I may not be a cop, but I know when something is off. I'm telling you, if those boys hadn't come into Marty's store, I believe something would have happened to Marty, anyway."

"How did you pull this theory of yours together?"

"I believe it's more than a theory. First, I want to know more about why people think Marty had something to do with Leon's shooting. Marty may be gone, but I have reason to believe there are others who know about what transpired between the two men. Marty and Leon had been close friends since high school. What would drive them apart like that and even make Marty mad enough to threaten Leon's life?"

Moses looked over at Baldwin, who by this time had ended his phone call and was listening to our conversation. The investigators exchanged looks, which I couldn't read.

"I will say it again, Ms. Manchester. We should look into getting you on the police force," Baldwin commented. "She has an uncanny ability to pick at interesting points to consider. Would you agree, Moses?"

"Don't encourage her." Moses cringed. "I will be back."

When Moses walked away from his desk, I turned to Baldwin. "You think that I'm crazy and that I don't have anything better to do with my time."

Baldwin responded, "You didn't hear me say any such thing, but I will say that you should leave the investigating to us."

"But you encourage the public to come forward with leads. What do you think I'm doing?" I argued. "Leon's case is unsolved. So what happened with Marty Davis being a suspect in Leon's shooting?"

Baldwin leaned back. "We brought Marty Davis in as a person of interest because he did threaten Leon a few days prior . . . during a fight. The man had a clear alibi. Marty wasn't even in South Carolina when Leon was shot."

"How convenient," I commented.

Moses returned to his chair with a cup of coffee.

I looked at him. "You didn't offer me a cup of coffee, Moses."

He didn't even look at me. "That's because you're leaving. I believe we answered enough questions for you today."

"One more question."

Moses glared at me.

I ignored him. He had invited me back here, and now he wanted me to go. "For a person to have an alibi, he needs people to corroborate his story. Who said Marty was out of state?" Moses opened his mouth, but before he could say one word, I answered my own question. "Let me guess. His brother. No half brother. Tone Davis."

Moses and Baldwin exchanged looks again.

I was about to shock them again, because I was starting to piece together a picture here. I just couldn't quite put it all together yet. It was purely guesswork. "I'm going to guess that Marty was supposedly in North Carolina at the time. Possibly in Charlotte."

Moses blasted me. "If you already knew this, why did you come here to ask?"

I jumped up from the chair. "I didn't know anything." I pointed at him. "You just confirmed some suspicions for me."

Baldwin asked, "What kind of suspicions?"

I wasn't ready to answer *that* question just yet.

Moses looked ready to pounce on me. "Don't go getting yourself into trouble, Manchester."

"Don't worry. I'm a big girl, and I promise I won't get in your way. But if I find something, I will let you know." I winked and walked toward the door.

It didn't matter if Marty was dead. Alecia and Chris needed to know that justice had been served. What was it Tone had said yesterday? Justice didn't always come in the form you expected.

There appeared to be a domino effect at work here. It had started with Leon's death. Based on the snippets I had overheard when Tone was whispering to Kenyon at Marty's funeral, I knew there had to be a prior event that was the starting point. After yesterday's conversation with Tone Davis, I was convinced he knew the whole story, and I wanted him to recant his statement about Marty's whereabouts when Leon was killed to the police.

I thought back to the photo I had found that was tagged on Chris's Facebook page. This was a piece of the puzzle that kept floating around. I was uneasy about Kenyon Cooper, and for good reason, since Trey didn't trust the man around his son. I wanted to know how Kenyon fit into the puzzle.

CHAPTER THIRTY-TWO

Saturday, April 26, 11:00 a.m.

I finally dragged myself out of bed on Saturday. I was starting to feel the weight of the past two weeks on me. While sipping my coffee, I looked outside the kitchen window and noticed the grass had grown since Chris came by to mow it. So much had happened in such a short time frame. There was a lot to absorb, but I was under no pressure to meet a deadline. This was a personal mission, and I knew I needed to take precautions, as I planned to approach two people, Tone Davis and Kenyon Cooper.

The doorbell rang, interrupting my thoughts. I put my coffee cup in the sink and walked around Callie, who lately seemed to like to hang out wherever I was in the house. The cat was teaching me to respect her presence, which was an interesting lesson for me.

When I opened the door, I fully expected to see Bev, since it was her thing to stop by without calling me. Instead, when I opened the door, I found Alecia standing there with her arms crossed. She seemed interested in the porch floor before she raised her head to look at me through the screen door. I was kind of hoping it was my younger sister instead, since my last meeting with Alecia had ended with me walking out of the hospital, hurt by her accusations. Even though Trey had tried to console me, I wasn't fully over my hurt yet.

Something provoked me to put on my big girl clothes. This woman had been my best friend at one time in my life. Though we had our separate lives, we were still connected by our pasts and by shared family members. I realized it was a big deal for Alecia to come to the house, so I opened my screen door. "Hey, girl. Come in."

Alecia hesitated for a moment, like she preferred that we talk outside, but then she stepped inside.

I said, "I was in the kitchen, but we can go into the living room to talk."

"What were you doing? I know you never learned how to cook," Alecia replied.

I rolled my eyes but smiled. "Oh, so you come with jokes."

I walked into the living room and plopped down on the couch. My head and my body were really tired, so I hoped the conversation would remain civil. I might just decide to crawl back under the covers for the day.

Alecia followed behind me but stood in the middle of the living room. "You haven't changed anything in here, even though it's your house now."

"This house still feels like Aunt C's home to me, and it always will be. It's comforting to have everything exactly the way she left it. I spent a lot of time in this house when I was growing up, so it feels like home."

Alecia sat down in the chair opposite the couch. "Which is why it was wrong of me to say what I said about you returning to Charlotte. Chris has lost his dad and his grandmother within a year. You're the only connection he has to his father's side of the family now."

I wasn't sure that was really an apology, but Alecia had never admitted when she was wrong. I was a bit curious about her change of tune. "Did you come up with that on your own, or did Trey have something to do with that revelation?"

A grin broke across Alecia's face, and she pointed at me. "I told you my cousin has feelings for you. He lit into me about telling you off the other day. I remember that when were younger, even if you were wrong, Trey would defend you. He's always believed in you."

That statement made me smile, but I knew not to read too much into what Alecia said. "Trey was very encouraging the other day, after he dropped me off. I see why he was called to ministry. He's very thoughtful and empathetic at the right moment." I thought for a few moments about my conversation with Trey. "You know, it's good you're not angry with me now, but your feelings may change before you leave here."

Alecia studied me. "What do you want to ask me now? You're always full of questions."

"Don't worry. My questions aren't about Chris. I decided you're right. I should leave his case alone. I'm sure Moses has a good handle on the boys involved. Now, what I can't do is leave Leon's case alone, because it has been unsolved for about a year now."

Alecia stiffened, but she didn't object to the fact that I was driving our conversation in a particular direction, so I pressed forward. "I asked Trey a bit about Leon's mindset before he was killed. He said Leon was acting nervous or as if he felt guilty about something. You were closer to him than anyone. How would you describe his frame of mind around that time?"

Alecia leaned back in the chair with her arms crossed. "I noticed something different about Leon's demeanor months before, while he had the job in Charlotte."

I asked, "What kind of job was it?"

"That's just it. I couldn't tell you. He was vague about the job. I knew it wasn't his usual construction work. When he worked in Charlotte, he would stay overnight there for a few days at a time, and he would come home on the weekends. It paid well. We paid off bills that I didn't see us paying off for a while."

"Really? Sounds like it was a good job. Why did it bother you?"

"He was excited about working, since he'd been unemployed for about six months. Then he started to become depressed, like he didn't really enjoy what he was doing. Then one day he came home and said he had been let go, but he didn't say why. The job lasted all of three months. Now, don't get me wrong. I was used to how Leon would sporadically get construction jobs. But with this one I got the impression that he hadn't been fired and that it was more like he had quit, for whatever reason."

"What made you think he just walked away from an opportunity that paid well? Leon did want to provide for the family."

"That's what I thought, and I was furious with him. He had a hard time finding another job afterward. I got the impression that he was feeling guilty about walking away from this job, especially the longer he remained unemployed."

"What was the company's name? May be it went out of business or something and Leon's pride was affected. Surely, there were pay stubs lying around?"

Alecia shook her head. "Leon always had a lot of cash. I saw no pay stubs."

That is curious, and it's not a good sign. "Tell me about his friends. Let's start with Marty. I met his brother, Tone, and he described Leon and Marty as being tight like brothers."

Alecia nodded. "I didn't approve of Marty, because he was always coming up with some get-rich scheme and pulling Leon into it. I heard a couple of times Marty almost lost the store. Anyway, they were all tight. Leon, Marty, Tone . . ."

"And Kenyon," I added.

Alecia was quiet for a moment. She finally said, "Kenyon isn't from around here. I want to say Tone introduced him to the group."

"I know you know about Iris wanting to take Joseph and move to Charlotte. How did she meet Kenyon?"

Alecia huffed. "Who knows with Iris? I always thought she was pretty insecure, but she seemed to get worse as she got older. I know it hurt Trey, but when she called the wedding off, I thought that was the smartest thing she's ever done."

I could see what Iris had said about there being no love between her and Alecia.

"Did Kenyon have any input in this job Leon was working, and what happened?"

Alecia shook her head. "I guess it's possible. Now that you bring it up, I think Tone must have worked at the same place for a while. Leon would go by to pick him up, and they would ride together."

"Interesting. Marty has always had the store. Was he going to Charlotte too? I'm trying to figure out what led up to this fight between Marty and Leon."

"I still don't know. I just know Marty started it. We were celebrating Chris's thirteenth birthday, and there were kids in the yard. This grown man drives up, gets out of his car, and throws a punch at Leon. Leon had no choice but to defend himself."

"Leon never told you what sparked the fight?"

Alecia got up and walked over to the bookshelf. "No. I tried to get him to talk, but he became more withdrawn. His mom tried to talk to him. It was like he was feeling guilty, but I have no idea about what and how he was involved with Marty. To be honest, we stopped talking. He would sleep in the living room on purpose. There was a time when I thought maybe it was another woman. I just didn't know."

I knew I was making this into an interrogation, but I really wanted to nail down more details. "Where were you when he got shot? I know Chris was in the house, and he heard the gunshots and was the first to reach Leon."

Alecia leaned against the bookshelf, looking visibly shaken, as if she was experiencing the entire event again. "I was on my way home from work. Just got off from my shift at the hospital. The ambulance was in front of the house. Chris was really brave, and he had called nine-one-one. It was like déjà vu on Sunday, except it was Chris instead of his father getting placed in the ambulance." Alecia wailed. "Why would this happen to my family? Twice?"

Her cries struck a chord in my spirit that made me feel a combination of anger and sorrow all at once. I reached over to the tissue box on the table behind me and pulled tissues from it. I walked over and handed them to Alecia.

"I'm sorry. If you want me to stop, I will," I said quietly.

Alecia wiped her eyes. "No, I'm not going to tell you to stop. Malcolm and his partner are focused on Marty and Chris's case now. I know they can't go back to Leon's shooting without a really strong new lead. You know, Leon's mother and I both felt like it was Marty who shot Leon. I saw the pain in your aunt's eyes when they let Marty walk away. The fact that Tone provided him with an alibi didn't feel right to me. But you have a theory, don't you?"

I stood and rubbed my hands on my head. "I do, but it's best that my theory remain inside my head for the time being. I need to sort out a few loose ends."

Alecia swallowed. "Do you feel like Marty killed Leon?"

I began to pace the floor. "I don't have enough information yet. What I know is Marty was nervous the night I walked into the store. I believe that before Chris and those other boys walked in, something or someone was working on Marty. I could be completely wrong. I could be trying to find some way for the police to refocus on Leon's case."

I stopped and held up my finger. "It's like this domino effect started when Leon was killed . . . maybe even prior to his death," I continued a few moments later. "I mean, would you agree that maybe Aunt C's health wouldn't have deteriorated as fast if she had not lost her one and only son? I believe that Chris wouldn't have gotten caught up with these boys in the first place if his dad hadn't been murdered."

Alecia nodded her head. "I have thought the same thing, but I guess I'm not seeing any connections. But you are, right?"

"I have been known to go on a wild-goose chase, but most of the time the dots eventually connect for me."

I rubbed my forehead. I was getting tired of the dots not connecting. Trey's words continued to hang over me. God had me back home for a reason. It was like I was supposed to pick up where Aunt C and Alecia had left off in their quest to find justice for Leon. I was the one who knew how and didn't mind digging further. The only problem was my stamina wasn't what it was before my injuries last spring. I hoped I wouldn't disappoint everyone, including myself.

CHAPTER THIRTY-THREE

Sunday, April 27, 11:00 a.m.

When Bev called me Saturday evening about going to church with her and the girls the next day, I agreed to attend. Bev still looked shocked but was overjoyed when I climbed into the passenger seat of her minivan less than twenty-four hours later. Brittany and Tiffany chatted with me from the backseat about all the things that had happened at school the past week. Of course, Chris's shooting was a part of the conversation. I watched Bev cringe as she drove. I told her that kids talked.

"Mama isn't coming to church today?" I asked her when the girls fell silent.

Bev said, "Mama wasn't feeling well. The girls and I will check on her after the service. I think she may be feeling the loss of the things in her house."

That was worrying me a bit. It was past time that I reached out to Mama myself. If I was going to be home for an extended period, the least I could do was mend our relationship.

We arrived at church right before the eleven o'clock service started. The morning service went by fast. I tried not to get too caught up in watching Trey, and instead, I really listened to the worship song. *I give myself away so you can use me.* The lyrics touched me again in a way I wasn't expecting. When I was in the choir as a teen, I sang merely because I was expected to participate. I couldn't say I really understood the lyrics.

Pastor Walker spoke about how God loved us before we first loved Him. Humans were pretty messed up. I knew if I waited for particular people to show me love, I'd be waiting for a long time. That God had this type of love was beyond my human understanding.

When I walked out of the church, I saw Trey standing next to his parents. I wasn't expecting either one of them to be as warm as they were. Mrs. Sharon Evans reached up to hug me. I bent down, because she was a petite woman, and her arms were strong around my neck. Though she was small, the former schoolteacher had a reputation that was similar to my aunt's. These women were from an era when folks did not take a lot of mess. I had always admired Mrs. Evans. Despite finding out about her husband's transgression early on in their marriage, she had stayed. I had heard that she didn't try to kick Mr. Evans out of the house, either. I was pretty sure I wouldn't have been as forgiving.

Mrs. Evans stepped back and looked at me. "It's so good to have you home. Isn't it nice to see these children returning to their roots?"

Mr. Donald Evans, who had been my father-in-law when I married Benny, had a sparkle in his eyes as he looked from me to Trey and back to me again. "Glad to see you and Trey together."

My face grew warm. I glanced at Trey. What did Trey tell his parents? I wondered. "Oh, Trey and I are . . ."

Trey chuckled and then finished my response. "Getting reacquainted again." He turned to me and asked, "Would you and your sister like to join us for lunch?"

I gave him a look. I wasn't amused, but I wasn't about to turn down lunch, either. I surveyed the crowd and found Bev. She was talking with a group of women. I went over to ask if she wanted to eat lunch with Trey and his parents.

My sister grinned. "I think you should eat with them. The girls and I are planning to visit Mama. I need to cook something special for Clay. He will be back from his conference later this afternoon."

The warmth I'd started feeling a few minutes ago had now spread from my face down my back. My nerves were sending my thoughts into overdrive. Maybe having dinner with Trey and his parents without my sister present wasn't such a good idea.

Bev must have seen the panic on my face. She touched my shoulder. "It's just lunch. Enjoy yourself and get to know them again. I'm sure Trey would appreciate your effort."

I stared at my sister. "You're right. I will. Tell Clay I said hello."

Bev winked and went to gather her girls.

Since I had traveled to church with Bev, I ended up riding in Trey's car over to the restaurant. I had been in his car a couple of times now, but it still felt awkward today. I made small talk.

"So Alecia and I talked yesterday," I revealed.

Trey smiled. "Good. You two made up. You both were like that when we were younger. You'd blow up, and then you'd be friends a few days later."

I laughed. "You're right. We did. It's funny how when you get older, not much changes."

"I agree."

I looked over at Trey, and our eyes met. I turned away, because that wasn't the reaction I wanted to see. Or maybe I did like that he looked at me like I was special.

We arrived at the restaurant after his parents. Trey seemed to have a better handle on the speed limit than his old man. The restaurant was a bit crowded as other Sunday service attendees had flocked there. While we waited to be seated, Trey's parents began to ask me questions.

Mrs. Evans asked, "Have you recovered from your accident last year?"

It was a bit more than an accident—more like a crazy man pushed me down the stairs on purpose—but I didn't want to bring up that unpleasant experience. "You know, I'm starting to feel like myself again. It was hard to cope with the memory loss, especially the short-term memory loss. Made me feel like I was going a bit crazy."

Mr. Evans commented, "I can relate. I had a concussion from a car accident a long time ago. Any brain injury can turn quite serious."

Trey grinned. "We're glad God has brought Serena through her health concerns."

My throat felt constricted all of a sudden as a flood of emotions swept over me. I smiled and looked into the crowd to try to compose myself.

Trey's phone rang at that moment. He reached into his suit pocket and pulled out his phone. After he answered it, I observed the frown on his face.

"Iris, is everything okay?" he asked.

Really? Iris would call right now? I listened closely to Trey's conversation, not feeling the least bit sorry for eavesdropping. I glanced over at his parents and saw a look of concern on both their faces. It was highly possible that they were not fans of Iris, since she had kept their grandson from them for so long.

Trey's voice lost its calmness. "How long has Joseph not been feeling well? Did you just bring him to the ER now?"

Oh no! It was Joseph.

"Okay, fine. I will be there in a bit." Trey hung up the phone and looked at his parents, then at me. "I'm sorry. I need to go to the hospital. Joseph is not doing well. He's in a lot of pain."

Mrs. Evans said, "Well, we can go with you."

Trey shook his head. "No, there's no need for all of us to go. The table will be available soon, so go ahead and have lunch. I will keep you updated."

It certainly didn't make sense for me to stay with his parents. "Well, you need someone to go with you. Plus, you're my ride home, so I will go with you."

Trey didn't protest. I said good-bye to both his parents and followed him out the door and through the parking lot to his car. We quickly climbed in, and Trey rushed out of the parking lot. His jaw was tight as he drove, but he managed to drive safely. If I were behind the wheel, I would've been pressing the accelerator pretty hard at this point.

When we arrived at the hospital, Trey and I jumped out of the car. I sprinted behind him as he marched into the hospital through the emergency room doors. Trey walked over to the information desk to ask about Joseph's location. A few minutes later a nurse buzzed us inside the area where Joseph's room was located.

As we followed the nurse, I saw various patients waiting to be seen in their rooms. When we arrived at Joseph's room, the nurse pulled the curtain back. I could tell by Joseph's face that he was clearly in pain. I was highly interested to see the man standing next to Iris. As our eyes met, I had the distinct sense that Kenyon Cooper had been expecting to meet me at some point too.

CHAPTER THIRTY-FOUR

Sunday, 3:30 p.m.

Kenyon's eyes moved from mine to Trey's. I sensed the tension between Trey and Kenyon, which was probably not good for Joseph. I knew Trey to be a pretty calm man, but his fists were now clenched.

Since only Joseph's biological parents needed to be in the room, I looked directly at Kenyon and said, "Maybe we should let Trey and Iris have time with their son."

Iris looked like she was going to protest if Kenyon left her side. I stared at her.

Kenyon had sense enough to agree with me. "Sure. I agree. Let's go to the waiting room."

I stepped out of the room and waited for Kenyon to follow behind me. I looked back and noticed that he was holding Iris's hand—or rather Iris was clutching his hand. She seemed to hesitate a bit too long before she let his hand go.

What is wrong with this woman?

Kenyon seemed supportive of Iris and Joseph, but Trey was a good man and he cared about his son. Why did Iris keep on denying him the opportunity to be in Joseph's life? That made no sense to me.

As Kenyon walked out of the room, Trey stepped closer to Joseph's bedside and did not look at the other man.

I headed out the door, toward the waiting room. Before I sat down, I turned to Kenyon and held out my hand. "I don't believe I introduced myself."

Kenyon ignored my hand and said, "You don't have to, because I know who you are, Serena Manchester."

I put my hand down at my side. I was slightly creeped out that he knew who I was, but then again, if Kenyon was familiar with the Charlotte area, he would know my identity, as I had a known face.

"I see. So I guess you lived in the Charlotte area before," I said.

He shook his head. "For many years. You have a recognizable face, though your hair is different now."

I smiled. "It was time for a change. So you're going to return to Charlotte?"

Kenyon narrowed his eyes. "Not much going on in this town."

"One of the reasons why I left after high school."

"Why did you come back?" Kenyon asked.

He was full of questions for me. "Family. Most of my family is here, and after losing a cousin of mine and then my aunt, it seemed appropriate to come home."

Kenyon crossed his arms. His arms were massive, as if he spent too much time pumping iron. I hadn't noticed until now that tattoos covered his forearms. He didn't respond to my statement, but there was something going on in his head as he looked at me.

Maybe I could prod his memory a bit. "Did you know my cousin Leon Robinson?"

Kenyon's eyes flashed at me. "I knew him. Sorry for your loss. Leon was a good guy. Had a great sense of humor. Sorry about your aunt too."

I didn't know whether to be touched or more creeped out when Kenyon expressed his condolences. "Thank you. It's a shame what happened to Marty and to Leon's son too. I'm really surprised to see this type of violence here. I guess I shouldn't be, though. Guns in the wrong hands anywhere are not a good thing."

Kenyon stared at me and grunted. Or it could have been more like a growl. Of course, that could have been my stomach talking, since Trey and I had missed out on a meal to come to the hospital.

"Nice to meet you in person. I need to go do something. Let Iris know that when she's ready, she can call me," Kenyon said. And as if he had just dismissed me, he walked out the door.

He was certainly a man of few words. I had a nagging desire to go after him to see where he was going. Unfortunately, I was here with Trey, which was actually a good thing for me. I felt like this wouldn't be the last time I saw Kenyon Cooper.

CHAPTER THIRTY-FIVE

Sunday, 4:45 p.m.

After Kenyon left, I returned to Joseph's room. I stood at the door and motioned for Trey to meet me in the hallway. When he stepped out of the room, I asked, "How's Joseph doing?"

"He's a bit calmer now," Trey replied. "They gave him some medicine, so he isn't in as much pain. They will move him to a regular room and will keep him here a few days."

"Sounds like you're familiar with the routine. Does his sickle cell condition flare up often?"

"Well, there's no cure for sickle cell anemia, but they have a good medicine that keeps the condition under control. I think he's been stressed about the upcoming move and Chris's shooting." Trey frowned. "Are you okay? You look a little bit shook up."

Trey had no idea what thoughts were going through my mind. I didn't want to alarm him, because he needed to focus on Joseph.

So I said, "I just talked to Kenyon, and he doesn't strike me as pleasant. I don't know what Iris sees in him, frankly. You and he are like night and day. Seriously."

Trey shook his head. "I don't know what Iris sees in him, either, but . . ." Trey pulled me a bit farther down the hall, away from Joseph's room. "I don't want Iris or Joseph to overhear," he explained. "I did talk to your brother-in-law this past week. I thought it was time to get legal advice."

I raised my eyebrows. "You're considering asking for custody?"

Trey nodded his head. "I hate to go to the courts, and Iris says Kenyon takes care of Joseph. It's just that . . ."

"He's your son."

Trey looked at me. "Yes, Joseph is my son. She's kept him from knowing me all this time. Not just me, but my parents. You know my mom knew Joseph when he was younger. She told me there was this boy in school who reminded her of me when I was the same age. Isn't it weird that Iris didn't consider that we would eventually run into Joseph?"

"I got the impression from talking to Iris that she didn't always have a stable life. You know her family had its issues, even though she was a popular cheerleader."

Trey nodded. "You're right. She had a lot of turmoil. For a few years she lived with her mom, and she's had a couple of different boyfriends around Joseph. I think Kenyon is the guy she's been with the longest . . . well, after she dated me."

"I'm glad you're moving forward with what's best for you and your son. Look, I'm going to run up to Chris's room. They may not have heard that Joseph is here, unless you talked to Alecia."

"You know I haven't had time to tell Alecia. Thanks. She would want to know how Joseph is doing."

I patted Trey on the arm and headed toward the elevators.

Once I stepped on the elevator, it hit me that two really sweet boys were in the same hospital, one stricken by a disease and the other recovering from a violent act. Despite my conversations with Trey about Iris as a mother, I had to wonder if God had shown me mercy by not making me a mom. I was not sure how well I would have walked in either Alecia's or Iris's shoes.

Once I arrived at Chris's room, I knocked on the door, and Alecia opened it. I peeked my head in. "Hey, you two. How are things going?"

Chris looked a bit better today and was even smiling. "I might get to go home next week."

Alecia didn't look as chipper. "Maybe. He has a long way to go. We're not rushing." From the unease in Alecia's eyes, I knew this whole ordeal was far from over.

"Well, I hate to come up and tell you this, but Joseph is here. He had another flare-up."

Alecia put her hands on her face. "Oh no! Is Trey downstairs with him?"

"Yes, he is here."

Chris's face was contorted out of concern. "He's always getting sick. I wish they could find a cure."

I nodded. "I'm with you. Hey, you mind if I bother your mom for a minute?"

Chris shook his head, indicating it was okay with him. Alecia looked at me. I nodded toward the door. She stepped out of the room behind me.

"Let me guess. You have more questions," she said.

"Yes, but this might be a different kind of questioning."

Alecia raised her eyebrows.

"Trey probably told you he is going to seek custody of Joseph."

"Yes. I've encouraged him to do it. That woman doesn't have much sense. I'm glad she did break off the wedding with Trey years ago, but I'm not sure what the deal is with keeping Trey from his son. Ever since she broke up with Trey, the men she's dated have been real pieces of work."

"Like Kenyon Cooper. I just met him and tried to have a conversation with him. He's not a very friendly guy, is he?"

"I would have to agree with you. I told you he started hanging around Leon and the other guys."

"It looks like Kenyon lived in Charlotte for some time, because he recognized me from being on television. I really do wonder if he helped Leon get this mystery job in Charlotte."

Alecia frowned. "You know, I don't know, but it might make sense. Leon started the job not too long after Kenyon showed up around here."

I had another question, but I needed to tread really carefully with this one. "Do you know what kind of car Kenyon drives?"

Alecia shook her head. "No. I'm never around him like that, and he never really came to the house, at least when I was there. I'm not going to ask why you want to know."

"Good. I'm still working on some things in my head." I looked up the hallway and noticed a woman coming toward us. I grimaced.

Alecia grabbed by arm. "Rena, are you okay? What's wrong?" Before I could say anything, Alecia turned around. I watched as Alecia narrowed her eyes. "What does *she* want?"

Iris walked up to both of us. While Joseph and Chris were pretty close friends, it was clear there was no love between these boys' mothers.

CHAPTER THIRTY-SIX

Sunday, 5:15 p.m.

I expected Trey to come up and check on Chris and give Alecia an update on Joseph's condition. I was really surprised when Iris showed up, since I knew she was not keen on Alecia. I imagined Iris understood that the boys' friendship was more important than any conflict among the adults.

Since Alecia wasn't trying to start a conversation, I said, "Hey, Iris. How's Joseph doing?"

Iris swallowed. "He's feeling better. I thought Trey needed more time with him, so I came up to check on Chris. Plus, Joseph asked about him."

Alecia's stance softened just a little. "I'm sorry to hear Joseph is here again. Chris is improving. His doctors are thinking that if he keeps it up, he can go home soon. He will still need time to heal fully from his wound."

Iris nodded. "I can imagine. I'm so sorry. This must be awful for you, especially with it being so close to the anniversary of Leon's death."

Alecia blinked her eyes. "I need to get back to Chris. I hope Joseph doesn't have a long hospital stay this time." Alecia left me in the hallway with Iris.

I stared at Iris, thinking she could have been a bit more tactful. Even I wouldn't have brought that up to Alecia.

Iris looked at the closed door as if she was offended. I did feel bad for her, because Iris's world seemed to be rather narrow and was mainly centered around Kenyon and her boys.

Iris started to walk away. I followed behind her. "So how did you meet Kenyon? He's an interesting guy," I said when I caught up with her at the end of the hallway. I thought it was better to say that instead of "Your boyfriend is creepy."

"Yes, he has had an interesting life. I met him at the Huddle House, of all places. Isn't that funny? He would come in and give me the best tips. One day he asked me on a date."

"Wow. Sounds like he courted you. Didn't know people still did that these days."

Iris giggled. "Me neither. Kenyon can be rough around the edges, but he's sweet."

I had to make a comment about that. "He seems so different from Trey."

We stopped at the elevators. Iris pushed the DOWN button. "Yeah, you're right. I guess so."

An elevator arrived, the door opened, and we stepped inside. As the door closed, Iris continued to talk. "He's a good provider and father. When we get to Charlotte, we're going to get married."

Marriage. Did Trey know about the pending nuptials? I imagined that could work against him some in the upcoming custody case. As I rewound the conversation in my mind, something Iris had said got my attention. "You said Kenyon was a good provider and father. Does he have other children besides James?"

Iris looked at me. "Yes, he has two other sons. He wants to have all his boys together."

The elevator door opened, and we both stepped off the elevator. A group of people was waiting to get on, and Iris and I were separated as the group pressed forward. I worked my way around the group and met back up with Iris.

I couldn't help but say to her, "Joseph isn't his son, though."

Iris stopped and turned to face me. "Trey's been talking to you, I see."

"Yes. Why would you not let him get to know his son?"

"He has been a part of Joseph's life."

"Not until recently," I argued.

"That wasn't entirely my fault."

I stared at her. "What? Explain."

Iris stepped back and shook her head, making her micro-braids swing toward her face. "I don't have to explain it to you."

"Oh, yes you do. You've hurt Trey enough, and the mature thing to do here is to be honest. You had a chance to marry him."

Iris eyed me, her lips pursed. "He never loved me."

This woman is tripping. "What? That's crazy! You were high school sweethearts."

"Yes. *High school.* When Trey went off to college, it was never the same. He asked me to marry him only because I kept pressuring him. I could tell, I wasn't in his league anymore."

I hadn't got that impression from Trey at all. Iris was trying to make excuses for her own choices.

She took a step closer to me. "Believe me, Rena. Trey wasn't that hurt when I broke off the wedding. He might have been more hurt that you were married at the time."

I tried to process what Iris had just said to me. What did my marriage to Benny, as pitiful as it was, have to do with her breaking off her and Trey's wedding?

"Is everything okay?" said a male voice.

I turned to see Trey out in the hallway. He approached us.

Iris gave him an accusatory look. "Who's with Joseph?"

Trey glared at her. "The doctor wanted to see him, so I stepped out of the room. Where were you?"

Seeing the tension being displayed amongst us it probably wasn't good for us to be out in the hallway causing a scene. I let out a deep breath. "Okay, maybe we should calm down. The most important person here right now is Joseph."

I watched Trey's shoulders drop. Knowing what Trey planned to do, I didn't want him to display any anger or do anything that could place the custody battle ahead in jeopardy.

Iris looked at both Trey and me. "Some things really do never change. I kind of figured you two were back in cahoots with one another." She marched back toward Joseph's room.

I did not understand why Iris had directed her anger at both me and Trey. My eyes widened. "Cahoots? Me and you?"

Trey sighed. "Iris has always been jealous of you. If it wasn't you she was angry at, it was Alecia."

Jealous? Iris jealous of me? I was jealous of *her,* the cute, perky cheerleader who had dated Trey. *Unbelievable*. Life is never quite the way one perceives it to be.

Trey turned to me. "I'm really glad that you're here, but if you want me to take you home, I can. There's no need for you to be held hostage here at the hospital with me. I'm sure you're not a fan of hospitals after last year."

I grinned. "No, I'm not, but it's okay. I hate seeing Chris and Joseph here. I hope both of them bounce back quickly and soon I see them playing video games together, like I did when I saw them a week ago."

Trey smiled. "I'm sure they will both get a chance to be boys again. Joseph is really mature for his age, and he handles pain way better than I do."

"Probably better than me too." It might not be my place, but I wanted to be sure Trey knew what Iris was planning. "You know, when I was talking to Iris, she said she may marry Kenyon."

Trey's smile disappeared. "I know. She told me that night you were at the house. That's why I'm going to move forward with hiring Clay to represent me in the custody case."

"Good for you. Besides, it sounds like Kenyon has other sons. Why would he take an interest in Joseph?"

"Yes, he does, but those boys are older. One may be close to Joseph's and Chris's age, but I don't think he has the best relationship with either one of them. Joseph said the boys have two different mothers."

I started thinking about that. *Kenyon doesn't have the best relationship with his sons.*

Trey put his hand on my shoulder. "Are you sure you're okay? I can take you home."

"Uh, yeah, it's probably good that I go home and lie down. I was really exhausted yesterday."

"Okay. First let me check with Joseph and find out what the doctor said. I will be right back."

As Trey walked away, I leaned against the wall. I started to think about my dad. We hadn't had the best relationship, but whenever Dallas had had the chance, he would buy me things, sometimes expensive clothing and jewelry. It had always felt as if my dad was trying to buy my love with those gifts, to make up for those times he wasn't there.

I wondered if Kenyon's sons lived in Charlotte or here in Georgetown. Did his boys inherit that hint of danger that seemed to surround him? I knew from experience that absentee parents purchased material items to make up for not being present. Sometimes there was another motive behind buying gifts. What was Kenyon's motive?

CHAPTER THIRTY-SEVEN

Sunday, 6:10 p.m.

Trey and I didn't talk much as he drove me back to my house. My head was full of ideas, and so I found it comforting to have him in the driver's seat. What Trey didn't know was my thoughts were taking me into areas that had DANGER ZONE stamped across them. I needed to have another talk with Tone Davis. He felt approachable to me, and I needed him to tell me the whole truth.

"You must be really worn out or deep in thought. Maybe you should slow down a bit."

I heard Trey's words and noticed he had turned into my driveway. I rubbed my head. "Oh, I didn't realize we were here already."

"Why don't you let me walk you inside?"

"I don't know. Is that appropriate? I mean, with you being a minister?"

Trey smiled and laughed. "I would have never imagined you trying to be modest."

"Not for me. For you. There's not much hope for me."

Trey's smile disappeared. "That's so not true. God doesn't expect us to be perfect. You may not have read the Bible in a while, but you know the stories. How many people did you find who never sinned?"

"True. I guess I still have Reverend Lawson in my head."

"You know, your stepdad was trying to protect a young girl the best way he knew how. I can't imagine having a daughter, especially today. The world is so different."

I knew what Trey had said meant sense, but I wasn't ready to let my stepdad off the hook yet. The man had been extra hard on me and harsh to me. Maybe his strict rules had been for my own good, but his overbearing personality hadn't helped me back then. We climbed out of the car, and I opened the front door.

Trey walked inside after me and looked around. "This place reminds me of when I visit my parents. It looks the same."

"Yeah, Alecia said that when she came by yesterday."

"I'm glad you two made up."

I walked in the living room and encouraged Trey to sit down on the couch. "She sounded like you provided some motivation."

Trey grinned as he sat down. "Life is too short to hold on to anger."

I had to agree with Trey, but I didn't say it out loud. "Do you want anything to drink?"

He shook his head. "No, I'm fine. I was thinking how, growing up, we used to hang out here more than at your house."

"Reverend Lawson didn't approve of me having a guy as a best friend. You do remember that time he scolded us at church, don't you?"

"Oh yeah. That was pretty scary. What were we doing to make him so angry?"

I grimaced. "Nothing. We looking at your yearbook and laughing at photos. You would have thought he had caught us making out or something."

I looked over at Trey and was a bit startled by his facial expression. Okay, maybe I shouldn't have invited him into the house. "Are you okay? Did I just embarrass you? You know I'm good at that, right?"

Trey shook his head and laughed. "I'm fine. You know one of the reasons why I wanted to talk to you is I started thinking more about your questions concerning Leon."

"You thought of something else? When I talked to Alecia, she thought his job was the starting point to his odd behavior."

"I have to agree. This is hard to say to you, but I think whatever Leon was doing those few months wasn't totally legit."

"I kind of thought that too, with him being vague about the job and with the cash flow he was bringing home. It was hard for him to keep a job, so Leon just quitting seemed a bit strange too."

"What I tell you is going to be even stranger, Serena."

I had purposely sat on the chair opposite the couch so I could keep some distance between myself and Trey, but I leaned in now. "Okay. Tell me."

He hesitated for a moment. "Remember I said Leon wasn't a church attendee? When he wanted to talk to me that Sunday, he also passed me an envelope and told me to make sure I gave it to the church."

My eyes widened. "Leon donated money?"

"A wad of money. I didn't count it, but when I passed the money to the pastor, it was at least a thousand dollars."

I frowned. "Did he give the money before or after he quit the job?"

"It was definitely after he quit."

At the heart of all this, I knew, money was involved. But how had Leon made money? My first thought was that he'd been involved in drugs, but Leon had been more of a drinker, like my dad. I had never thought that drugs had been part of the picture with him. So how else had he made money, which later made him feel guilty?

"Money is the root of all evil," I announced.

Trey looked surprise. "Look at you, quoting scriptures."

I shook my head. "Ignore me. I didn't mean to say that out loud. I'm processing. I have another question. Were you at Chris's birthday party when Marty showed up?"

"Yeah. I was one of the ones trying to pull Leon and Marty apart. Marty came out of nowhere. I remember Leon really had to recover enough from the first punch Marty threw before he thought to get up and fight back."

I stood. "Did Leon give you the church donation before the fight?"

Trey wrinkled his forehead while he pondered my question. "I want to say it was after the fight. He had quit the job a few weeks before Chris's party."

I started to pace. "Did Leon seem like he wanted to confess something? Maybe giving the money was to ease his conscience. But it wasn't enough. He could have been shot just so he wouldn't come forward and confess his involvement in something illegal."

"Very similar to Chris's shooting," Trey commented. "Someone wanted to make sure Chris didn't talk, either. There are too many coincidences for me. So, Serena, what are you thinking?"

I was so glad to have Trey here, but I knew I couldn't tell him what was on my mind. If what I was thinking was closer to the truth, then Trey and his son were too close to the man I suspected. "I'm still trying to figure it out."

Trey stood, began to pace, and then stopped in front of me. "This may be pointless to say, but I feel like I need to ask again. You will be careful, won't you?"

I opened my mouth, but I realized I couldn't guarantee that I would.

Trey took both my hands in his hands. "I'm going to do what I know how to do. I'm going to pray for you. Bow your head."

Conscious of my hands in Trey's hands, I didn't protest. I listened to his voice.

"Father God, we ask for you to send your angels of protection to surround Serena as she moves forward to find the truth. We ask that she be provided wisdom to know when she's reached her limits and she needs law enforcement. While I ask for protection for her, I also lift up my son so that you will take his pain away and protect him. Thank you for watching over Chris and Alecia. May justice be served for all. In Jesus's name. Amen."

I repeated, "Amen." As Trey took his hands away, I looked up at him and said, "Everything's going to be fine."

He nodded. "I believe that too. Get some rest, Serena. Don't wear yourself out."

We walked to the front door, and then I watched as he made his way back to his car, started the engine, and drove away. I closed the door and leaned against it, still smelling Trey's cologne, which lingered in the air. Trey holding my hands and praying over me had taken me in another direction. I'd never had a man show that type of concern for me.

Thoughts of my earlier conversation with Iris made me slide to the floor. I remembered her words about Trey and my marriage. *He might have been more hurt that you were married at the time.*

Neither Trey nor I was married now. But I had been married twice already and really had no intention of trying to settle down again. Besides, Trey was smarter and wiser now. He was a godly man.

Me . . . I was still complicated. Trey didn't need complicated.

CHAPTER THIRTY-EIGHT

Monday, April 28, 2:00 p.m.

Last week I was full of questions. This week I was determined to find answers. It took me some time, but I found Tone by looking up names in a phone directory online. There were a lot of Davises in the area, but I narrowed my search down to an Anthony Davis. Tone's house was only about a few houses down from Mama's house. I remembered Tone saying that Reverend Lawson used to give him work at the church and at the house.

I decided to touch base with Mama. It was long past time for us to talk. I walked into the living room and picked up the phone by the couch. I dialed Mama's phone number.

Mama sounded sleepy, despite it being the afternoon. "Hello?"

"Hey, Mama. It's Rena. How are you feeling this afternoon?"

"Okay. I'm still going through some things in the house. I might be able to give them to the church missions."

"That sounds good, Mama. I want to stop by later to talk, but I'm wondering if you're okay with me leaving my car at your house."

"Sure, Rena. Why would you need to do that?"

"I'm visiting with someone nearby, and I could use some walking. I just didn't want to leave the car at the house and not tell you."

"Okay. That's fine. I will see you later."

So about thirty minutes after I talked to Mama, I parked my car in front of her house. I was grateful for all the volunteers last week, because the place looked like a different house and like someone cared for it. I locked my car door and saw that Mama was looking out the window. I didn't want her to know who I was going to visit. I waved to her and pointed in the direction in which I was walking. I caught her nod and then watched the curtains fall back in place.

As I walked, I recognized some of the other houses. Strange what memories came to me while I was walking, versus cruising by in a car. I started to remember all the neighbors, some now long gone like Reverend Lawson.

Tone's house was on the left, about two blocks down. His house looked a bit worse than Mama's had. In fact, I wondered if he needed some intervention. There were at least three vehicles—or rather, car parts—in the front yard. I recalled that Tone had said he made a living as a mechanic, and from the looks of his hands last week, I knew it was true. That thought brought to mind again the issue of how he was involved with Kenyon. Leon had worked construction mostly, and Marty had owned a corner store. What was it that had drawn these men to the opportunity presented last year in Charlotte?

I walked up the porch steps, which creaked, and then knocked on the door. Tone opened the door, and he didn't appear happy to see me. Dressed in a sleeveless white T-shirt and jeans, he stepped out of the house and looked up both sides of the street.

"What are you doing here?" he muttered.

"I have some questions. Are you busy?" I peered beyond the front door and into the house and saw a table strewn with beer bottles.

Tone jammed one of his hands into a jeans pocket. I looked and noticed how skinny he really was with his arms exposed. He waved me inside with his other hand as his eyes darted around. "Hurry up. You have to make your questions quick."

I walked across the threshold quickly, and he slammed the door behind us. I jumped a bit as my eyes tried to adjust to the dark room. The only light came from a larger flat-screen TV set and a window by the couch. The couch looked like it needed to be thrown out. It sagged badly on one side. As I observed Tone's surroundings, I realized that the television was probably the only luxury item he had in the house. I wondered if Tone had made any money along with Leon. Had he got his fair share? Why had he questioned Kenyon at Marty's funeral?

Tone pulled out a chair at the table and sat. "Sit down over there. Just make your questions quick."

I pulled out another chair at the table. As I sat down, I noticed that there were pizza boxes stacked on the table, next to the beer bottles. I didn't want to be here that long, so for both our sakes, I hoped Tone cooperated.

"I just want the truth, Tone. I know you provided Marty with an alibi for the night Leon was killed. I needed to know the answer to one question. Was Marty really in North Carolina with you that night?"

Tone looked at the floor. He picked up a half-empty bottle of beer off the table and drained it before answering me. "No."

I sucked in a breath. "Why did you lie?"

"You said one question," he barked, reprimanding me.

"I wasn't expecting you to tell me the truth, so now I have another question," I shot back. "Where was Marty that night?"

"I can't tell you that."

"Did he ask you to lie for him?"

"No. I knew what people were saying. I know they would blame him. Marty would never intentionally hurt Leon. He just got really mad. People say stupid things when they're mad."

I felt like Tone was trying to defend Marty. "Why was Marty so angry with Leon?"

Tone shook his head. "I can't say."

Or he won't say. "Did he have something to do with the job Leon was doing in Charlotte? He made a lot of money, and then, all of sudden, he quit. What kind of job would give you a guilty conscience?"

Tone jumped up from his chair and walked over to the window. "We had nothing against Leon wanting to pull out, but he was going to mess it up for the rest of us. Marty just wanted him to keep his mouth closed."

"About what?" I asked. "Why can't you tell me the truth? Leon's gone. Marty's gone. Don't you think something is wrong with that?" I stood up from the table. "Are you scared?"

Tone stared at me like a deer caught in headlights. I could smell the fear rising up from him. He turned away from me and toward the window and shoved his hands into his pockets. I was really hoping he wanted to clear his conscience. I was so close to getting answers.

"Oh no! No!" Tone jumped back from the window and then turned around. His big eyes had grown larger. He pointed at me. "You need to get out of here!"

I felt Tone's panic, and my own heart started to race. "Why?"

Tone flailed his arms and whispered loudly, "He can't see you here! Just go! I will let you out the back door."

Tone flew past me at a speed that made me dizzy. He yelled, "Come on!"

I ran toward the kitchen area, where Tone had the back door open. I felt like the mistress being thrown out the back way. It occurred in my warped mind that I would have much rather hidden in a closet, but Tone motioned for me to move, so I did.

Once I was outside, Tone said, "Don't come back here. We're done." He slammed the door closed.

I looked around the backyard. It had some overgrown areas, but it looked relatively normal, with chairs, a table, and a barbecue grill in the corner. I inched my way around the side of the house, where tall shrubbery lined the foundation, to catch a glimpse of Tone's visitor.

Then I understood Tone's panic. I recognized the Crown Victoria, and I was thankful I'd parked my car at Mama's house. My intention was to gather evidence, and if Kenyon was a part of this, I wanted to tell the police. From Tone's reaction just now, I conjectured that Kenyon was not a man to take lightly.

I had no idea why Kenyon was here, and I wanted to find out. I wondered if Tone had locked the back door and if I could sneak back inside the house. But I didn't get a chance to, because just then the back door flew open. I dropped to the ground behind the overgrown bushes, and I watched as Kenyon shoved Tone out the door. The branches scratched my arms and the sides of my face as I tried to make myself smaller among the shrubbery. My discomfort would not be a problem as long as I was out of sight.

A moment later, Kenyon swung around, and I could tell he wasn't happy. I was glad that I wore an olive-green T-shirt over my jeans. I didn't think about camouflage wear when I put it on this morning, and now I prayed it was working for me.

I watched as Kenyon grabbed Tone by the neck. "I don't know why I ever brought any of you into this. All of you are messing up. What does she know?"

"Nothing," Tone choked out.

Is he talking about me? I was in enough danger. I sat pressed against the house, praying I could make it out of the yard. I no longer needed to hear another word.

Kenyon let go of Tone and began pacing the yard, as though he was counting to ten and trying to calm down. Tone hit the grass, gasping and coughing for air. Kenyon appeared to be looking around the yard. Did he know I was still here? Better yet, how did he know I was here? It wasn't like I had made an appointment with Tone. I had just shown up.

Kenyon stepped over Tone and went back into the house. I turned and looked toward the front of the house and then along the side. I had no idea if Kenyon was looking around the house for me. I needed to get out of this yard.

Just be patient, Serena. No sudden moves.

So I waited as Tone went back into the house. I peered up at windows above me, trying to figure out exactly where I had talked to Tone inside just a few minutes ago. Then I looked at the house across from me. I couldn't tell if anyone was home, but if I could climb the neighbor's fence, I could probably make my way up the street, or through a couple of neighbors' yards, and back to Mama's house.

Thoughts of long ago, of when I was a young girl in this neighborhood whirled around in my mind, and I remembered doing the exact same thing once. I didn't know why I did it, but at that time it was Alecia and I who were cutting through people's yards. Maybe I was avoiding the eyes of those who would tell my whereabouts to Reverend Lawson. Right now I needed to avoid Kenyon.

I stayed put for another ten minutes and listened to see if I could hear any conversations coming from the house. I peered up and over the bushes and saw Kenyon climb into his car. I ducked down and watched Kenyon drive out of the driveway and in the opposite direction of Mama's house.

Thank you, Jesus!

I watched as Kenyon drove out of sight, but then I wondered if it was a trap. *Should I go back to check on Tone?* No, Tone might want to hurt me the next time he saw me. He was scared for his life now. I was scared for him and me.

So I waited another ten minutes, sweat pouring down my back. I took a breath and climbed the neighbor's fence out of precaution. I looked around, forgetting there could be a dog. No canine was in sight, but I knew not to press my luck. I ran around the side of the neighbor's house and peered out, feeling like a burglar. The street seemed clear, so I walked as fast as I could down the street, toward Mama's house and my car.

Once I was inside my car, I gulped for air like I had been running a marathon. Not seeing any cars or anyone around me, I slowly drove off. As I went, I tried to figure out my next step, which I would take after I recovered from today. I also wondered how long I had before someone came after me.

CHAPTER THIRTY-NINE

Monday, 4:00 p.m.

I didn't go home, mainly because I didn't want Mama to worry. I did tell her I was going to stop by and visit with her too. Then I started to worry that Mama's house was too close to Tone's house. So I circled the neighborhood, looking for Kenyon's car. I couldn't understand where he could have been that enabled him to know that I was visiting Tone. Unless he had some spies around Tone's house. What would make a man that paranoid? Was that why Leon and Marty had had this nervous energy about them? Was that why Tone had it now too?

Leon and Marty must have known Kenyon was watching them, and Tone surely knew it now, but why?

I decided to go back to Mama's house. This time I parked the car in the backyard so it was hidden for the street. Mama didn't ask me any questions, like why I looked so sweaty, why I was scratched up, or why I seemed scared. I was feeling pretty exhausted, and right now being at Mama's house was all right with me. I needed to think.

Mama went into the kitchen. I was still shocked at how good it looked compared to last week. The table had nothing but a napkin holder and a pair of salt and pepper shakers. Last week it was covered with papers and knitting supplies.

"Would you like something to drink? You look thirsty," Mama said.

That is an understatement. "Yes. Water would be great." Mama and I hadn't been alone together in quite a while, so this was an adventure.

She poured some water from a jug in the refrigerator and sat the glass down in front of me. I guzzled the water down like I'd been out in the desert or something. Mama placed the jug of water on the table, and I gratefully poured more and then drained the glass again. When I put the glass down, I suddenly realized how shaky my hands had become.

"Rena, are you feeling okay? Bev told me she's been trying to get you to go to the doctor."

"Yes, I'm fine. This has nothing to do with my injuries from last year."

"Did things go well at your friend's house?"

I wanted to laugh, but all I could do was shake my head. "He isn't a friend, and I don't know."

Mama nodded, as if it was okay for her firstborn to be acting a bit mental. She said, "I have some things for you." She walked out of the room and came back with a box. "I saved these for you."

I didn't really like Mama using the word *saved,* because that was how the house had become such a mess. Then I saw what was on top of the box. It was the framed picture of my Dad and me that I saw the first time I walked into the house. I stood and started to pull other items out of the box, like a baseball cap, more photos, and a baseball signed by a player I had never heard of. Then I started to understand. "These are all my dad's things."

Mama nodded. "I know your aunt Claudia had some of his stuff, but he left some things here too. I boxed them up, but I forgot to give them to you."

Probably because I didn't come home that often, and I certainly didn't step foot in this house all those years, I thought to myself. I sat down, a bit overwhelmed from my earlier run-in at Tone's house and from seeing items that had belonged to Dallas Robinson.

"I always thought it was my fault that he left," I said.

Mama stared at me. "Why? You were five years old. You had nothing to do with him leaving. I used to think it was *my* fault, but I knew what I was getting into when I married your father."

I studied my mom, but I didn't comment. She had never been open with me like this.

Mama continued talking. "You know, I dated Thomas first."

I cringed. "What? I didn't know that. You and Reverend Lawson were a couple first?"

Mama nodded. "Then I met your dad. Dallas was so different, and I'd never had a man that good-looking notice me."

I was still shocked by the fact that Reverend Lawson was really Mama's first love. "So after my dad left, Reverend Lawson was just there waiting?"

Mama smiled. "He waited for me to come to my senses. Although I didn't. Your dad did that for me. He told me the night before he left that he wasn't good enough for me or you. That he would always mess up. We didn't need that kind of instability."

I looked down at the photo in my hand. "Aunt C couldn't keep him in one place, either. I would go over to her house, waiting to see if he would show up. Sometimes he did, and sometimes he didn't. Why did you let me spend so much time at her house?"

Mama shrugged. "A girl needs her daddy. Thomas tried to be a father to you. You may not believe me, but that man did love you like his own daughter. He didn't like when I would let you spend so much time at your aunt's. He would say all the time, 'That girl will get her feelings hurt.'"

I hated to admit how right Reverend Lawson had been.

"So who was the love of your life? My dad or Reverend Lawson?"

Mama smiled. "Both. I had two loves. I think that's possible. I have two girls to show for both loves."

Tears rolled down my cheeks. I wanted to blame it on being exhausted, but I was touched. Touched by a man I couldn't stand, a man who had loved Mama enough to take her and her hardheaded daughter. Touched by the notion that he hadn't wanted me to get hurt. Trey had said Reverend Lawson was trying to protect me. Maybe he was too harsh in his methods, but he was the real father figure in my life.

We sat in silence in the kitchen for some time, Mama with her memories and I with mine. She eventually got up and asked if I wanted something to eat. I was starving.

Mama went to the refrigerator and pulled out breakfast food, which was a favorite of mine on days like today. She quickly scrambled eggs as a pot of grits bubbled on a back burner and bacon sizzled on a front burner. As Mama cooked, I ventured down the hallway and stepped into the bathroom. My face and arms were starting to sting. I had quite a few scratches on my cheeks that were already developing scabs. I was surprised Mama hadn't questioned me about it. Of course, while I was growing up, I was a pretty tough cookie. My banged-up look might still seem normal to Mama.

I decided to visit my old room while I was here. When I opened the door, I could tell Mama had moved some of the boxes around, because I could see the twin bed now.

"I will get this cleaned up soon," Mama said. She had come up behind me.

I turned. "I plan to be around for a while, so maybe I can help you."

Mama smiled. "Let's get you some food to eat."

So we ate and talked more. All the while we talked, my heart was warmed by the conversation. It was like a new leaf had been turned over with Mama and me.

In the back of my mind I still wondered about Tone's confession. However, with Kenyon showing up on the scene, I hadn't got all my answers. What a help it would be if Tone recanted his statement. That would be a start. Maybe it wasn't up to me to try to get all the answers from Tone. When I got home, I would call Moses. He wouldn't be happy with me, but I had never told the investigator I would stop hunting down leads.

I helped Mama wash the dishes. After I dried the last dish and put it away in the cabinet, I said, "We need to do this more often. Next time, let's have Bev and the girls come over."

"I would like that. I missed not having people come over. I was so ashamed of how the house looked."

I reached down and hugged Mama. My conversation with Trey came to mind. *Everything will be all right.* I could feel that now. Mama walked me to the door.

As soon as my feet hit the porch, I heard a bang not too far away. My instinct was to duck. I felt the floorboards beneath my feet and whirled around. "Mama, close the door and get inside!"

"But you need to get in here," Mama whispered loudly.

"Don't worry. Just get inside!" I leaned toward the edge of the porch and looked down the street. Did we really just hear a gunshot?

Bang. A second gunshot.

Mama reached for me. "Get in here, girl!"

"No. I'm okay. Close the door." I pulled my phone out of my pocket. "I'm going to call for help."

I waited for Mama to close the door, and then I dialed 911. I crept down the porch steps. The bulldog next door was having a fit. A dispatcher answered. I struggled to recall the street name and then said, "I just heard gunshots on Liberty Street. Two gunshots. Can you send the police and an ambulance?"

The dispatcher asked, "Who was shot, ma'am?"

I answered, "I don't know yet."

I hung up the phone and started toward my car in the backyard. Those gunshots had come from the direction of Tone's house.

CHAPTER FORTY

Monday, 9:10 p.m.

I started my car and drove it through the open gate and down the driveway. This time I didn't want to be on foot. I drove in the direction of Tone's house, not sure what to expect. As I approached Tone's driveway, I had to hit my brakes because my headlights illuminated a young man running from Tone's house. Something was oddly familiar about his face. The boy disappeared into the darkness on the other side of the street.

Was that boy doing the shooting? I wondered.

I looked over at Tone's house and gasped. "Oh no." It was just as I had feared. I saw a man, who had to be Tone, lying on the front porch. The front door was wide open. Tone must have opened the door and been shot point-blank. I assumed the young man running away from the scene had done it. *But why?*

I pulled my car over and cut the engine, but I kept the headlights on, since they illuminated Tone's house. As I jumped out of the car and ran over, I could tell Tone was wounded in the abdomen area. Blood had spread across his white T-shirt, the same shirt he had been wearing earlier, when I saw him. I bent down and heard his moans of pain. He was barely conscious.

"Tone, I called for help. Hang in there."

"We . . ." His speech was slurred.

I shook my head, though he probably couldn't see me. His right eye was closed shut, which made me think I should have checked on him earlier, before I fled on foot. Kenyon must have punched him in the face a few times before he left. *All because of me? But why do this much damage and then come back to finish him off?* That was extraordinarily cruel.

But then I realized that wasn't Kenyon whom I had seen running from the crime scene. Was this another gang-related incident, like Marty's shooting?

Tone tried to talk again. I could hear sirens in the distance, so I bent down closer to his lips, which were turning purplish, to catch what he was saying.

"We should've . . ."

I looked at him and repeated in the form of a question what he was trying to say. "Tone, what was it y'all should've done?"

I could see the flashing red and blue lights of approaching vehicles. I jumped up and waved my arms until the ambulance pulled up in front of the house. I bent down again to reassure Tone. "Help is here. Okay, hang on."

Tone grabbed my hand, and with all his strength, he said, "We should've said no. It wasn't worth it."

Tone was squeezing the life out of my hand, and I was sure he was clinging to me for dear life. I patted his hand. The paramedics came up to us. I recognized the female paramedic from a few weeks ago. I removed my hand from Tone's grip.

"He's been beaten and shot," I informed them.

The male paramedic said, "We will take over from here, ma'am."

I moved out of their way, feeling a deep sense of guilt. I still didn't understand how Kenyon had known I was here. And I didn't know why he would go after Tone so viciously. Had he done the same to Leon? What had he got these guys into?

I looked up the street and noticed that, while it was quiet before, now the neighbors were coming out of their houses. Then it dawned on me that I needed to go check on Mama. She would be worried. I also was not comfortable with her being in this neighborhood alone. I had seen too much today. I walked back over to my car and turned off the headlights before I completely drained my car battery. I reached for my phone and thought it best to get my sister to come get Mama.

Before I dialed my sister's number, I made a call to someone else. I knew that it was past time to talk to him about everything I had learned.

It didn't take long for Moses to answer his phone.

"Moses, it's Manchester."

"Let me guess. You wouldn't happen to know about a disturbance on Liberty, now would you?"

"Are you on your way?"

"Baldwin and I are en route, Manchester. Don't go anywhere. You have some explaining to do."

"Okay. I will be here waiting." I clicked the phone, wondering what Moses was talking about. What did I do besides my usual being in the wrong place at the wrong time? I was a credible witness, and this time I could tell the investigators exactly what I saw.

I needed to make sure Mama was safe first, so I dialed Bev's number. I didn't know what time it was currently, but my sister answered, her voice sounding sleepy. "Hello?"

"Bev, it's me. Can Mama spend the night with you? There's been a shooting not far from her house."

I heard Bev ask, "Did someone get hurt?"

I turned to see the paramedics lift Tone's limp body onto the stretcher. I feared the worst for Tone.

"Serena?"

"Yes, one of her neighbors was shot. Can Clay come get Mama? I have to wait for the police."

"Sure. We will get someone to watch the girls and will come as soon as possible. Serena, what were you doing at Mama's?"

I sighed. "We were getting reacquainted. We made some good progress tonight. Bev, you would be proud of both of us."

"That's good to hear. We will be there soon."

I said good-bye and hung up the phone.

There were silver linings in the midst of the tragedies around me. There was a time in my life when I would have overlooked them. Now I was thinking that life was too precious not to look hard for the good amid all the evil.

I noticed there were more people on the street now. A police cruiser with flashing blue lights was in the middle of the street.

Thanks to the flashing lights, I caught sight of the one person who should be hauled off to the cops. Kenyon Cooper. He was looking right at me. That man had some nerve. Though I was uncomfortable, I refused to flinch. I was too angry to be scared.

But I had seen a young man running away from Tone's house. Was he the shooter? Another theory started to swirl in my mind. When my headlights had shone on that young man's face, he had reminded me of Kenyon. Was he Kenyon's son? Was his son working alongside Kenyon, doing his dirty work for him?

CHAPTER FORTY-ONE

Monday, 10:25 p.m.

My phone rang when Bev and her husband arrived to pick up Mama. I told them not to look for me, but to get Mama out of the area. I didn't trust Kenyon Cooper for one second and didn't doubt that he had his sights on me now, although he had disappeared into the crowd. It was time to tell the police all that I had found out, and to hope that they could arrest the man. Even if Kenyon wasn't the shooter, I was sure he had assaulted Tone earlier. That had to be enough to arrest him.

A car came up behind my car. I turned and watched as both Moses and Baldwin exited the vehicle. I gave a sigh of relief upon seeing them. I noted that my reaction was quite different from the first time I saw them two weeks ago. Then I'd wanted to get as far away from that crime scene as possible, but this time I walked toward them. I felt like I was responsible.

I had heard Tone say that he could be next. I had seen a man in fear earlier today. Maybe if I hadn't shown up at his house, none of this would have happened.

Baldwin shook his head. "Really, Manchester? You at another shooting?"

I threw up my hands. "Just minding my own business."

Moses came up to me from the other side of the car. "Are you sure about that, Manchester? I want you down at the station for your statement."

I frowned. "Why? I can talk to you right now."

"You have a lot of explaining to do," Moses barked. "So if I were you, I would be at the station when we get there."

I turned around and stared at the back of Moses as he walked away. Why was I suddenly being treated like a criminal? I didn't want to argue. Frankly, I just wanted to go home. I climbed into my car and shut the door. I tried putting my key in the ignition, but for a few seconds I couldn't. My hand was shaking too badly.

Come on, Serena. Pull yourself together. You got to see this through.

With some effort, I turned the car on and pulled off. When I arrived at the station, I sat in the same chair I had occupied previously, waiting for the investigators to return. I was sleeping pretty well in the chair, and probably drooling, when Moses shook me awake.

I rubbed my eyes. "Do we really have to do this now?"

Moses said, "Yes, we do. A man's life hangs in the balance, and you were there, at the crime scene. Let's go."

I struggled up from the chair and followed Moses down the hall to a room marked INTERROGATION. I stopped outside the door and spun around to face Moses.

"Am I a suspect or something?"

Moses opened the door. "Look, the sooner you answer our questions, the sooner we can all go home. Or at least some of us."

I stared at him, feeling a bit unsure about what was going on. I glanced over at Baldwin, who had walked up, and his face was just as solemn as Moses's. "Fine. Let's just do this." I entered the room, sat down in a chair, and wiped my face, trying to make myself feel more awake.

Moses asked, "Do you need some coffee?"

"Please." The least they could do was give me a cup of crummy coffee and let me talk.

Moses walked out, and a few minutes later he returned with a steaming cup of black coffee. I sipped the bitter coffee as both detectives sat across from me. This really wasn't feeling right to me.

Moses started the questions. "How do you know the victim?"

"I met him a few days ago," I answered.

"Did you talk to him recently?"

I might as well let them know everything. "Yes. I stopped by Tone's house earlier today to talk."

The investigators looked at each other.

I eyed Moses. "What am I missing?"

Moses pulled out a photo from a folder he had sitting in front of him and placed it on the table. It was a photo of me taken earlier today.

"What? Where did this come from?"

Moses answered, "You were caught on a neighbor's camera, climbing their fence and then running across the yard."

"Really? They have a camera in the yard?" My mind started racing. What else did the camera pick up, besides me running scared?

"What were you doing?" Moses quizzed.

I looked at Moses. "I was trying to get out of there."

He frowned. "Out of where? Did you and Mr. Davis have an argument?"

"No. We didn't. In fact, he was making a confession, or at least trying to tell me the truth."

Baldwin held his pen in midair, abandoning his note taking. "What was he confessing about?"

"The alibi for Marty. Tone lied. Marty didn't have an alibi, because he didn't go to North Carolina with Tone." I started waving my hands. Maybe the coffee had kicked in, because all of a sudden I felt like the Energizer Bunny. "I was trying to get him to tell me more, but then he looked out the window and he got nervous. He told me I had to go."

Moses asked, "Why did he tell you that you had to go?"

"Because someone was coming. Someone who wouldn't like that I was there, asking questions."

"Who?" both investigators asked in unison.

I sighed and took a breath. "The man I have been suspicious of for days now. Kenyon Cooper."

Both men looked at each other. Baldwin nodded to Moses and then grabbed his notepad and left the room.

I watched Baldwin leave and then turned back to Moses. "You know about Kenyon Cooper?"

Moses watched me. "We have had our eye on him for a while. My concern is, what do you know about him?"

I shook my head. "Nothing much. I know he's responsible for getting my cousin Leon, Marty, and Tone into some quick cash flow scheme. I know both Leon and Marty—but hopefully not Tone—lost their lives in some strange related way." I took a deep breath. "I have a theory."

Moses asked, "You do?"

"Hear me out, because it sounds crazy. I learned the other day that Kenyon has sons, but I didn't ask about where the sons lived."

"What are you getting at, Manchester? You're babbling."

"Tone's shooter. It was a young man. It might have been the same guy who shot Marty."

"How would you know this? You couldn't identify this guy before."

"You're right. The guy had shades. Tonight it was dark, but my headlights definitely caught his face. Now that I think about it, he reminded me of Kenyon. A *younger* version." I leaned forward. "I'm not a gambling woman, but I would guess that the minor you have in custody is

Kenyon's youngest son, and the oldest son is the one you really want."

Moses shook his head. "Let me get this straight. You think Kenyon has a son who's basically playing assassin. Why?"

"I know that sounds crazy, right? You wouldn't think a father would let his son do that, but I don't think Kenyon is any ordinary dad. I think he likes to be in control. The fact that he got not one, but three grown men, and maybe others, to follow some crazy scheme . . . Who knows what type of influence he has over his own sons?" I leaned back. "I don't know. Maybe the son is going half-cocked on his own, because it doesn't make sense. What would be his motive?"

Moses scribbled something on the notepad in front of him. "How are you making this connection to one of Kenyon's boys?"

"I'm just guessing based on something my dad used to do. Suppose Kenyon has some guilt about not being a good father. Say he bought his sons these expensive, exclusive jackets with cash. You know what? I know there may not be surveillance camera footage in that Atlanta store, but what if you could take a photo of Kenyon and show the employees? He's not a man you would forget. Those jackets were on sale what? Six months ago? That's not too long ago."

"That's a long shot, Manchester, and it's not enough for me to move on. Kenyon may not be father of the year, but we can't prove he had anything to do with Leon's, Marty's, or Tone's shooting."

"But he was there at Tone's house earlier." I picked up the photo. "Do you know why I climbed the fence? Do you know I haven't climbed a fence in years? Kenyon was throwing Tone around like a rag doll. He definitely assaulted him earlier. Isn't that enough to bring him in for questioning?"

"Yes, but he could come in here and lawyer up. He already has a lawyer for his kid."

I smacked the table and stood. "Make that kid talk, Moses. That boy might have been there at the store that night, but he's not the shooter. "

Moses cringed. "Sit down, Manchester."

I sat down. "You need to get the other son. He's the really dangerous one. I wouldn't even be surprised if he had something to do with Chris's shooting. Chris is still in danger until you get this crazy dude."

Moses stood. "Calm down, Manchester. I'm on it. Get out of here and go home."

"What? You're going to let me go?"

"Of course. What did you think we were going to do?"

"I don't know. You were acting like you were going to throw me in a cell!"

"Considering all the trouble you have gotten into, maybe I should," Moses shouted. "I am going to request that we have someone watch your house tonight."

I was kind of glad to hear that, but I asked about it, anyway. "Do you really think Kenyon or his son would bother me? I really don't know anything. I still have questions. Like what did Leon and the other men sign up to do?"

Moses nodded. "I'm familiar with that part of your cousin's case. Your aunt told me that something was different about Leon after this job."

"Any ideas about someone who gets paid a lot of money, gets a guilty conscience, and decides it's time to beg for forgiveness from God?"

"I'm thinking definitely not any kind of legal work. Let's get you home. We will take over from here, Manchester. I need you to lay low until we can make some moves. We don't need you in the middle of any more crime scenes. Do we have an understanding?"

I raised my hand. "Understood."

CHAPTER FORTY-TWO

Wednesday, May 1, 7:25 a.m.

I had a fitful night's sleep. Leon, Marty, Tone, and Chris were all in my dreams. Even Trey and Joseph. When I saw Trey in a dream, I jumped up from the bed in a sweat. Moses had told me to lay low, but it had occurred to me, I needed to warn Trey. Iris needed to come to her senses about moving to Charlotte with Kenyon. I knew she had had a child with Kenyon and he had promised her marriage, but it wasn't good for her young son, and certainly not for Joseph.

If Moses arrested Kenyon, Iris would see Kenyon's true self. But then I started thinking that a woman couldn't be around a man like that and not know he had some major issues. I mean, was Kenyon's son really that evil? I couldn't feel sorry for the boy, because he was a cold-blooded killer.

There was no use trying to go back to sleep, because now I was alarmed that so many people had been or could be affected by this one man. I wanted to check on Tone, so I grabbed my cell phone off my nightstand and dialed the hospital. No one on the hospital staff would tell me anything since I wasn't a relative. I looked at the clock and thought of a person who could find out. I dialed her number and waited. Alecia answered my call on the second ring.

"I guess you're awake," I said.

"I haven't slept. Moses called to tell me he was putting a man on duty at Chris's room. Why now? What's going on?"

I told her, "I will tell you everything, but I really need you to do me a favor. As a nurse, you might be able to find out information about a patient."

Alecia asked, "Who?"

"Tone Davis. He was shot last night." I heard Alecia suck in a breath. I quickly said, "I promise I will tell you all I know. I just have to know if Tone made it through last night. Tone is the one person who can tell the whole truth. He has to live."

"I will see what I can find out."

After disconnecting the call, I walked to the front of the house and looked out the window. True to his word, Moses had an unmarked police car out front. While I waited on Alecia to call back, I went into the kitchen to start the coffee. While I waited for the coffee to brew, I sat at the kitchen table and called Bev.

"Are you okay?" Bev asked. "Mama has been worried. She didn't go to sleep for the longest time, hoping to hear from you."

"I'm sorry, and I'm fine. I had to make a statement to the police. I was exhausted when I got home."

"Are you going to tell us what happened?"

"Not yet. Just please keep Mama at your house. I will tell you everything later."

"Serena, you have me worried. Let me pray over you."

I wasn't going to refuse. I was starting to feel responsible for Tone, even though I didn't understand how Kenyon had known I was at Tone's house and why he thought I was such a threat. "Please do."

Bev prayed for protection and wisdom. It struck me that Trey had prayed a similar prayer a few days ago. A beep came through my phone.

"Bev, I need to take this call."

I hung up and switched over to see Alecia's name on my caller ID.

"I'm sorry, Rena. Tone is in the ICU, in a coma. He has major damage to his liver, and there is a search on for a donor. They're not sure if he's going to make it if his liver fails."

I cried out, "He has to make it."

Please, Lord. Don't let Kenyon get away with what he's done.

"What is going on in our town with all these shootings?" Alecia asked. "It doesn't't make any sense."

I agreed with Alecia. "Is Chris awake?"

Alecia's voice rose a bit. "Why?"

"Alecia, Chris needs to confirm something for me. This is more than about him."

Alecia was quiet.

I nudged her by saying, "This could affect Trey and Joseph. Kenyon Cooper is at the center of everything. I know it, and I told Moses last night."

"Kenyon? You think he had something to do with Leon's death?"

"I can't go into specifics, but Kenyon definitely had something to do with where it all started. Look, if you don't want Chris saying anything, tell me what you know about Kenyon's sons."

"They're troublemakers. They moved to town last summer to live with Kenyon. Trey's complained that they have bullied Joseph and they have bothered Chris."

"So Chris knows them."

Alecia sighed. "Chris had started hanging out with the youngest one. I think his name is Kelvin. I don't know why. He was one of the boys at the church that day we were there."

"What?" That boy was Kenyon's son. "Why didn't you say something?"

"Why does it matter? Moses arrested him."

"No. No. No." I started breathing hard. My head was starting to hurt. I should have been asking more questions before now.

Alecia asked, "Rena, what's wrong?"

I gulped, trying to calm my breathing. "There is another son? An older boy?"

"Yes. He may be eighteen or nineteen years old. I think he dropped out of school. Why?"

"Did he hang around Chris or Joseph?"

"I don't know. It's possible. Serena, why are you asking these questions?"

"I should've been asking these questions before," I shouted, straining my vocal chords.

Alecia was quiet on the other end after my outburst. "Are you trying to say Kenyon's oldest boy is responsible for hurting Chris? Is that why Moses put an officer outside Chris's door? What? Hold on, Rena."

I heard Alecia talking to Chris. I shouted into the phone, "Alecia, what is Chris saying?"

"Rena, Chris said that the oldest boy is KC. He drove them to the store that night. He told his younger brother to stay in the car and be the lookout." Alecia's voice faded.

I strained to hear Chris's voice in the background. Alecia came back on; her voice was hoarse. "Chris said that when the boys came to church, they warned him not to say anything to the cops. But he wasn't going to say a word." Alecia's voice cracked.

I nodded as everything started to fall into place. "KC. That must stand for Kenyon Cooper, Jr. Alecia, listen to me. You need to tell all of this to Moses. KC sounds like a really troubled young man."

"Rena, how do Tone, Marty, and Leon fit into this?"

"I'm still working on that part. I will check in with you later. Please talk to Moses."

I sat for a moment after I hung up the phone. My head was hurting worse now. I looked up at the counter and realized I had forgotten about the brewed coffee. I stood and reached for a cup and poured some coffee. My head was throbbing now.

I sucked down the coffee as my thoughts whirled in my mind. I had sensed something was wrong the moment I walked into the convenience store that night. I had driven up, completely clueless, and had left that crime scene a coward.

I placed the coffee cup in the sink. I needed to sit down. I plopped down on a kitchen chair, aware of Callie floating around my ankles. I had to ignore the cat's needs for now as I was mulling over all the wrong actions I took weeks ago.

Chris had been in the back of that Crown Victoria that fateful night at the convenience store, as KC plotted what he was going to do. I should have made Chris talk to me that day I went to find him. I should've told his mother, and we all should have talked to Moses. That very night I should have sent the investigators to Chris's home, whether I could tell if it was Chris or not in the store. It would have been fine if I was wrong. My instincts had been on point the whole time.

Even more importantly, maybe it had been more than instincts. What if God had been trying to tell me something and I hadn't been listening? I had been typical Serena Manchester, in her own world. I slammed my fists down on the kitchen table. Out of the corner of my eye, I saw the cat flee from the kitchen and my wrath. I didn't know how long I sat there as the tears rolled down my face.

It was time to make it right. I had to find out the last bit of missing information. There had to be more evidence for building solid cases. I started at the beginning. Maybe the plan that night had simply been to commit the robbery, and the shooting had been a fatal mistake. No. Something had felt off. As my mind went back to that night, I reminded myself that I hadn't been up front to see what was going on, but it had seemed like KC shot Marty after he had already opened the cash register. I'd always thought that second shot was the act of a really ruthless person. The investigators had said that Marty didn't have a weapon. So why did the boy feel threatened?

If KC was the one who shot Chris, I understood his diabolical reasoning for going after Chris. He needed to keep Chris from talking to the police about the robbery gone wrong. What I didn't understand was why KC went after Tone last night. KC might have known that Kenyon had visited Tone and assaulted him earlier in the day, but it seemed a bit much that KC would go back and finish Tone off. Did KC act on his own, or was his father pulling the trigger by influencing KC's actions? It seemed hard to believe that a father would condone or even encourage that type of violence. If Kenyon had wanted Tone dead, he would have killed him earlier in the day.

The biggest question was, who really shot Leon? Tone had said he'd lied about Marty's whereabouts on the day in question, so Marty had no alibi for the time of the murder. Where was Kenyon Cooper, or KC, for that matter, last spring, when my cousin was left to bleed to death in his front yard?

CHAPTER FORTY-THREE

Thursday, May 2, 3:25 p.m.

I knew I had told Alecia to talk to Moses, but I needed to make sure something was happening. In the afternoon I called him to be sure they were searching for Kenyon and his oldest son, KC.

"We have an APB out on Kenyon Cooper, Jr.," Moses assured me. "We looked back at the surveillance camera footage, and we talked to Kelvin Cooper in the presence of the lawyer. It appears we might be able to work out a deal. I think the younger brother no longer feels like taking the rap for his older brother."

"Good. So you think Kelvin and Chris will help at a trial?"

"For Marty's death," Moses said. "We are also checking the ballistics from the gun. If the same gun was used in Chris's and Tone's shooting, that helps build evidence for those cases. I have to tell you the motive for this kid is a bit sketchy when it comes to Tone."

"I thought the same thing. I want to look more into what Tone was trying to tell me last night." I was haunted by Tone's words as he was clinging to his life. Now he was in the ICU. What did Tone mean by "We should've said no. It wasn't worth it"? If I could figure out what this group of men had done, it might lead to motives.

Moses broke my thoughts. "I told you to lay low. You're in enough hot water, Manchester."

"I didn't know you cared," I responded sweetly.

Moses growled something at me that I was sure it was best I didn't hear.

"I'm keeping an officer on you and Chris. Don't make this difficult."

"I promise I won't. Thank you, Moses. I know you don't have to share or bring me in on these cases."

"It's the least I could do for your aunt, Alecia, and Chris. Just please nothing else crazy."

I ended the call. The last thing I needed was to get myself in any deeper. I knew Aunt C had been having trouble accepting her son's death. I felt like Aunt C's life had been taken far too quickly. It was like she'd been ready for God to take her home now that her son was gone. I owed my family, especially Aunt C, after all the years I'd been gone.

That was when it hit me. I'd been asking questions, but it was time to put my skills to work. I went into the bedroom and pulled out my laptop. It was time to go back to some of my old haunts. While I was in the hospital last year, what was going on in Charlotte that I had missed?

I walked into the living room and sat down on the chair opposite the couch. Then I placed the laptop on the coffee table and turned it on. While I waited for the laptop to boot up, I jotted a list on a notepad, starting with Leon's name. Both Trey and Alecia had said that Leon had shown signs of guilt and nervousness before his death. Then I wrote Marty's name and then Tone's. Both men must have been feeling similar pressure before they were shot. Finally, I wrote Kenyon's name and circled it. Tone clearly was scared of Kenyon, and I had seen firsthand Kenyon's threatening manner.

Whatever the source, money had flowed easily into the pockets of the men involved. I believed Kenyon had bought high-priced items for his sons. Alecia had said that Leon had paid off debts. Had Marty and Tone made money? Tone's living conditions didn't seem to point to much money, but Marty had clearly been angry with Leon about something. Was the anger due to Leon developing a conscience and quitting? Maybe Leon had thought it best to turn himself in, which would have affected the others involved.

I started my search online back at my former TV station, WYNN, and I also searched other stations, as well as the newspaper the *Charlotte Observer*. Hours later, with tired eyes, I was about to call it quits when I came across a headline in the newspaper's Crime section: CHARLOTTE STORE OWNER ARRESTED FOR ILLEGAL GAMBLING, LARGER OPERATION POSSIBLE.

As I scrolled down and read the story, a few things popped out, such as the name of the man who was arrested for the crime. His name was Kenneth Cooper. As I looked at his photo, I couldn't help but think he looked familiar. Was he a relative of Kenyon Cooper? According to the article, there was quite an illegal gambling operation within Kenneth Cooper's store in Charlotte, and there were even some illegal gaming machines at his home. The article stated that this was part of a larger operation and that the FBI had been brought in to search for other suspects. The arrest took place last April, possibly around the same time Leon supposedly quit his Charlotte job. Was this something Kenyon was a part of, and had he brought in the other men?

Alecia had said that Marty had introduced Kenyon to the group. Marty had had a store like the one of this man who had been arrested. Most stores were equipped with surveillance cameras and alarms. Marty had had all the necessary equipment to ensure his store's security. Had Marty done anything else with the store? Why had he really been angry enough to threaten Leon in front of so many people?

I leaned back in the chair and thought about what I knew so far. Kenyon had come to Georgetown for a reason. Since he and Iris had had a child, that could be one reason, but he'd brought his two oldest sons here too. *Why?*

Moses wouldn't want to hear from me twice in one day, but I needed to know more about Kenyon's and Marty's past and if there was any connection to this illegal gambling case. I decided to call Moses again. He picked up immediately.

"This is Moses."

"So good to hear your voice again, Moses. What can you tell me about Kenyon Cooper? Would you say he is the entrepreneurial type and engaged in entrepreneurial activities?"

Moses breathed in deeply. "Manchester, what have you gotten into now?"

"Well, I have a lead for you, and it's in a place we know and love. Charlotte, North Carolina."

"I'm listening."

"I've been doing some research, and I'm just curious about this arrest last spring in Charlotte. There may be no connection at all, but this guy named Kenneth Cooper was arrested there for illegal gambling. . . . I'm just wondering if there's any relation to Kenyon Cooper? Do you know if Kenyon has been involved in any criminal activities?"

Moses didn't respond.

"Moses, are you still there?"

"Yes, Manchester. I'm really baffled about how you're able to dig up dirt in a few days or hours. I don't know of any relation to Kenneth Cooper, but I'm familiar with Kenyon Cooper and his felonies. He's done prison time for what you describe as 'entrepreneurial activities.' He's a smart and resourceful man. He just decided to pursue illegal matters instead of obeying the law."

I jumped up from my chair. "Are you serious? How long ago did Kenyon get out of prison?"

"I remember when he was arraigned. I happened to be a part of the sting operation. He served at least ten years in prison. He's been out maybe for the past two or three years."

"So, tell me, can a lot of cash be generated with illegal gambling?"

"Yes, especially with sports gambling. It could be something up Kenyon's alley. We got officers looking for Kenyon. This is certainly something to add to the list of questions."

"What about illegal gambling here? This is a prime area for tourists, which means good business. I do know Marty met Kenyon and introduced him to the other men. Could Marty have been using his store for other matters? I know he was a good, upstanding member of the community, but suppose there was another side to him."

"That could be possible," Moses replied. "You've given us a lot to look into, Manchester. I will get someone to check out Marty's store operation."

"So I don't get any thanks for the leads?"

"Manchester, remember what I said earlier."

"Yes, sir!" I hung up the phone.

I knew I had told Moses I would lay low, but I wondered if Iris knew her boyfriend was a convicted felon. She certainly should be aware of what Kenyon and his sons had done. I decided I would pay her a visit. But first, I needed to touch base with Trey. I needed to tell him that all his fears about Joseph living with Kenyon Cooper were warranted. He certainly had more ammunition for his custody case now.

CHAPTER FORTY-FOUR

Thursday, 5:15 p.m.

I left a voice mail for Trey to let him know I was going to talk to Iris. I told him to talk to Clay about Kenyon's prison record. Everything would probably work out fine once Kenyon was brought in for questioning. With Kenyon and his son off the streets, a sense of normalcy should return. Who was I kidding? I didn't know what normal meant. Maybe *peace* was the word I was seeking.

I looked out the window to see if Moses still had an officer outside my house. I figured the police had more to do than sit outside my house, especially during the day. When I peeked out, I saw no officer. The coast was clear for me to go. I wasn't exactly sure how I was going to convince Iris not to make the biggest mistake of her life, but I had to try.

When I arrived at Iris's house, I was really surprised to see a moving van in the yard. After I parked my car in front of the house, I walked over and peeked inside the open truck. Furniture and boxes were piled up inside it already. Someone had been working hard all day. I wouldn't be surprised if they planned to pull out tonight.

I didn't recall Trey saying that Iris was leaving so soon, though. Joseph still had a few weeks of school left before the summer break. What was she thinking? I walked up to the front door, which was open. I knocked and shouted, "Iris, are you here?"

A few seconds later Iris poked her head out of a nearby room and came down the hall. Her hair was tied up with a scarf, and she looked really tired. "Rena, what are you doing here?"

I stepped inside and looked around. The house had undergone quite a transformation since I was here last. "You've been busy. I didn't know you were moving so fast."

Iris swallowed. "Well, I didn't, either, until yesterday. We got a good deal on a house, and Kenyon thought we should move in and get settled before it gets too hot."

Yesterday. I wondered why Kenyon really wanted to get out of town so soon. "That's still pretty fast. I mean, once you buy the house, you can take your time to move in . . . you know, to decorate it the way you want."

"I won't have a job for a while, so I will have plenty of time to work on the house."

I frowned at her. "You already quit the Huddle House?"

Iris's shoulders seemed to droop more. "This morning. I was kind of sad, especially since I wasn't able to give two weeks' notice. I told you I worked there longer than anywhere else. I guess I can stay home with James for a while. No need for babysitters."

This woman was really naive or clueless about the man she was planning to move to another state with and also marry. She made what she was doing all sound so normal.

"So will Kenyon's sons being moving in with you? They are staying with him now, right?"

Iris looked puzzled by my questions. "No, I don't think so. The oldest, KC, will probably get his own place. He's not even going back to Charlotte. I think he's going to Florida or something."

Really? Sounds likes some guilty people are on the run. I wondered if KC had made his way out of the state already, after last night's shooting. "What about Kenyon's youngest boy, the one in police custody right now? Kelvin may not be going anywhere, either."

Iris stared at me. "Kenyon said he will be fine. He just got into a bit of trouble."

I walked closer to Iris. "I would say. He must really love his older brother, since he took the heat for *his* crimes. I hear that all that might change now, though. I mean, would you want Joseph and James to be doing that? If one of them committed murder, would you want the innocent brother to be locked up, while the guilty one ran free?"

"What are you talking about? What are you really doing here, Rena? How do you know so much about Kenyon's sons?"

Iris was really being too naive for me. "I haven't even started on Kenyon. You're leaving town to live with a convicted felon. You would rather take Joseph from his dad, a really good man, and have him live with a criminal."

"Stop it. Kenyon is a good man, and people make mistakes. You don't have any business judging."

"I'm not *judging* anyone. I'm stating the facts. People have lost their lives or been hurt, and that can't be ignored. Kenyon steals, kills, and destroys other people's lives to provide for you. Do you really think that's fair to *your* sons?"

"Get out! Did Trey put you up to this? He doesn't think I know, but I know he wants to get custody of my son."

"You mean *his* son, right?"

Iris shook her head. "I'm sorry for my past decisions, but it's my time to be happy."

"Are you really happy, or are you fooling yourself, thinking you will be happy?"

"Rena. Get out!"

I stepped up to her. "Your family had the same reputation as mine. Dallas Robinson was known for his shenanigans, and so were the Jenkins boys. We know when people are doing wrong, but we get used to turning our heads. That's what you're doing right now."

Iris pushed me toward the door.

I stood my ground. "His sons are dangerous, and so is Kenyon. You can go anywhere you want and have the life that you want. But you can't put your boys at risk. A mother would protect her children. Children are gifts from God."

Iris pointed at me. "Now you sound just like Trey. You tell Trey, if he doesn't stop this, I will never let him see Joseph."

I looked at Iris. "Trey has nothing to do with me coming here. I came to talk some sense into you, but apparently, it's not working out too well. I feel sorry for you. I just hope you and your boys don't pay the price for your stupidity."

Iris looked at me, and then she looked past me. By the way her face contorted and she sucked in her breath, I guessed who was behind me. When I turned around, I was pretty sure Kenyon had heard the last part of my comments to Iris, as he closed the front door behind him.

I hoped I wasn't about to pay the price for coming over to talk sense into Iris.

CHAPTER FORTY-FIVE

Thursday, 5:45 p.m.

As Kenyon walked toward us, a few things occurred to me. I started to have that same feeling the night I entered Marty's store. Why hadn't Moses already taken Kenyon in for questioning? This whole situation at Iris's house looked like a man getting ready to run. The problem with this picture was that he was taking a woman and her children with him. Why was the move happening so fast? Where were Joseph and James? School should have been out by now for Joseph, and I hadn't seen either boy since I arrived.

As if she had read my mind, Iris asked Kenyon, "Where are the boys? Why didn't you bring them back with you?"

That alarmed me even more. What kind of game was Kenyon playing?

As Kenyon stood in front of us, his right eye twitched rapidly.

What is he nervous about?

Ignoring Iris's questions, Kenyon focused his attention on me. His voice was low and deep when he said, "Ms. Manchester, you just don't know how to stay out of people's business. Ever since you got here, you have been starting trouble."

I stared back at Kenyon. I had been here a whole three months, minding my business, before I walked into Marty's convenience store a few weeks ago. "Well, I see it a bit differently. When my family is being targeted, it is my business, Mr. Cooper. Seems to me like ever since you and your sons showed up, there's been trouble."

Kenyon growled.

Iris flinched.

I could blame my boldness on stupidity, but I really wasn't trying to be intimidated by this man. Kenyon and his oldest spawn had done too much damage. "You should get the father of the year award with the way your son played a part in all this. I'm not talking about Joseph or James."

My bravado faded as I watched Kenyon lift a gun from the waist of his pants. He didn't point it at me, but I didn't need any convincing that he would use it, so I stepped back. *Like father, like son.*

Iris looked like she was getting ready to hyperventilate. "Kenyon, what are you doing? Where are my sons?"

"Shut up, Iris! They will be fine," Kenyon yelled. He shook his head as he faced me. "I should have known when I saw you at your aunt's funeral and you decided to stay in town, you would eventually be trouble. Your reputation followed you from Charlotte."

"I guess yours did too," I couldn't help but comment.

Kenyon laughed. "You're a real piece of work. Leon was so proud of his cousin, the reporter. He bragged about how you brought the mayor of Charlotte down last year and how you were tight with the cops."

I shook my head. "You have destroyed good people's lives with your schemes."

Kenyon shook his head. "I did nothing but offer people a way out of their situations. People always need and want money. They don't think about the costs as long as the money allows them to have what they want."

I looked over at Iris, who was standing there like some puppet, waiting for her strings to be pulled. Hadn't she seen all this before?

Kenyon swung the gun up toward my forehead. "Move. We're going for a ride."

A wave of fear, along with a distinct desire to cry out, assaulted me at once. I sucked in a breath. "Where am I supposed to be going with you?"

"No more questions from you. I have something for you to do."

I swallowed my fear, remembering the prayers of protection from Trey and Bev. *God, please protect me.* I put my hands up and turned around. I didn't want to have my back to Kenyon, but I didn't have much choice.

When we reached the front door, I heard him say, "Iris, get everything finished in the next hour. We will roll out of here tonight. If you think of calling the police on me, you can forget seeing either of your boys again."

I gasped and turned around, despite the gun pointing at me. I looked back at Iris, who was visibly crying. "You're holding her kids hostage against her?"

"Move it now!" Kenyon shouted, his voice booming. "We don't have much time here."

I turned and opened the door, not sure what he meant. Kenyon pressed the barrel of the gun into my ribs, to make me walk faster, I guessed. The gun in my side didn't alarm me as much as seeing Trey getting out of his car. He must have gotten my voice mail. I didn't mean for him to come here.

Kenyon saw him too.

Trey stopped and started to run toward me.

I yelled, "No! Trey, don't!"

Kenyon wrapped his large arm around my neck, choking me. In slow motion I watched him raise the gun. I couldn't let him shoot Trey. I kicked Kenyon as hard as I could and elbowed him in the ribs, below his raised arm. I heard him grunt, but I also heard the gun go off.

I saw Trey go down, but I had no idea if he had been hit or was just ducking down to get out of the line of fire.

Kenyon still had a death grip on me as I felt him dragging me away from Trey. I didn't understand why he just didn't kill me too.

CHAPTER FORTY-SIX

Thursday, 6:10 p.m.

"What did you do? Let me go!" I screamed.

Kenyon's grip on me was so tight that I couldn't see if Trey was still on the ground. I didn't know if he was hurt or worse. Iris finally had sense enough to cry out behind us. Kenyon swung the gun toward Iris.

After all this, I sure hope she has changed her mind.

Kenyon stuffed me in the passenger seat of a truck I'd never seen before. I saw Iris run toward where Trey had fallen. I saw no signs of him on the ground. Maybe he had ducked down and then had run behind the truck.

Kenyon jumped into the driver's seat, turned on the ignition, and roared out of the driveway.

"Are you crazy?" I yelled at Kenyon. "You shot at the man who's the father of your girlfriend's son. What kind of sense does that make?" I didn't care if Kenyon had a gun or not, I was ready to pummel him. I wanted to rip the car's steering wheel from his hands.

Kenyon kept his eyes peeled to the road, although he hadn't let go of the gun. "I didn't shoot him."

"How do you know?"

"Because I wasn't trying to kill him. I only wanted to scare him away so we didn't waste any more time. I need your help," he yelled back at me.

To scare him away. "What's so important that you need me?" I stared incredulously at him. "Why would I help you? We've already established that you brought evil with you when you came here and you've been wreaking havoc ever since."

Kenyon sighed. "I may have done some things, but I haven't killed anyone."

"No, you didn't beat up Tone."

Kenyon said between clenched teeth, "I didn't kill him. He talked too much, and I needed him to know I didn't appreciate it."

I looked at the gun in his hand. "Well, you own a gun. Are you sure you didn't ask somebody to finish Tone off for you?"

"I told you, I'm not a killer. I wanted to make a point."

"Sounds like a lot of people like to walk around and make points. Marty did that to Leon. After they fought, Leon was killed later."

"When Marty shot Leon, it was an accident. I told him to cool off before he went over to see him. Marty was scared Leon was going to blow the whole thing, and he wanted to scare Leon."

"Scare him? That didn't end too well. Marty said he would kill Leon. He said it and did it. I don't know what's going on, but I don't have a reason to help you."

"What if I tell you what you want to know?"

"What is that?"

"The whole reason why you're snooping around. Marty really didn't mean to shoot Leon."

"He left Leon there to die. He could have confessed, instead of coming up with some concocted alibi."

"Marty owed a lot of money and was trying to save the store. He didn't want Leon's conscience to get in the way. Leon was all in at first, because he needed money too, and he gladly participated. Then he got religion or something and thought it was best we stop before we got caught."

If only Aunt C knew that her prayers had finally worked on Leon all the way at the end.

"Why are you telling me this, and where are you taking me?"

Kenyon didn't answer me and instead kept his eyes on the road.

I noticed we were getting farther outside the city limits and into more rural territory. We even passed the church where Marty's funeral services were held last week. My mind tried to wrap itself around where we could possibly be going.

Kenyon finally answered me. "I need you to get the boys."

"Joseph and James?"

"Yes. I need to distract him while you get the boys out of the house."

"Distract who?" As soon as I said it, I knew. "KC has them." Then I remembered Alecia saying that Kenyon's boys had teased Joseph and Chris. "Jeez, Kenyon. Poor Joseph must be scared to death. This isn't good for him and his body."

"I know. Look, I will talk to KC. I need him to turn himself in. I just don't want him to hurt the little guys and . . ."

I waited for Kenyon to say more, but instead he slowed the truck down and made a right onto a dirt road. I started praying, because I had no idea where we were going and how anyone would find us back here.

God, what's the plan here? I wasn't a superhero. How was I supposed to rescue two boys?

"You said you need me to get the boys," I commented. "Can you start explaining to me what it is I'm supposed to do?"

Kenyon drove up to a small white house that had come into view. The dark Crown Victoria was parked in front of the house. As we got closer, I saw a familiar person on the porch. It was Margaret from the Huddle House. She was sitting on the porch, rocking in a chair, but she didn't appear to be relaxed. Sitting in her lap was James, and next to her, with his hands wrapped around a Gameboy, was Joseph.

Kenyon stopped the car and cut the engine. I looked over at Kenyon and noticed he'd slipped the gun back in the waist of his pants and had placed his shirt over the weapon.

I asked, "Is Margaret your mother?"

He nodded. "She wasn't supposed to know anything. Tone saw her the other day, and he said too much. He upset her, and she said something to KC. That set him off. That boy has never been quite right in the head."

Now I was starting to understand. When Kenyon went to Tone's house yesterday and had a fit, he was upset about his mother. He was furious that Tone had clued his mother into what was going on. KC had got mad and had shot Tone, and now he was holding his grandmother, James, and Joseph."

I would say this boy is definitely crazy. Dangerous and crazy.

I swallow and asked, "How exactly will this work? You want me to walk up to the house and get them off the porch? I'm assuming KC is inside the house or somewhere else on the property."

Kenyon looked at me. His forehead was covered with perspiration. "I need you to play along with me. You're my hostage."

I stared at him. "Yes, I'm your hostage. You forced me into your truck."

Kenyon removed the key from the ignition and handed the set of keys to me.

I looked down at the keys and back at him. He was serious. I took a deep breath and grabbed the keys and stuffed them in my jeans pocket. *Looks like this former reporter is making her first rescue attempt.*

He stared at me. "When I give you the signal, you get everyone off that porch and in the truck. You go!"

I kind of didn't like this idea. It sounded like it gave him and KC the opportunity to run. "What are you going to do?"

"I'm going to reason with KC. If that doesn't work, I want my boys and my mother as far away from this house as possible."

"That's why you came to Georgetown. Your mother."

"I don't have time to get into my history with you, but that's my heart. She's a God-fearing woman who I should have listened to more. It had been a long time since I'd seen her. Now I brought danger to her house." Kenyon took a deep breath. "I will move KC away from everyone. When you see that I have him far enough away for you to get everyone out, don't hesitate." With that Kenyon got out of the truck.

I didn't know how to process his instructions, so I climbed out of the truck too. When I looked up, Margaret smiled at me. James had begun to cry a bit, but Margaret held him tight.

"It's going to be all right. You will be with your mama soon," she said, comforting him.

I observed Kenyon. He appeared sad as he watched the older woman comfort his son. I didn't doubt the fact that Kenyon had messed up with his older boys, but he did seem willing to be a father to his youngest and had even accepted Joseph. I remembered the way Kenyon had supported Iris and had stood by Joseph's bedside at the hospital while the young boy was in pain.

I studied Joseph's face. Joseph looked calm, but I could tell by his wide eyes that he was scared. This kind of stress wasn't good for Joseph's condition. I hoped he would remain okay. Seeing Joseph made me hope and pray that Trey was okay. This father and his son needed to be together.

The screen door on the front of the house flew open. My eyes saw KC's face clearly for the first time. I'd seen him only with shades in the daylight, and then last night he had run in front of my car. He was a younger, more handsome version of his dad, but his mouth was currently in a sneer.

"What's she doing here?" he grunted.

Kenyon looked at his son. "I needed some way to keep the police off of us. She's going to help."

KC looked skeptical. "How?"

That is a good question.

Kenyon just answered, "Trust me. This lady will be our ticket out of this place. Let's talk about the plan."

The plan. What in the world is Kenyon talking about?

I looked down at KC's pants. This young man was all ego. His gun was stuffed in his sagging pants, but it was in plain sight. I wondered how often KC had fired that same gun in the past few weeks.

Then I remembered Kenyon had stuffed his gun in his pants too.

This was a father and son showdown like I'd never seen before. I wasn't thrilled to be a part of it. Not at all.

CHAPTER FORTY-SEVEN

Thursday, 7:20 p.m.

I should've known this wasn't going to be easy. It got dark pretty rapidly, and I was starting to doubt Kenyon. We had moved from the porch to inside the house, which made my rescue effort a bit more perilous. Kenyon had claimed I was to protect the younger boys and Margaret. I had the truck keys in my pocket, but my imagination spun a scenario in which both Kenyon and KC took me out to the woods and finished me off. I knew too much. What did Kenyon think was going to happen by telling me what he did earlier? I guessed he thought giving me information I wanted to know would make up for everything else.

If Kenyon really was going to give me a signal, he was taking his time delivering it. I had a feeling that any attempt on my part to make a run for it with two boys and an older woman might not go well. Both father and son had guns. It was a scene right out of a Western movie, with the possibility of one of them being quicker on the draw than the other. Would Kenyon shoot his son? What if KC fired a shot at the man he had already killed for? Could I move the boys and Margaret fast enough?

Little James was restless again. He was really missing his mother, but I could tell the toddler was used to being around his grandmother. I was wondering if Margaret was as clueless as Iris when it came to Kenyon and KC or if she had chosen to turn her head and not acknowledge what her son and grandson were doing. *God, I need some wisdom here.* I continued to pray. I had no clue how this story was going to end, but I was strangely calm, as I was certain that God knew, and that was all that mattered.

I made eye contact with Margaret. "Do you babysit him a lot?" I asked.

Margaret peered at me, her eyes still wide with fear. "Yes. When I'm not at work. I take turns with Iris's grandmother."

So if we were to run, how much commotion would little James make? I looked to the door, which was across from the couch. KC and Kenyon were standing out on the porch. KC's back was to me, but Kenyon was facing us. He was talking to his son, who seemed to keep waving his arms, like he was agitated. What exactly were they talking about? Was Kenyon helping his eldest son escape, or did he really want me to get everyone out of here in the truck?

I looked at Joseph. I moved next to him on the couch. I needed him to be ready. I observed KC and his father, noting that they were still talking, and then turned to Joseph. "How are you doing?" I whispered.

Joseph nodded. "I'm fine."

I said to him, "I need you to be brave. Okay?"

"I am."

"Good. When I say so, I need you to run to the truck. You will need to move really fast. Can you do that?"

He looked at me. I pulled the truck keys out of my pocket so he could see them. Joseph nodded. "I can."

I put my arm around him and squeezed his shoulders.

Margaret was across from us, holding James. She had been watching me with Joseph. I pointed to the door, but Margaret frowned. I looked outside and saw that Kenyon and KC were no longer on the porch. Where did they go? Kenyon had said he would draw KC away from us. His disappearance didn't seem like a very good signal, but I stood, nevertheless, and inched over to the screen door.

I tried to look out into the yard, but it was really dark out there, except for the glow from the porch light. If it wasn't for the truck being white, I might not have seen it. What I really wanted to know was where the father and son had gone. I stepped closer to the screen door and put my hand on the door handle and gently pushed.

KC showed up and banged on the screen door. "Where are you going?"

I jumped back and heard Margaret screech. Her screech set off James, and he started crying.

I shook my head. "Nowhere. I was just looking out-side."

Where is Kenyon, and how is this going to work? This was taking way too long.

KC opened the screen door and walked in with his hand on his gun. I moved back to the couch and sat down next to Joseph. A minute later Kenyon showed up on the porch and walked inside.

I flashed my eyes at Kenyon, wondering when he was going to help us make the move. *Would anyone know to come out here to look for any of us?*

"You need to take care of her. I don't trust her," KC said.

Kenyon shook his head. "Boy, I told you to cool it. We got enough trouble breathing down on us now. If you plan on getting out of here, you need to get your stuff ready. It's just about dark out there now. You need to move."

Was Kenyon helping his son escape? How was that helping anyone? That boy needed to be locked up.

KC hesitated and looked over at me. He turned to his grandmother. Margaret looked up at her grandson with what I would describe as pity and disappointment. This young man had brought her pain, maybe more than her own son had.

I thought, *Sins of the father.*

KC glared back at me and then sauntered off to the back of the house. Kenyon looked at me. He didn't say a word, but I knew this was our chance to escape. I nudged Joseph so that he would move to the door, and then I walked quickly around to Margaret. I pointed at the door.

She looked confused at first, but when she looked over at Kenyon, she seemed to realize what was happening. I just hoped that James, who appeared to have settled back down, would remain quiet.

I pulled the truck keys out of my pocket and moved toward the door. Once Joseph and Margaret had walked outside and were on the porch, I quickly followed, without even looking at Kenyon. We didn't have time to be looking back.

It was really dark out, but the porch light cast just enough light on the truck. I sprinted off the steps and ran to the passenger door of the truck. I opened the door slowly and hoped it didn't squeak. I turned and saw that Joseph was right beside me.

"Hurry up! Climb in!"

As Joseph scrambled into the truck, I turned and looked for Margaret. She appeared to be tiptoeing toward us as she struggled with James. I didn't know how long it would be before KC noticed we had slipped out, and what his reaction to his dad would be at this betrayal, so I needed Margaret to pick up her speed. I didn't want to take James from her for fear that he would start hollering at a stranger's touch.

"Margaret, hurry!" I whispered as loud as I dared.

She finally got to the truck. I realized I had to take James so that Margaret could climb into the truck. Once she was seated, I handed her the sleepy boy. I gently closed the truck door and ran around to the other side of the truck.

Once I climbed in, it took me a moment to catch my breath. I looked at the house and saw Kenyon standing in the doorway. I pushed the key into the ignition, and my heart fluttered as the engine cranked to life.

Once the truck started, I glanced at the house and saw a commotion near the front door. I watched for only a split second. I needed to move this truck, like, now. I switched on the headlights, and I turned the steering wheel, maneuvering the truck around in the yard as best I could. As soon as I had turned the truck around, I heard gunshots. Definitely more than one bullet pinged off the truck. When I looked up in the rearview mirror, I saw Kenyon with his gun in his hand.

Why would he be shooting at us? I had no idea why, but I wasn't going to stick around and think about it. I pressed the accelerator and drove the truck swiftly down the dirt road.

I prayed for Kenyon and KC, because I had a distinct feeling that I might never see one or both of those men again. I also prayed that I could find help, because I had no idea how to get us out of here in the darkness.

God must have heard me, because before I heard the police sirens, I saw blue flashing lights coming toward us.

CHAPTER FORTY-EIGHT

Thursday, 9:05 p.m.

I had never been so glad to see Trey in my entire life. I had no shame about hugging him hard. Of course, I had had to wait patiently as Trey hugged Joseph first. I'd wiped the tears from my eyes as I watched the two males hug each other fiercely. Then Trey had grabbed me and pulled me into his arms. All my tension melted away as we hugged.

When Trey released me, Iris was kissing James, who was still sleepy and was clueless about what had happened a while ago. Margaret stood to the side, looking lost and scared. I walked over to her.

"Are you all right?" I asked her.

"No." Tears were forming in her eyes. "I need to know what happened to my boys."

I nodded. I wanted to know too. My last image before I gunned the engine and shot down that dirt road was of Kenyon pointing his gun at us, but that didn't make much sense. When I'd seen the police cars, I'd pulled over to the side of the road. I'd told them what was going on at the house. One police car had stayed behind with us, while the other police officers had continued up toward the house. Trey and Iris had followed behind the police in Trey's car.

I looked up to see a familiar unmarked vehicle coming down the road. Moses stopped the car and climbed out. "Everyone all right here?"

I tried to smile, but I felt like crying. "Yes. I think there is a horrific crime scene up that way, but I can't be sure. Can you tell me what happened?"

Moses touched my shoulder. "I will as soon as I can process it. Let's get everyone checked out at the hospital, okay?"

We were driven to the hospital. I felt fine and refused care, but I paced the floor in the ER waiting room, waiting to hear how Joseph was doing. Trey felt that Joseph wasn't doing well, but that he had been too scared and shaken up to reveal his pain. He was a brave boy.

As promised, Moses came and found me in the waiting room. He pulled me over to the side, and we both sat down. He sighed. "You are a ballsy woman. You rescued Margaret Cooper and the boys after being taken hostage yourself."

I shook my head. "I had help from Kenyon. I was kind of in the right place at the right time."

Moses said, "Explain."

"Kenyon must have realized when I was at Iris's house that I could help. On the way to the house on the dirt road, Kenyon came up with this crazy plan. He would distract KC, and I would take everyone away in the truck. He gave me the truck keys. While we were trapped in the house, I just couldn't figure out if he was trying to get KC to turn himself in to the police or to help him escape."

Moses cleared his throat before he spoke. "When I got there, a man was down. A young man. He died at the scene."

I'd heard the gunshots. I frowned. "KC must have been shooting at the truck. Kenyon must have stopped him."

Moses asked, "Is that what you think happened?"

I nodded. I felt really sad all of a sudden. All of my questions had gotten answered except for one. I asked Moses, "What did you find out about KC?"

"We don't need to go into it now."

"Yes, we do. He's the mystery piece in this puzzle. Why did he deliberately shoot Marty when he didn't have to? Why go after Chris and Tone?"

"KC had some issues. He wanted to please his father, and at the same time he was a bit of a sociopath. We had some talks today with a few people who knew him. He was charming in his own way, but very calculating, especially if he perceived someone as a threat. I think Kenyon might have moved both sons here to avoid some trouble back in Charlotte. It appears KC might have been involved in some open homicide cases in Mecklenburg County too."

"Wow! So, was justice really served tonight?"

Moses shook his head. "I don't know. Unfortunately, a man lost his son, and it was at his own hands. Kenyon was very somber when we arrested him. This may finish off any of his entrepreneurial pursuits for good. The consequences were too costly this time." Moses patted my shoulder. "Good work, Manchester. Maybe now you are satisfied and can figure out your next steps. Hopefully, nothing involving a criminal case."

After Moses walked away, I looked up to see Trey and Joseph walking down the hallway. I assumed Joseph had received a clean bill of health from the ER doctor. That was good, because I would hate to see the boy cooped up in the hospital again.

The picture of the father and son walking toward me stood in sharp contrast to the crime scene I'd left tonight. It was a beautiful sight, and if the God allowed me to, I wanted to stick around and watch that relationship grow.

I also wanted God to work on me a bit more so I could be ready for what was next.

CHAPTER FORTY-NINE

Six months later, Thanksgiving Day

So many memories of my past at Aunt C's home had been folded together with my present. I, Serena Manchester, was hosting Thanksgiving dinner, like she would do every year when I was younger. Of course, I couldn't pull off the cooking without Bev's and Mama's help. Alecia showed up with some pie. While everyone ate around the dining room table, I had to admit it was good to be around my nuclear family and my extended family. My lonely existence as an obsessed-for-the-story reporter had almost been forgotten. I said "almost" because I still liked to do a little investigating.

After everyone was finished eating, Bev helped me clear the table. Then I sat back in Aunt C's favorite chair in the living room and reflected. In the past six months I had gone to Charlotte and had taken my things out of storage and had brought them here. The decor was now a mixture of my eclectic taste and Aunt C's traditional bent, though I had kept the house pretty much the same.

I smiled as I watched Brittany and Tiffany hanging on to every word Joseph and Chris exchanged. It was so good to see those two boys blossoming again. Both their grades were up in what was now their sophomore year. Joseph was adjusting well to his new medications. He hadn't had a single flare-up of his sickle cell since last spring.

I had invited Iris over and had asked her to bring James, but she still was mad at me for some reason, so she didn't show up. I wasn't sure why, since it was her now incarcerated boyfriend who had brought all the trouble. Still, I guessed that in time we would talk again. I did know she was back working at the Huddle House, or at least that was what Margaret had said when I talked to her earlier this week. I was still amazed at the calmness of that woman.

I'd also invited Margaret to Thanksgiving dinner, but she had gone to be with some other relatives. Evil might have invaded her home, and she might have lost her grandson and, in some ways, her son, but goodness and mercy had prevailed that night.

I looked over at Alecia and Moses. I was glad those two had finally decided to let their relationship grow. Moses looked back at me. I grinned at him.

He eyed me. "That smile is a sign of trouble, Manchester."

I stood up and clapped my hands. "Not trouble, Moses. Everyone, can I have your attention for a moment?"

Bev and Mama came out of the kitchen. Clay and Trey stopped their conversation and looked over at me. I caught Trey's eye. He grinned at me. He already knew my news, because I had jumped up and down like a little girl when I told him. At the moment I received my news, I felt like God made all that I had been through in the past two years worthwhile.

"First, let me say to my brother-in-law, I'm so grateful that you hired me as an investigator on your staff. Being employed at Clayton Matthews Law Firm will be a great experience. I appreciate you helping me transition from my former career."

Moses sighed. "Thank goodness you deal only with civil cases, Clay."

Clay laughed. "I'm sure the caseload may prove to be a little boring for Serena sometimes."

I grinned. "Well, I might have a fix for that. I'm happy to announce I received my approved application from the South Carolina Law Enforcement Division and Manchester Private Investigation is officially open."

Moses covered his forehead. "Oh no. Here we go."

Alecia patted Moses on the knee and beamed at me. "You go, girl!"

Everyone stood around me, and I gladly accepted the hugs. After Mama hugged me, Trey came closer.

"I guess this means you're permanently planted back here at home," he said.

"Yes, I guess Georgetown isn't bad." I smiled at him.

Trey and I had rekindled our friendship. I wasn't sure if we would ever cross the line into a relationship. Right now I was developing another relationship. God had brought me full circle to the place I had run from years ago.

Just then Proverbs 22:6 came to mind. *Train up a child in the way he should go: and when he is old, he will not depart from it.*

I had to give old Reverend Lawson some credit. I looked at Trey. "You know, I never thought I would say this, but it's really good to be home."

DISCUSSION QUESTIONS

1. At the beginning of the novel, Serena is depressed about the changes in her life and contemplates her regrets about her failed marriages, about being motherless, and about her former career. Have you ever been at a crossroads in your life where your decisions and your regrets caused you much frustration?

2. Serena had been gone from her hometown for quite some time. She had occasionally come to visit, but she had become distant and estranged from her family and friends by choice. Have you ever walked away from any relationships, and have you found yourself wishing to rekindle those relationships or revisit the past?

3. Serena felt that her aunt C (Claudia Robinson) was like a second mother and that Aunt C's home was her sanctuary while she was growing up. She feels strongly that she should honor her aunt by protecting the people her aunt loved. Do you have a special or a favorite relative or caregiver who is now deceased? What has that person brought to your life? How has that person influenced you?

4. Serena is surprised by her attraction to Trey Evans. She feels that this childhood crush should have gone away after she graduated from high school and left town. It seems like other people remember Serena and Trey's relationship differently than Serena does.

Have you ever had a second chance at love that was lost or at an opportunity that you let get away? If so, what did you do? Did you pursue it or let it get away again?

5. Iris Jenkins is an interesting character in that it seems that she did not grow up as much as her high school classmates did after graduation. Why do you think Iris pursued men like Kenyon Cooper? Do you know women whose insecurities influence their choices?

6. Serena often contemplates not being a mother, but she gets along well with Chris and Joseph. She grows very protective of both boys as the novel progresses. Her nieces love being around their aunt, and Serena in turn basks in the joy the girls bring her. In your opinion, what makes a true mother?

7. In the novel Serena comes to the realization that she has lived selfishly, and she bases this on how she perceived her upbringing under Reverend Thomas Lawson. Her skewed perceptions of Reverend Lawson's parenting affected her for most of her life, to the point where she refused to be involved in church or had some dislike for ministers. Have you ever been in a place in your life where you felt individuals who were Christian affected your views? When did you realize Christianity was about a relationship with Christ?

8. This novel explores the relationships between children and their fathers, stepfathers, and father figures, and the ways in which these relationships impact children's lives. Did you relate to any of the characters more than you did to the others? How has the presence or absence of a father in your life affected your journey?

ABOUT THE AUTHOR

Tyora Moody is the author of Soul-Searching Suspense novels in the Victory Gospel Series and the Eugeena Patterson Mysteries Series. As a literary-focused entrepreneur, she has assisted countless authors with developing an online presence. Her design and marketing company, Tywebbin Creations LLC, offers such popular services as online publicity, social media management, and the creation of book trailers and book covers.

Tyora is also the author of the nonfiction series *The Literary Entrepreneur's Toolkit* and the host of the Literary Entrepreneur Podcast. Tyora's debut novel, *When Rain Falls,* was a second-place finisher for the 2014 Yerby Award for Fiction. She is the winner of the 2013 Urban Literary Award for best debut author and the 2013 Urban Literary Award for best mystery/thriller/suspense for *When Rain Falls.*

Tyora is a member of Sisters in Crime and American Christian Fiction Writers. For more information about her literary endeavors, visit her online at TyoraMoody.com.

UC HIS GLORY BOOK CLUB!

www.uchisglorybookclub.net

UC His Glory Book Club is the spirit-inspired brain-child of Joylynn Ross, an author and the acquisitions editor of Urban Christian, and Kendra Norman-Bellamy, an author for Urban Christian. It is an online book club that hosts authors of Urban Christian. We welcome as members all men and women who have a passion for reading Christian-based fiction.

UC His Glory Book Club pledges its commitment to providing support, positive feedback, encouragement, and a forum whereby members can openly discuss and review the literary works of Urban Christian authors.

There is no membership fee associated with UC His Glory Book Club;however, we do ask that you support the authors by purchasing their works, encouraging them, providing book reviews, and, of course, offering your prayers. We also ask that you respect our beliefs and follow the guidelines of the book club. We hope to receive your valuable input, opinions, and reviews that build up, rather than tear down, our authors.

What We Believe:

—We believe that Jesus is the Christ, Son of the Living God.

—We believe that the Bible is the true, living Word of God.

—We believe that all Urban Christian authors should use their God-given writing ability to honor God and to sharethe message of the written word that God has given to each of them uniquely.

—We believe in supporting Urban Christian authors in their literary endeavors by reading their titles, purchasing them, and sharing them with our online community.

—We believe that everything we do in our literary arena should be done in a manner that will lead to God being glorified and honored.

We look forward to online fellowship with you.

Please visit us often at:

www.uchisglorybookclub.net

Many Blessings to You!

Shelia E. Lipsey,
President, UC His Glory Book Club